Malawi's Sisters

Also by Melanie S. Hatter

The Color of My Soul
Let No One Weep for Me: Stories of Love and Loss

Malawi's Sisters

Melanie S. Hatter

Four Way Books

Tribeca

Library of Congress Cataloging-in-Publication Data

Names: Hatter, Melanie S., author.
Title: Malawi's sisters / by Melanie S. Hatter.
Description: New York : Four Way Books, [2019]
Identifiers: LCCN 2018028723 | ISBN 9781945588303 (pbk. : alk. paper)
Subjects: LCSH: Domestic fiction.
Classification: LCC PS3608.A8656 M35 2019 | DDC 813/.6--dc23
LC record available at https://lccn.loc.gov/2018028723

LOVELY DAY

Words and Music by BILL WITHERS and SKIP SCARBOROUGH

Copyright © 1977 (Renewed) RELANA DENETTE FLORES PUB DESIGNEE, CANDACE
ELIZABETH SCARBOROUGH PUB DESIGNEE, PLAID FLOWERS MUSIC, SWEET
COOKIE MUSIC and GOLDEN WITHERS MUSIC All Rights for RELANA DENETTE
FLORES PUB DESIGNEE, CANDACE ELIZABETH

SCARBOROUGH PUB DESIGNEE, PLAID FLOWERS MUSIC, SWEET COOKIE
MUSIC Administered by WARNER-TAMERLANE PUBLISHING CORP.

Used by Permission of ALFRED MUSIC
All Rights Reserved

This publication is made possible with public funds from the National Endowment for the Arts

and from the New York State Council on the Arts, a state agency.

PROUD MEMBER

We are a proud member of the Community of Literary Magazines and Presses.

To the countless children, women, and men of color, who lose their lives every day because of fear and racism.

Prologue

Malawi felt good about Connie, a ruddy-faced white woman from Alabama with a Southern accent that made Malawi laugh. She drank gin straight-up and said the word "fuck" so often no-one would ever guess she was a high-school math teacher. She'd taught in the Palm Beach County school system for almost as long as Malawi had been alive. That first week at school, when she heard the woman give a belly laugh in the teacher's lounge, Malawi instantly adored her. And Connie had felt the same about Malawi, inviting her to dinner and sharing dirt on their colleagues. Malawi had only a handful of white friends, most of them liberal hipsters around her own age. Connie was well into her fifties, had voted for McCain in 2008 and for Mitt Romney in 2012. Malawi forgave her for that, putting it down to her Alabama upbringing.

They gathered at Connie's house once a month. Sometimes they played Scrabble or watched a movie, but mostly they drank gin (Malawi added Coke—she liked being different) and talked about their students, good teaching strategies, their co-workers. Malawi could ask Connie advice on just about anything related to teaching. She made Malawi's decision to move to West Palm Beach worth it. A spur-of-the-moment decision she had worried was the wrong move. But, so far, her new life was working out. She could imagine settling down here, making a home for herself. Maybe even having a family. With the right guy.

Malawi had driven to Connie's house in Greenacres on Saturday night, calling her sister, Ghana, on the way there. They talked at least three times a week and texted almost every day. Malawi shared everything with Ghana—even the real reason she'd moved to Florida, though she didn't reveal his name. That was a secret she'd take to the grave.

Ghana hadn't talked to Mama or Kenya in months. Malawi understood perfectly well why. Yet a feeling, small, like one of those tiny chocolate eggs at Easter shifted in her stomach—a discomforting recognition that those cracked spaces between them all shouldn't be left to grow. She'd needed to get away from the family, but the distance— while it had given her some clarity—had become greater than the miles. They should be better to one another. She would make an effort when she went back for a visit. Malawi made a promise to herself to bring everyone together.

For now, though, she'd met a new guy and wanted to get to know him better. Wanted to enjoy being in a relationship she didn't have to hide from everyone. Her new man was a physical therapist at the medical center. Tall, brown-skinned, and fine as hell. Marriage material, even. Malawi had a thing for older men, but he wasn't that much older, at least not compared to some of the others. He was smart and ambitious—traits she found sexy in a man, and he seemed to carry little baggage—no wives or other girlfriends, no kids, no strings she'd detected in the few months they had dated. Yeah, she could see this as a long-term thing.

He was disappointed she wasn't spending the evening with him and asked her to come over later, no matter how late it was. When Malawi left Connie's house well after midnight, she called to tell him she was on her way. "I got something for you," he said, and she squirmed in her seat. He wouldn't say what it was. "Just don't take all night."

The GPS on her phone kept cutting out and she suspected she'd made a wrong turn somewhere, but with each turn she seemed to find her way deeper into a neighborhood she didn't know. The signal was weak and when she tried calling her man, the call dropped before she could say hello. One hand on the steering wheel, the other moving the phone around, trying to get a signal, and when she looked back at the road ahead something ran out in front of her. Looked like a bobcat. Just the other day she'd read about a recent sighting in the area. Instinctively, Malawi swerved and next thing she knew the airbag exploded in her face. Stunned, she sat for several moments as the airbag deflated, shaking, thinking maybe she shouldn't have had that last gin and Coke. She'd been sipping water throughout the night and didn't consider herself drunk, but couldn't remember exactly how many drinks she'd had.

Malawi rubbed her palms across her hot face. Carefully, she opened the car door and grimaced at the sight of the buckled front end of the Camry lodged against a light pole. Her immediate thought was to call her father, but instead she dialed her guy's number—still no service. Frustrated, she stood looking up and down the street. No traffic. No lights in any windows. It was after one a.m. She started walking, hoping to either get a signal on her phone or find someone still awake who would let her use theirs. Holding the cell phone out in front of her, she wandered a few minutes down the street until she saw a light in the front window of a small bungalow.

Malawi gave a sigh of relief and walked up the path.

The trilling of the phone stirred Bet from sleep, but it was the thudding of her heart that opened her eyes. An inexplicable dread rising in her chest before she looked at the clock to see the time—three in the morning. She glanced at Malcolm, who had pushed the covers to the bottom of the bed as he often did in his sleep, especially in the summer. He lay on his side, his face turned away from her, his snore chugging into the air. She offered a silent prayer that the call would be nothing bad. Leaning on her right elbow, she reached with her left for the phone on the bedside table, another prayer for a wrong number, that she could snuggle into her husband's back and savor the memory of last night's kisses.

She grabbed the phone just before it rang a third time, her heartbeat erratic in her chest. "Hello?"

"Mrs. Walker?"

"Yes."

"This is Sheriff Wheeler of the Palm Beach County Sheriff's Office. Do you have—"

His words faded and Bet pressed the phone closer to her ear. The voice was low and deep. She reached over and turned on the lamp, the light pinching her eyes.

"What? What did you say?"

"Do you have a daughter named Malawi Walker?"

"Malawi? What happened? Is she all right?"

"Mrs. Walker, there's been an incident. Your daughter has been shot."

"What?" Bet swung her legs off the bed and sat on the edge of the mattress pressing the phone into her ear. "What?"

She couldn't breathe, yet a scream burst from her throat. Malcolm jumped up, his arm automatically reaching out to her. "It's Malawi," she yelled. "She's been shot."

Malcolm took the phone from her hand. "Hello? This is Judge Walker, Malawi's father." He listened and stared at Bet for what seemed an age, before responding. "Thank you, Sheriff. Yes, we'll get on the first flight we can." He touched her arm and the pressure of his hand was reassuring. "She's at the Palm Beach Hospital. The sheriff said it's a shoulder injury. You pack a bag. I'll call the hospital. Maybe they can give us an update. I'll find a flight."

Malcolm rushed downstairs to his office while Bet remained seated on the bed, struggling to bring into focus what he'd said. She had to pack. They were going to Florida. They were going to see Malawi. Pushing herself to move, she ransacked closets and drawers for necessities. She stumbled over the cat as Kitty silently appeared from one of her hiding spots, meowing at the sudden disturbance in the house. In a moment, Malcolm advanced back up the stairs, shouting that he'd booked an early flight leaving National in a few hours. He handed her the phone. "I'm on hold with the hospital." He gestured for her to take over listening to the tinny elevator music and stepped into the adjoining bathroom, closing the door behind him. She tried to picture her daughter being shot in the shoulder—over-dramatized scenes from movies clouded her mind; not images of Malawi. Bet took a deep breath.

She padded downstairs and put on a pot of coffee. Kitty followed and sprang from the floor to the chair, then up onto the counter and daintily pranced across to Bet, who tut-tutted and dumped the cat back on the floor with unnecessary force. She switched the phone from her right to her left and adjusted the salt-and-pepper shakers, aligning them just so. Her fingers were shaking. A voice came on the line and Bet threw out her daughter's name, stumbling through an explanation that her daughter had been admitted a few hours ago, a gunshot wound. The voice couldn't find Malawi's name and suggested Bet call again in an hour. Bet huffed and glowered at the phone as if the voice could see her irritation, but the line was dead. She dialed Kenya's number and her oldest answered after the third ring, her voice muffled and sleepy.

She tried to explain, but her words got tangled around her tongue as if fighting against her mouth.

"Mama, slow down. What happened?"

Bet's head felt like it was in a tumble dryer and she was about to vomit. "We don't know yet. I'll call you when we know. I just—just wanted to let you know we're going down there."

"Do you need me to do anything?"

"Call Ghana for me. I can't— I just—" Tears blurred her vision. Before hanging up, she repeated her promise to call when they got to Florida. "Oh, and stop in and feed Kitty, will you?"

The room was thick with shadow, only a glow of light came from the bulb above the stove. When the coffee was done, she poured a large mug and sat at the breakfast table trying to stay calm.

2

Kenya poured a second cup of coffee knowing she would be wired all day, but what do you do at four in the morning after your mother calls to say your sister has been shot? She had tried to go back to sleep but had lain with the weight of her thoughts pressing on her, closing her eyes just to have them open again. So she got up quietly, trying not to disturb Sidney, put on her robe and tiptoed downstairs, her head wrapped in a silk scarf to keep her hair smooth. She left a message for Ghana, emptied the dishwasher, took out chicken pieces to thaw, and sat at the breakfast bar nibbling at a hangnail as daylight gradually filled the kitchen.

As she gazed through the window at the bushes in the yard, irritation nipped the back of her neck at having to postpone the surprise party. And what to do with the huge sheet cake decorated with her parents' smiling faces and the words "Happy Anniversary" in purple icing? Kenya bit harder at the skin around her nails. She wanted to be magnanimous toward her sister, and yet this feeling that Malawi always ruined everything kept shoving its way into her thoughts. She didn't want to think this. Malawi was in pain, suffering a gunshot wound, for God's sake. It's not that she wasn't worried about her baby sister—of course she was—it was just that Malawi had always been a drama queen. Always had to be the center of everyone's attention. This was just another stupid cry to be noticed. Probably not even a shooting, but something else entirely.

She remembered missing her first-ever girls-and-boys party because Mama went into labor with Malawi. Instead of wearing her new dress and kissing her first crush, Kenya spent the night at Grandma's house with Ghana. She had imagined dancing the night away in her crush's arms, but instead, when she got to school the next day she heard he'd danced with Bethany Gilbert and kissed *her* goodnight. The kiss should have been Kenya's. From that night on Malawi became the center of their lives—and the bane of Kenya's.

Mama and Daddy always ran to her rescue, even now that she lived in Florida, off they went. They'd find she hadn't been shot. Just Drama Queen creating a crisis. Malawi moved south claiming a desire to be free of the family. As if *the family* was some kind of mafia she needed to escape. But Malawi wasn't the good girl their parents thought she was. For one thing, she was no stranger to smoking weed, and Kenya wondered if her sister had been experimenting with something stronger. Had fallen in with a bad crowd. Didn't seem that long ago Malawi had called their parents in the middle of the night from West Baltimore because she'd hit a stop sign, apparently trying to reach her phone on the floor. So she said. She couldn't start the car and needed money to get it towed and repaired. When asked what she was doing in West Baltimore in the early hours of the morning, all she said was, "just visiting friends." Of course, Daddy immediately drove in the middle of the night from D.C. to save her, as if she couldn't have called Triple-A.

Kenya's coffee was cold now and she frowned at her thoughts. Everything would be fine. This was just Malawi being ridiculous, as usual.

Sidney came into the kitchen and murmured, "Good morning." She could tell he was tired from his slow gait and low voice. His hair had grown into a short afro and she wished he would get it cut, yet couldn't find words to say anything. She shifted her gaze to the window as he settled on a stool next to her, wearing white shorts and a striped Polo shirt, his skin tanned to almost black. He slurped his coffee—a sound she hated—and read the Post while waiting for a bagel to pop out of the toaster. He had returned yesterday from a business trip to South Africa. She knew that much to be true. As far as she could tell, he had never lied about where he had been, just who he'd been with.

The bagel popped up and Sidney remained still, reading. She wouldn't spread the cream cheese for him. She knew that's what he wanted, because that's what she usually did. The cheese should be spread as soon as the bagel popped up so it melted. She hated for anything toasted to sit and get cold. But she refused to do it today. Not anymore.

He glanced at her. "You okay, Babe?"

"Um hmm."

She took a sip of cold coffee, aware of his eyes on her, then he got up and spread the bagel himself. Between bites, he said, "I'll be heading out soon. Meeting Jon for a round of tennis."

Flooded with a combination of thoughts and emotions she didn't know what to do with, Kenya said nothing. This morning, everything was irritating her. She decided not to mention her mother's call until she heard more. She acknowledged his comment with a nod, her teeth still nibbling at the skin around her nails, her mind on having to call everyone on the invite list to cancel the surprise party—surprise!—and thinking about her parents rushing off to Florida to rescue her sister. She listened but didn't hear the crackling pages of the newspaper, Sidney crunching the bagel, the hum of the refrigerator.

After a while, Sidney said, "Okay, then," and placed his mug on the empty plate, the clink bashing her ears. "I'll see you later." He left her with a kiss on her forehead.

3

Malawi has been shot. The words rolled and collided like marbles on a wooden floor; Ghana could make no sense of them. She deleted Kenya's rambling message then called Malawi's number but it went straight to voice-mail.

She sat on the couch in the dim morning light, her locs tied up with a scarf into a loose pile on top of her head, her latest tattoo, a vine of flowers curling over her shoulder and along the back of her neck, peeking around just below her right ear. She had wandered, naked, into the living room in search of her phone. The dull ache of a hangover squeezing her brain as she listened to her sister's message. Grabbing Ryan's T-shirt from the cushion next to her, she covered herself then pulled her feet up onto the couch, straining the cell phone's charging cord. She leaned her arm on her knees and listened to the phone ring so many times, Ghana expected to get voice-mail, but her mother finally answered.

"Mama. What's going on?"

"We're in Florida. Me and your father." Her mother sounded weary. "Malawi's in the hospital. We've just landed at the airport. Once your father gets a car we'll go straight there."

Ghana tightened her knees into her chest. "Is she okay?"

"They said it was a shoulder wound. Look, I need to go. We'll call when we know for sure what's going on, okay."

Ghana ran back to the bedroom and jumped on the bed. Ryan lay on his stomach and shifted his head from left to right, but didn't open his eyes. He'd worked well past his regular evening shift and hadn't gotten home until after two a.m. She hesitated to wake him, but needed to talk. As a cop, he might have some perspective to help her understand what was happening with her sister.

She touched the milky-white skin right below his hairline, skin that gradually darkened to a golden brown along his shoulders and down his back. For a white boy, during the summer, he got as dark as she was. "Baby." She nudged his shoulder. "Wake up!"

He made a grunting noise, rolled onto his side and reached out for her, wrapping his arms around her waist and snuggling his face into her thigh. "Come back to bed," he said, his words muffled. She pushed him back so she could see his face.

"Malawi's been …" She paused thinking maybe she was dreaming. *Malawi's been shot.* The phrase seemed absurd to say out loud.

Ryan's eyes flickered open; he squinted at her, his face soft and sleepy. "Huh?"

Clutching his forearm, her mind began to race, a barrage of questions filling her head: Should she fly down there, too? Was it a drive-by shooting? Could a shoulder injury be fatal? Was she overreacting? Daddy would be there soon to make sure Malawi was okay. And they'd call. Everything would be okay.

Ryan's eyelids slowly closed and his face fell into the pillow. She stared at him, feeling her throat tight, her pulse throbbing in her head. His arm made one more attempt to pull her back to bed; she shoved him away and went to the bathroom to shower. Maybe she would fly down there.

Waiting for the water to warm, she thought about calling Kenya to see if she knew anything more, but decided against it. Ghana hadn't talked to her older sister in months. Not since Christmas when everyone was home.

"You're not living up to your potential," Kenya had said. The family was gathered, as always, at their parents' home in Crestwood. Kenya loved that they grew up in the bourgie neighborhood, nicknamed the Gold Coast. That her daddy was a prominent judge, that she'd married a successful businessman, and that she went to law school and lived in a swanky house in Potomac, Maryland.

"Is that what *you're* doing?" Ghana had asked. "Living up to your potential with your two perfect kids and your big house and Louboutin shoes."

"I don't wear Louboutins." Kenya had looked at her feet, and with a straight face said, "These are Fendi."

Ghana looked to the ceiling. "Whatever."

"I'm serious, Ghana. Look at your life. You do massage. You do graphic design. You're all over the place. You live in a pitiful apartment in Anacostia."

"Yeah, and you wouldn't set foot on that side of town, right?"

"That's not what I mean."

"You don't know anything about the people who live there, so shut up."

"I'm not talking about the people who live there. I'm talking about you and your lack of focus. You need to go back to school. Finish your degree."

"Go to hell, Kenya. My business is my business. Besides, I'm moving in with my boyfriend next month."

Before Kenya could say anything more, Li'l Sis had stepped in, as she often did. "Jesus, you two. Knock it off."

Malawi was the peacemaker. The one who wanted everyone to

get along. And Ghana loved her desperately. They had talked yesterday evening. Malawi seemed happy to be in Florida, though she had confessed she missed everyone. She had met a guy and said they'd been dating for a few months. Last night, she was headed to a colleague's house for dinner, a woman who also taught Math at the same high school. Ghana couldn't remember the woman's name, but she had become somewhat of a mentor to Malawi. At least that's how Li'l Sis had described her. Malawi had called from her car, on her way to the woman's house. She'd been in good spirits and they'd laughed about her maybe stopping by her guy's house after dinner for a booty call on her way home. Ghana wondered if her sister had visited him and he'd gotten angry and hurt her somehow.

She turned off the water and stepped out of the shower, wrapping a large green towel around her. In the steamy bathroom, the blood left her head and she sat on the edge of the tub.

"Good god, I hope not."

4

It was just after eleven in the morning and the air was muggy and hot. Malcolm drove the rental straight to Palm Beach Hospital. The Taurus handled well enough but the GPS seemed to lack an accurate image of the terrain and they made several wrong turns causing Bet to fuss about taking too long. Malcolm kept quiet—anything he said would result in an argument. The flight had lasted just over two and a half hours, but had seemed to take forever. He hated flying, but Bet was worse so he feigned indifference to keep her calm. As the plane's wheels hit the tarmac, she gripped his hand so tightly the tips of his fingers turned white.

The massive parking garage had no open spaces until the fifth level, and all the while Bet fussed. "It's too hot. Why are so many people at the hospital already? Are these spaces for both staff and visitors? Shouldn't they separate them and have them marked? Visitors should get priority."

He knew she was anxious but he needed her to stop talking. He couldn't think. "Bet, just give it a rest for a minute. Please!"

He backed the car into the space, exited and walked around the front to open her door. He took her hand and she huffed, but fell quiet. He looked for directions to the emergency room. After an agonizingly slow ride down on the elevator and a short walk, they found the ER crowded with a long line leading to the intake desk. Bet exclaimed, "Oh, Jesus Lord."

Of course, he thought, the chaos and madness of a Saturday night spilling into the emergency room on a Sunday morning. Malcolm told Bet to wait in line while he skipped to the front. "I need to see my daughter. She's been shot."

The heavyset woman behind the desk didn't look up. "Sir, you'll have to wait in line."

Ready to do battle if need be to get in immediately to see his daughter, he raised his voice fully aware of the effect his baritone could have in a courtroom. "I'm not here for service. My daughter is already here. In surgery."

The woman had blotchy pink skin and small blue eyes. She glanced at him and insisted, "You have to wait your turn."

"I am not waiting in line," he said. He didn't like to use his authority outside court, to throw his weight around, as Kenya liked to say. But he did when it was warranted. "My daughter has been shot and I need to speak to a doctor. Now!"

An orderly approached, a young Indian man maybe twenty-five at most, tall and skinny meeting Malcolm eye-to-eye, and asked the name of his daughter. This was a good man, Malcolm thought. Helpful with kind eyes. The young man disappeared behind sliding glass doors but only a few moments passed before he reappeared.

"Let me take you up to surgery," he said.

Malcolm waved to Bet who was already rushing to him. They followed the young man to an elevator. The doors slid closed, sealing them in, shutting out the cacophony of the waiting room, and Malcolm took a breath. He would see his daughter. He would take her hand and tell her he loved her. He couldn't remember the last time he'd spoken those words or held her hand. Perhaps when she was little. They exited on a floor marked Surgery and the orderly took them down a short corridor with pale pink walls to the nursing station and explained that these were

Malawi Walker's parents. The nurse behind the desk had blonde hair tied back and looked young enough to be just out of high school. A momentary frown crossed her brow, making the hair rise on the back of Malcolm's neck.

She looked at Malcolm. "I'm so sorry," she said then closed her eyes as if she'd said something she shouldn't have.

Bet began to moan, "Oh my God. Oh my God."

So sorry. These words were not enough for Malcolm. He needed to hear why she was sorry. He needed to know what had happened, though didn't want to think of the possibilities. But he asked anyway.

"You should talk to Dr. Kosi. He can explain." The nurse beckoned the orderly who had been standing a few feet away, at the ready if needed. Malcolm heard a child heaving rasping coughs and a flash of Malawi as a baby, wheezing and coughing, making painful noises only babies can make, noises that grasp the heart and squeeze. Malcolm was ready to search for his daughter in the recovery room leading off to the right of the nurse's station, glass partitions and modest curtains giving little privacy to the afflicted. He wanted to find Malawi behind one, sitting up in the bed, giggling and rolling her eyes at her stupidity for being in the wrong place at the wrong time. Not shot at all, but merely scraped from a fall requiring a few stitches. Not surgery.

Dr. Kosi strode up to the counter with a calm sense of urgency, clipboard in hand, passing it to the nurse with the confidence that she knew what to do with it, ready to rush to the next in line with a medical complaint.

"Dr. Kosi, this is um …" The nurse paused, as if trying to remember Malawi's name. "These are the girl's parents, the girl who was …"

"Mr. and Mrs. Walker." Dr. Kosi made eye contact with Malcolm. "Please, follow me."

He led them into a small office, walls lined with certificates, and offered them a seat but everyone remained standing, an awkward silence freezing the air. The doctor said, "I'm sorry …" And there it was again, that phrase, *I'm sorry*. For what? Malcolm wanted to yell, but he held the doctor's gaze and waited.

A screech, short and high-pitched escaped Bet and Malcolm felt her fingers clawing at him, her weight growing heavy on his arm as she interpreted the doctor's apology. A step ahead of Malcolm, already accepting what he was not willing to accept. He needed to hear the words to believe what had, so far, been unsaid. "What do you mean?"

Dr. Kosi wavered but only for a second, a slight flicker in the eyes, then he said, "She died during surgery. We did all we could and worked on her for several hours, but she lost too much blood."

"I don't understand. The sheriff said she was shot in the shoulder. Just a shoulder injury."

"She was shot twice, Mr. Walker." He looked at Bet who was almost doubled over now moaning into Malcolm's forearm. "She was taken downstairs. Nurse Templeton can show you."

Malcolm looked at the blinds covering the window. He knew what was downstairs. The word "downstairs" was better than the word "basement," which was where most hospitals housed the morgue. He and Bet were here now to identify their baby girl, not to console her and pay the hospital bill, though that would come later in the mail. Malcolm wasn't sure his daughter had health insurance. He should know these things. As her father, he should know whether or not his daughter had health insurance.

"Why don't you take a moment and sit down," said Dr. Kosi, extending his arm to the chairs behind them.

Malcolm gripped Bet by the shoulders, almost dragging her to a standing position. He thought the words, let's sit, but nothing came out of his mouth. He tried to take a step but his feet were weighted with invisible blocks and his knees began to shake. He almost dropped Bet in an effort to grab the desk to stop himself from falling. "Please, Bet," he said, feebly. This was not the judge's voice. It was the voice of a tiny man afraid of having to identify his daughter's body.

* * *

They stared at her. Her skin was a sickly pale brown. Taupe, Bet thought. She wanted to say it wasn't her. Not her baby girl, her Mowie. The floor seemed to buckle and the walls bent and the entire room swayed. Like a carnival ride that shook you up and left you nauseous and upset, unable to stand straight for several moments afterward. Bet placed her hands on her knees and stared at the floor expecting her entire insides to be expelled all over the linoleum. She closed her eyes and, as if whispering a mantra, said, "Don't make this be real," several times, then she felt Malcolm's hand on her sacrum. Everything stopped swaying, and it was real. She looked again at her baby's face, so serious and composed. The doctor had said she was shot in the chest and right shoulder; her body was covered with a pale green cloth that showed only her neck and face. With the back of her hand, Bet touched Mowie's cheek and inhaled sharply at the chill of it. She leaned forward and kissed where her hand had been. Though cool, the skin shifted slightly under her touch. Real, yet not real, like a clone made without Mowie's vibrancy. Without life. She placed her head next to Mowie's cheek and began to cry, tears that trickled quietly across Bet's nose.

She shouldn't have gone to Florida. Bet knew it had been a mistake. All that talk of needing real independence. Ghana and Kenya had real independence and they hadn't moved out of the area.

"You're being ridiculous, Mowie," Bet had said during one of her daughter's Sunday visits. Before moving to Florida, Malawi often came to visit on the weekends, bringing laundry because she disliked being in the dirty laundry room of her Baltimore apartment building; the machines were slow and unreliable. Bet would miss those visits, though sometimes they had annoyed her. An irritation she couldn't quite express. Malawi had been overly attached to her parents, or rather to her father. In three more years, the girl would have been thirty; she should have been making more of an effort to find a husband.

"Times have changed Mommy," she'd said, rolling her eyes at Bet. "I don't need to have a man to get along in this life." Perhaps not, Bet thought, but it wouldn't have hurt.

Her daughter had sat on the settee in the studio while Bet worked on a painting; the smell of a roast in the oven filled the house. Her legs curled under her, Malawi pulled the ear buds out and announced she had accepted a job offer. No warning. No lead-in. Just, "I've gotten a job in Florida. At a high school in Palm Beach."

Bet was unsure what to say while her daughter's large eyes watched, waiting for some overreaction from her mother before continuing. "I just, like, need to be in a place where, you know, no one knows our family. Everybody here knows Daddy."

"That's not true, not everyone. What a silly thing to say." Bet didn't know why she had been so contrary. It did seem that everyone knew Malcolm. His father had been a city councilman for a number of years back in the seventies and eighties and his mother had worked with Mary McLeod Bethune and Dorothy Height at the National Council of Negro Women. The family was well known in D.C. But still, she told her daughter, "You're being ridiculous."

"Well, it's a good job opportunity," Malawi said.

"Teaching high school math? How many schools do we have here in the D.C. area?" Bet rapidly swirled her paintbrush on the palette, mixing yellow and blue to create a swampy dark green. "You really couldn't have gotten a job here?"

"Seriously? Baltimore wasn't good enough. Now Florida isn't good enough."

"There's a lot of crime in the city of Baltimore. Even the surrounding county would have been a safer choice."

Malawi stood up then, stretched her arms above her head and offered a bored sigh. "Where's Daddy?"

"In his office, I suppose." Bet jabbed the canvas with blotches of almost-black green blobs, spoiling the forest landscape. "He won't be happy with you leaving."

"He'll just have to get over it," Malawi said and ambled to the stairs, taking them two at a time up to the main level of the house. Bet listened for her daughter's feet to cross the landing to Malcolm's office, but instead she heard the hardwood floor creak in the den and a burst of noise from the television.

Malawi's dismissal that day had hurt Bet, but she never spoke of it. They didn't always talk but Bet had enjoyed those moments when Mowie chose to sit with her over being with her father. Sometimes, Bet would sketch her daughter curled on the settee, bopping her head, listening through earbuds to some kind of music Bet found wretched on the ears, all thud, thud, thud with words she couldn't understand. Now, she regretted not making more of those times together, not going after her that day to convince her to stay near home, not hugging her more and revealing how much those moments in the studio had meant to Bet.

With her head resting on her daughter's cheek, Bet whispered the words now and they fell silent on Malawi's cold skin. "I always loved you as much as your daddy did. I should have made sure you knew."

5

The sheriff should have come to the hospital, Malcolm thought as he drove through sunny flat streets of Palm Beach County to the Sheriff's Office. The A/C blasted cold air on his face but didn't seem to have much of an effect; his eyeglasses slipped down his nose and sweat ran down his neck. Bet was curled away from him, her head cradled between the headrest and the passenger window. Occasionally, a groan rumbled out of her and rolled to the car floor. Malcolm kept his eyes on the road, glancing at the GPS poised on the dashboard, passing palm trees, low single family homes, and occasional shopping plazas. Finally he saw a squat sign announcing the Palm Beach County Sheriff's Office. He pulled into a visitor's parking space and helped Bet out of the car. Her grip was tight in his hand and she stumbled forward as if she'd had one glass of wine too many. Bet giggled like a little girl when she got drunk. Her eyes would sparkle and tiny dimples appeared in her cheeks. He loved her for that. But today she was not drunk. She was injured, stumbling from a blow he wasn't sure she would ever recover from. A blow that had hit him equally as hard in the gut, yet someone had to be coherent, ask questions, and discover what happened. The coroner would do an autopsy and only after that was completed and a report filed would Malawi be released to go home. Not Malawi, he thought. Her body. Her body would be released for shipment like a package. Malcolm pushed back the nausea with a deep breath.

Inside they waited at the reception desk until the sheriff came out to greet them. He was a short man with a large belly protruding over his belt and red cheeks. Malcolm thought, with the right beard, the man would make a great Santa Claus. His handshake was firm and his expression serious, a slight frown creased his forehead. He led them down a short hallway to his office. The space was small with piles of folders on the desk and a coffee pot in the corner next to the swivel chair that creaked as the sheriff sat down. He motioned for the Walkers to sit. Two large wooden-framed chairs with vinyl cushioning were positioned at forty-five-degree angles just in front of the desk, cut perhaps from the same wood.

Bet sat on the edge of the chair and stared at the floor.

"Mr. and Mrs. Walker, please accept my condolences on your loss." Malcolm was aware these words were likely ones the sheriff had said more times than he could probably count, but they fell flat on Malcolm's ears.

"You said it was just a shoulder injury," he said. "When you called the house, you said she'd been shot in the shoulder, not the chest."

"Yes. That was the information I had received at the time. Again, I'm sorry for your loss." He cleared his throat. "We have interviewed the owner of the home where Miss Walker was shot." Bet groaned and shifted in her seat. The sheriff continued. "The owner, Jeffrey Davies, said Miss Walker was snooping around his home just before two in the morning. He thought she was an intruder and shot in self-defense."

Malcolm stared at the sheriff, not comprehending the man's words. He didn't like his use of the word *snooping*. After a moment of silence, he leaned forward. "That doesn't make sense. What was threatening about my daughter? She's one-hundred-and-twenty-five pounds at most."

"Well, now, that's what Mr. Davies is saying."

The sheriff watched Malcolm who felt the thump of his heart in his throat and a headache beginning at his temples. "Who is this man, Davies?"

Again, the sheriff cleared his throat. "He's been living in Lake Worth all his life, a good hard-working man with no arrest record. He has no reason to lie."

"I'm not saying he's lying. It just doesn't make sense to me why he would be threatened by my daughter. Why would he shoot her?"

"What you have to understand, sir, is that Mr. Davies heard the door handle rattle and heard tapping on the front window."

Malcolm's dislike for the sheriff rose with the hairs on his neck and he resented the man's use of the word, *sir*, like he was patronizing Malcolm.

"Folks don't do that sort of thing in the middle of the night. Not in these parts. Mr. Davies was simply watching television when he heard suspicious activity outside his door."

Malcolm's breathing shortened as his anger expanded. "Suspicious activity? Since when was knocking on someone's door suspicious?" He shook his head. "Do we know why she was there?"

"Well, sir, that's what we're trying to figure out. We're investigating and will let you know what we find." The phone rang and the sheriff rested his hand on the receiver. "I need to take this." He picked up and asked the caller to hold on.

The sheriff stood up but Malcolm remained seated. "What was she shot with?"

"I'll make sure you get a copy of the report once it's completed."

"This Mr. Davies. Is he a white man?"

"What difference does his race make, Mr. Walker?"

"I want to know."

"It's irrelevant."

"Not to me. Is he white?"

"As it happens, yes, he's white, but that's—"

Malcolm stood up. "Has he been arrested?"

"Well, no, sir. He was well within his rights."

Malcolm leaned toward the sheriff, who also rose to meet his stare. "I want him arrested."

"Mr. Walker, I don't know how they do things in the nation's capital, but down here, we don't go arresting people for activity that's within the law. I'm sure you're aware of our Stand Your Ground Law—"

"I am well aware of it, Sheriff. But I'm having a hard time understanding why this man felt threatened by a young, unarmed woman. Now, you will arrest this man or I swear to God, I will call the U.S. Attorney's office to investigate this as a hate crime." Malcolm paused then said, "And it's Judge Walker."

Sheriff Wheeler's tongue created a momentary lump in his cheek and his lips pressed together. "Like I said, *Judge Walker*, we are continuing to investigate and if we see cause to make an arrest, we will. Now, if you don't mind." He sat back in his chair and began to speak into the phone, turning his back to the door.

Just home from the grocery store, Kenya refilled the shelves—frozen items first into the freezer, canned items on the lazy Susan, fresh vegetables and snacks in the pantry. She wanted to get this done before the kids got home from their respective play-dates. When the house-phone started ringing, she almost didn't answer, fearing a telemarketer. But the call was from her father, his voice soft and strained put her on alert. "Daddy, what's wrong?" A rush of sensations hurtled through her body, a tightening in her chest, her windpipe constricting, eyes blinking rapidly. "Daddy?"

"She didn't make it, Sweetheart. Your sister didn't make it."

Kenya contemplated what her father was telling her. "I don't understand," she said finally.

The line was silent and then she heard him clear his throat. "Sweetheart, Malawi is gone. She didn't survive …" His voice broke and the line again went quiet. Kenya's heart bumped in her throat. She clutched at her collarbone.

"But Mama said it was just a shoulder injury."

"Sweetheart, I'm sorry. She was shot twice. This man, he … she was in surgery, but didn't …" Kenya realized her father was crying and she froze, gripping the phone to her ear, her other hand fixed to her neck. Her sister had been shot twice. Finally, he said, "I'll have to call you back. When I can talk about what happened. I love you. I need to call Ghana. Take care of each other, okay."

"Is Mama okay?"

"Not really. She's ... Look, I'll call you back, okay? I love you, Sweetheart."

"Love you, too, Daddy," she said, but he had already hung up.

She sat on the edge of the couch and stared at the rug. Specks of dirt were scattered here and there. Everyone took off their shoes at the door. No dirt should be on the sitting room rug. She jumped up and dragged the vacuum cleaner from the closet, plugged it into the wall and violently shoved it back and forth across the rug, the noise reverberating through her head and tears streaming down her cheeks.

* * *

Her cell phone vibrated and her father's face brightened up the screen. Ghana had snapped the picture, catching him laughing at something she had said. His eyes, almost closed with laughter. She grabbed the phone. "Hi, Dad! Everything okay?"

"Ghan-Ghan, Sweetheart," he said softly into her ear and the hairs rose all over her body, a surge of energy shooting up her spine. He didn't have to say anything more. She knew. Her sister was gone.

"Oh my god! Daddy! Please. No no no." She wanted to know what happened, yet didn't want to know. Ryan stepped out of the kitchenette where he was making quesadillas for a late lunch and sat next to her, mouthing, "What happened?"

Ghana listened to her father stammer on. "She was in surgery, but ... Your mother ... she's a wreck." He paused. "I ... I just wanted you to know. I called Kenya already. I'll explain everything later. Listen to me now. You two need to take care of each other. You hear me, Ghan-Ghan?

You take care of each other. You hear me?"

"Yes. Yes, I hear you." Ghana was shaking, her arms and hands twitching uncontrollably.

"Okay, I gotta go. I love you, Sweetheart."

As soon as the phone went silent, she screamed at a pitch that hurt her throat. Ryan wrapped his arms around her, squeezing and she fought him but he held on until her body flopped in his arms like a soft toy. "She's gone." Her voice was hoarse and she pressed her face into Ryan's arm. "Li'l Sis. She's gone."

Moments later, her big sister's face appeared on her phone. Kenya: her only sister now. Despite her father's insistence, she couldn't bear to talk to her. Not yet. Ghana turned the phone over and curled back into Ryan's arms. He rocked her gently and she clung tighter not letting him move away.

7

Malcolm picked up the *USA Today* from the floor outside his hotel room door. It wasn't likely there was any news about Malawi there, so he took the elevator down and got a local paper from the mini market in the reception area. The lobby was bright, people were smiling, the weather was sunny outside. The clerk wished him a nice day. A nice day. He didn't respond, merely took the newspaper and left. Today was far from a nice day.

A story was on the lower right of the front page, "Palm Beach Resident Shoots Intruder." Malcolm began to seethe. How dare they say she was an intruder. As he headed back to his room, tension grew in his jaw and he rubbed at a headache beginning a slow beat on his temples. He was breathless when he closed the door behind him and sat down at the desk, adjusting his glasses on his nose and spreading the paper before him. Bet lay motionless in the bed, having taken three or four sleep aids the night before. Malcolm was glad for this reprieve from her tears and moaning.

A 27-year-old teacher from West Palm Beach was shot and killed in the early hours of Sunday morning by Jeffrey Davies, a long-time resident of Lake Worth, according to a police report. Malawi Walker, a math teacher at the West Palm Beach High School, was shot in the chest and shoulder on the 6000 block of Orange Drive. She died at Palm Beach County Hospital shortly before 8 A.M. on Sunday.

Good God, she died before we even got on the plane. Malcolm took a breath.

Davies said he heard noises outside his home at about 2 A.M. Someone rattled the door handle and knocked at the front window. "I thought someone was breaking in. We've had a rash of break-ins around here these past few weeks, and I wasn't about to let it happen to me," he said in a telephone interview. "I didn't mean to shoot no woman."

Walker's car was located half a block from Davies' home on Orange Drive, according to the police report. It appeared she had swerved and hit a light pole. The police report indicates that Walker's blood alcohol level was 0.5 and the accident was likely the result of intoxication.

"Bullshit!" Malcolm brought his fist down on the newspaper. "No way in hell my daughter's blood alcohol was that high." He read the last line of the story: *No arrest has been made.* "That bastard will pay for murdering my daughter."

He grabbed the car keys and paused before opening the door. Turned and sat on the bed beside Bet. "Honey? Honey, you awake?" Bet moaned and her body shifted under the blanket but her eyes remained closed. "I'm just going to run a quick errand." He ran his fingers over her short hair, the gray reappearing at the roots. "I'll be back soon."

He drove to the medical examiner's office, and paced back and forth in the small waiting room for the coroner. A stocky Asian man in a white coat approached him with his hand extended. "I'm Gene Kim. How can I help you?"

Malcolm gave a short firm handshake, then held the newspaper up and pointed at the story. "Tell me this is not accurate."

Gene Kim squinted at the story, politely asking to take the paper from Malcolm's hand. "May I?" Malcolm waited while the coroner read the piece. "Um, I don't think that is correct. We did find alcohol in her system, but I don't believe she was this intoxicated."

"Can I see the report?"

"You're the judge from D.C., right?"

"Yes."

"Come this way."

Gene Kim led Malcolm down a long corridor with bright fluorescent lighting. "I'm sorry for your loss," he said as they walked, their shoes tapping just out of sync on the vinyl floor. Malcolm felt flustered and said nothing, but appreciated the man's words. At the end of the corridor he turned left into an equally bright office. Kim flipped through a pile of folders and pulled one out with WALKER, MALAWI marked on it. He slipped out a typed page and glanced over it before saying, "Yes, I thought so. They made a mistake. It should say point zero-five. A considerable difference and below the legal limit here in Florida."

"What did he use?"

"The weapon? A four-ten gauge shotgun. What we call a backpacker. Hit her once in the right shoulder and once in the chest, just right of the sternum."

Malcolm winced and tried not to picture his daughter stumbling backwards, hitting the ground and struggling to breathe. She would have been in shock, he thought. He reached for the desk and gripped the edge of it.

"Do you want some water?"

Malcolm shook his head. "Can I get a copy of the report?"

Gene Kim handed him the typed page. "You can have this one. It's preliminary. The official report will be finalized later."

Malcolm folded it in half then a quarter. After a moment, he thanked the coroner for his help and headed back down the long bright corridor.

In the hotel room he called the newspaper and asked for the journalist who wrote the story. "I want a correction," he said. Ready to do battle, he was surprised at the amicable response from the reporter—a man, young-sounding—who apologized profusely and pointed out that the change had already been made online and a correction would appear in next day's newspaper. Malcolm hadn't thought about the online stratosphere and hoped the story hadn't gone beyond the local community. He didn't want his daughter all over the news.

He called the sheriff's office and talked to a deputy, having been told the sheriff was unavailable. The deputy told him that Jeffrey Davies had not yet been arrested.

Malcolm stared at the wall, considered all the people he had yet to call, and then dialed his colleague, Joe Willis, who probably had already heard the news from Malcolm's assistant, Cynthia. Joe could help recommend a Florida lawyer who could file a lawsuit against this man Davies.

8

Kenya studied the ceiling, a white expanse, gray in the dim light of the early morning, so calm and peaceful, not reflecting the turmoil that ensued every day below it. Sidney had stared at her for a long time when she told him Malawi was dead, and he cried as if she had been *his* sister. He's such a fake. Kenya took a deep breath. The therapist said to breathe when those angry feelings flared, and she could feel the anger rising again in her throat. He had tried to kiss her, comfort her and she'd held her breath as his arms enfolded her. Her body had been numb. The bewilderment on Charlene's and Junior's faces. The flow of tears choking Kenya so that all she could do was clutch her children to her body.

She and Malawi had never been especially close, not as close as Malawi had been to Ghana. But she should have called more often and made an effort to spend time with her. Malawi had been such a spoiled child that it riled Kenya to see her father smothering the little girl in a way he had never done with Kenya. Jealousy clouded Kenya for most of Malawi's life, and now the guilt coiled through her body like another set of veins.

Sidney stirred next to her, and she wondered when she'd feel okay with him again. He had cheated on her twice that she knew for sure. The first time was several years ago with an employee who eventually left the company. He promised then he would never stray again. But he had. Awhile back, a flashing icon caught her eye as she passed by his laptop, sitting open on the dining-room table for anyone to see. She wasn't sure now why she had stopped—she'd never been in the habit of checking his laptop and phone—but the blinking had caught her attention. A bright yellow chat box winking at her, revealing a conversation between him and a woman, identified as AfricanQueen. The words were explicit and sexual; the woman ended by saying, "cant wait to c u again." Again. Kenya read and reread the text as the blood drained to her feet, and whatever food had been in her stomach began to curdle. She'd hoped it was a joke. When he came back from the bathroom, she was still standing by the laptop and he stopped a few feet from her. "Baby," he'd said, his body softening, his feet moving cautiously toward her. He knew. "It's not what you think," he'd said. "It's just sexual banter to pass the time when I'm away. It's nothing."

Without a word she walked away unable to express the rising rage, wondering why he needed to talk sex with some other woman, yet knowing the answer.

He'd promised to stop, but recently she'd found a pair of silk panties in his suitcase from a business trip to Miami. Clearly, the online banter had evolved into a real-life repartee. The humiliation strangled her and she demanded he move out to give her time to think things through. He'd spent two weeks with his brother in Falls Church and called her every day. They met for lunch one day to talk and he confessed that he had, in fact, slept with the woman, this "AfricanQueen," a woman he said he'd met in an airport; they'd slept together twice. Just twice, he said. Just.

"I disrespected you and our union," he'd said, his eyes filling with tears. "I'm sorry," he said. "Truly," he said. "Please don't let this stupid mistake end what we have," he said. "Please take me back." He said. He said. He had kept saying all these words that made Kenya weary. But she forgave him. Again. The uncertainty of her decision still gnawed at her bones.

Kenya slid out of bed. She unwrapped her hair and pulled it back in a ponytail, dressed in her active wear, tied her sneakers firmly, and headed out.

In the weeks since her discovery, he had been trying, but in all honesty, the thrill of sex with him had faded after the children were born. And now, his infidelity had caused her to dry up completely. He rubbed between her legs as if a genie would appear, rushing her through the motions. She used to moan to make him think she enjoyed what he was doing, but the last time, she practically held her breath until it was over. All she could think about was how he had kissed and touched this AfricanQueen—what a ridiculous name—if he'd prodded and rubbed with the same urgency or if he'd taken his time the way he used to do when they were first married.

Outside, she walked briskly at first, feeling the warm air on her skin. Another hot day in store. She preferred springtime over summer, but though it was early June, blossoms still held on to their trees, and the azaleas and rhododendrons offered beautiful splashes of color as she picked up speed and ran through the neighborhood. Manicured lawns. Expensive vehicles behind two-car garages. No sidewalks. She ran faster and faster along the road until she stopped, doubled over, breathless. This was the life she assumed would be hers, the life she deserved, but what did anyone deserve? Not death. Not death at twenty-seven by some maniac. Kenya fought back tears. Not here. Not on the street where anyone might see. She adjusted her ponytail, stretched her hamstrings and her calves then took off, heading back home.

Sidney was in the kitchen making coffee.

"Good morning, Babe." He peered at her as if assessing her

mood. "How are you?"

"I'm fine," Kenya said with a forced smile. She didn't want his sympathy. Everything would be normal. She wanted everything and everyone to carry on as normal. That was the best thing to do. Keeping to her routine, she prepared cereal, mini muffins and orange juice for the kids. She sprinted upstairs and yelled into their rooms for them to get up. Junior and Charlene were in their last two weeks of school. They were sleepy and, like most mornings, slow to get ready. Finally, they appeared at the breakfast bar. Junior gulped down his food and Charlene picked at the muffins. Kenya didn't know how to tell them her sister had been shot by a white man (she'd told them it was a car accident), didn't know how to explain their charmed life wasn't immune to the dark side of the world.

"Chop, chop," she said, smacking her hands together. She got the kids into the Mercedes. As the oldest, Junior sat in the front. He was stocky and Kenya worried about his weight. Though his father was fairly slender, Sidney's mother was obese and Kenya feared Junior had inherited her mother-in-law's genes. She would never use this word *obese* in front of Sidney or his mother, but Kenya was always astounded by the size of his mother's backside, which seemed to have a life all its own, swaying casually even when the woman was standing stock still.

Kenya backed out of the garage and collected two more girls: Lilian from Tracy's house around the corner and Kesha from Christine's the next street over. Kenya took them in the mornings, and Christine and Tracy took turns bringing the kids home after school. The three of them—Charlene, Kesha and Lilian, who was a year older than the other two—sat sleepily in their smart school uniforms, staring out at the passing houses, an occasional giggle erupting from them. Kenya eyed her daughter in the rear-view mirror. "Everyone okay back there? Charlie?"

Charlene nodded without taking her eyes from the window. Such a quiet, thoughtful girl, Kenya thought. Too shy, though Kenya wasn't sure how to get her daughter to be more outgoing. She fell into the stop-and-start line of cars as parents dropped their kids at the school's entrance and noticed up ahead, Maxine Bailey had a brand-new Lexus. She wondered if it was time to get a new vehicle herself. When they reached the drop-off point, everyone tumbled out, rocking the car slightly as they slammed the doors closed. She watched Junior immediately separate from the girls, finding and giving a fist bump to one of his friends. They laughed and disappeared inside. The girls huddled together, heads close, perhaps whispering about something they hadn't wanted to share in the car. Sadness and panic flooded Kenya as her children disappeared from view. Here one moment, gone the next. She tried to remember when she last saw Malawi. Christmastime, she thought. They had said little to one another. Kenya had admired her new hairstyle, braids in a bob that curled into her chin.

"Don't you look good," she'd said giving her sister a loose hug. Malawi had come bustling in with Daddy, who had picked her up from the airport. Her bags were strewn across the foyer of their parents' home and Kenya wondered if she was coming back for good with so much luggage. Malawi responded with a grin and a quiet thank you, touching the tips of the braids with her fingers. They chatted a little about her new job and how much she was enjoying Florida, but not much else. A pang of regret filled Kenya as she passed plush lawns and large deciduous trees in the throes of summer green. She struggled to recall when she had last invited her sister to her home. Must have been last year for the annual

Fourth of July cookout she and Sidney had hosted. Kenya pulled into her driveway and remembered her little sister arriving to the cookout alone. She had welcomed her but had been so caught up on being host that Sidney had been the one who kept her company, talking with her on the patio. Malawi stayed late and helped clean up, yet even then, Kenya had spent little time talking with her. She should have been a better sister to Malawi. Over the years, she had blamed the nine-year gap between them for their disconnection. Still, that wasn't a good reason.

Inside the house, Kenya cleaned up the kitchen and gathered dirty clothes for laundry. She separated and organized each item into color and textures, washing light colors together before moving to dark, and delicates before heavier fabrics. She called her father to make sure he and her mother were okay. He was subdued on the call but talked about what happened, anger tinging each word. Malawi had run off the road and hit a light pole—there was nothing to indicate what caused her to swerve. She had gone to a nearby home for help and the owner shot her without question.

"Didn't even ask what she was doing or what she needed," he said. "Son-of-a-bitch just shot her in the chest."

Kenya was speechless, the weight of his words pressing on her shoulders. "My God," she said, finally. "Whatever I can do, Daddy. Just let me know how I can help."

"Of course, Sweetheart." He ended the call saying he would ring again soon. She sat for a long time thinking about her sister seeking help and getting killed as a result. It was a news story that happened to other people, not to the Walker family, blessed and honored in their community. They gave to charity. They volunteered. They served the public as teachers and lawyers. They raised good, productive citizens. They didn't get shot.

Kenya dialed Ghana's number and listened to her voice-mail, but left no message. She wandered through the house checking for dirt and dust then decided to organize her bedroom closet. Her shoes had gotten terribly out of order and there were likely several pairs she could donate to charity. Sitting on her knees, she dragged the ones from the floor out of the closet and made several piles on the rug by the dresser—slingbacks, wedges, peep toes, flats. A sickly feeling swelled in her stomach as she worked. She hadn't believed that Malawi had really been hurt. Tears came sharp and sudden and Kenya crumpled into a ball on the floor.

9

Ghana lifted the lid of the warming pan, dipped the wooden draining spoon into the steaming water, and scooped out two medium-sized basalt stones. She cooled them slightly in a bowl of cold water then covered them in oil. Her client, a white middle-aged woman, laid face down on the table but kept adjusting her position, shifting her hips, then her arms, then her feet.

"Are you comfortable?" Ghana asked.

The woman lifted her head and said, "Yes."

This was her fourth and last client of the day. She slid the stones across the woman's back and immediately stopped when the woman's body jerked.

"Too hot?"

"No, it's fine."

Ghana resumed, feeling for areas of tension. She slid one stone around the shoulder, pressing into knotted muscle, but as if pulled by an invisible energy, the stone slipped from her hand to the floor, landing with a disturbing thud. Her client's body stiffened and Ghana whispered an apology, nudging the stone aside with her foot. Reaching for another, she touched the water and felt the tips of her fingers burn. With a deep breath, she tried again, this time with the spoon. Her boss had urged her to stay at home, but Ghana needed the sanctuary of the massage room, the focused movement, the connection with another without conversation or revelation, the simple action of healing. Yet she couldn't stop her mind from wandering through memories of her sister. Her laugh. Her passion for shoes, purses, and all things Idris Elba, all day, every day. Ghana's mind drifted to last night's dream, where she was sitting with Malawi on a beach somewhere tropical. Both sitting cross-legged on the sand looking out at the ocean complaining about the heat, which was odd because they both loved the sunshine. That's why Malawi had moved to Florida. And to get away from some guy she had met. Ghana wasn't to tell anyone that part. Malawi didn't want Mama or Kenya asking questions, digging up her feelings about the mystery man.

"I love him so much, but …" Malawi had paused then and Ghana felt chills. "But he's married." She revealed this news a month before she moved to Florida as they sat drinking tea in a cafe on Capitol Hill. They had met at Eastern Market one Saturday morning and giggled their way through the vendors, then wandered along the uneven, narrow sidewalk to Pennsylvania Avenue and settled at a table in the back, treating themselves to sweet pastries.

"Who is he?" Ghana asked.

Malawi talked in that slow thoughtful way she had when sharing a secret. And she had shared many with Ghana, who had been her little sister's confidante on just about everything.

From the time she came to Ghana when her menstrual period first began to when she received sex ed in school—Malawi had huddled in bed with Ghana, asking question after question about getting pregnant and what sex was like. "It's different for everyone," Ghana told her. "But you have to be sure you're with someone you care about, because if you're not, it doesn't feel as good. It's all tied to what you feel inside yourself. For women, anyway. I don't know what boys feel when they have sex. I do know that's what motivates them when it comes to girls, though." Malawi soaked in every word, wide eyed and giggling. Sometimes Malawi shared much more than Ghana wanted to know—she knew when Malawi first kissed a boy in middle school, when she fell in love with a different boy in high school, when they had sex for the first time, and when that same boy broke her heart, dumping her just before graduation because he wanted to be free in college. Ghana always felt protective, yet encouraged Li'l Sis to express herself and explore the world in all its light and darkness. Still, she hadn't needed to know *every* detail. Although now, Ghana wanted to crystallize those secrets, those intimate confessions of love and betrayal, and cherish them forever.

When her sister revealed she was in love with a married man, Ghana made no judgment though silently worried about where it would lead.

"I don't really wanna talk about him," Malawi said, "but he's, like, all I can think about."

Ghana smiled. She knew that feeling all too well. "How long's it been?"

Malawi took a leisurely sip of her tea. "Kinda off and on for, like, three months. I was just, like, I can't do this anymore. I feel so guilty, but, like, I just can't stop myself." She shook her head. "I need to get away."

The client jerked up and yelled, "You just burned me!" The fresh hot stone hit the floor and Ghana checked the skin where she'd touched the client, relieved there was no mark, only a fading flush of redness from the stone's heat.

"Sorry about that," Ghana said as the woman settled back on the table. She got fresh stones and waited a little longer for them to cool, but the woman rose onto her elbows and said, "Why don't you just do a regular massage. I don't like these hot stones." Ghana reined in a surprising urge to scream at the woman, and said, "Of course." She apologized that the hot stone massage wasn't to her liking and felt the ache of tension in her own shoulders. She finished the session by massaging the woman's skull. Softly, she asked her client to take her time getting up, and was relieved that it was time to go home, maybe to bed.

That evening, her father called, apologizing for not calling back sooner. But she understood. In a soft and shaky voice, he explained that Malawi had been shot twice and Ghana began to sob. She thought about recent headline news of black men who had been murdered at gunpoint by police or vigilantes. Riots in cities across the country erupting because yet another young black man had been shot by police.

"Was he white?" She whispered the question, almost afraid to say it aloud.

His response was just as quiet, "Yes."

She didn't like this feeling, this slow, thick gurgling through her insides, like sour milk on her stomach. Her sister was not a statistic. She would not be another headline. This was not happening.

"What do we do, Dad?"

The phone was silent for several heartbeats, then he said, "I don't know, yet."

10

Bet heard Malcolm tell her he loved her. She wanted to respond but couldn't make her body move to face him. She couldn't make her lips form any words. She laid under the covers, heavy with an unbearable sadness, unsure of the time or even the day, as if caught in a sudden avalanche of amber now solid. Her baby girl had been murdered. Murdered. Her baby girl. The last child, who was supposed to be a boy.

She remembered being violently sick those initial weeks with her first pregnancy. Couldn't keep food down, and just looking at meat made her queasy. (If they hadn't conceived during their honeymoon, it must have been soon after they returned.) Once the sickness passed, she enjoyed being pregnant, watching her body change, feeling the initial flutterings of life and then the full-blown somersaults of a child at six, seven, eight months. Malcolm's kiss on her naked belly, his hands cradling her like a basketball and the voluminous joy in his eyes, she savored every moment. Convinced a boy frolicked in her, Malcolm was ready with the name Sudan.

In all seriousness he said, "All our children will have names of countries on the African continent to connect them back to the motherland, the birthplace of humanity. And our first born will be named Sudan."

"What if we have a girl?"

He thought for a moment, as he stood by the window in the newly-painted baby's room.

"We'll call her *Ethiopia*."

"What kind of a name is that?" she asked, horrified.

"It's our homeland. It's where life began."

Sitting in the bentwood rocking chair, she shook her head vigorously. "No, I am not naming my child Ethiopia. I get the sentiment, but that's not happening."

He hurried out of the baby's room and returned with a map of Africa, unfurled it on the changing table and began reciting countries he thought would make a good name. When he said Kenya, Bet felt a tingle run through her that seemed to indicate *Kenya* was the right one. At that moment, she knew she was having a girl. Kenya Marie. The middle name honored Bet's mother.

Malcolm, of course, adored his first-born, but desperately wanted a boy. Four years passed before she felt the stirring of a new life inside her, and again, Malcolm insisted she was pregnant with a boy.

"You know, Sudan could work for a girl, too," he said. Bet wrinkled her nose. She wasn't thrilled about the name, even for a boy. In what was becoming a tradition, he ran through a list of countries on the African continent. Chills confirmed *Ghana* was the right name and Bet knew this was another girl—Ghana Caroline, to honor his mother. His disappointment was slight, though Bet could see it in his eyes.

"One more," he pleaded. Two was enough for Bet. She had dreams of art school, of getting a master's degree in art history and perhaps teaching at the college level. She had the potential. That's what the instructor at the community college had said. Before Ghana, Bet took an oil painting class and the instructor asked if she had thought about a graduate degree in Art. Blushing, she nodded, "Why, yes. That's my dream." Before marrying, she had taught Art at a private middle school and fantasized about continuing her career once her daughters were in their teens. With a third child, however, her chances of getting back to school would evaporate. But that was her role. To raise the children, be wife to the hotshot attorney on a fast track to becoming a judge.

Kenya was almost nine and Ghana was four when Bet got pregnant for a third time. Convinced the baby was a boy, Malcolm didn't look for any other name besides Sudan. When a baby girl was pronounced, she remained nameless for three days until Malcolm finally pulled out the map—Bet adamantly refused to name the child Sudan.

"Why can't we give her a regular girl's name?" Bet asked, already worn out from caring for two children.

"That would ruin it," he said. "All the children have names from the continent. Why stop now?"

There were no chills or any sign at all with any name he shouted out. He held the baby in his arms and repeated a name two or three times, staring into the baby's face while Bet struggled to keep Ghana from running out of the room. He said *Malawi* and nodded in confirmation, looking at Bet with an expectant expression. "Yeah? Malawi Elizabeth, after you."

Bet shrugged. She was tired and frustrated, unconvinced a third child was the right thing for her. As with each baby, he raised Malawi above his head and said her name three times, pronouncing a future of prosperity, knowledge, wisdom and love, a ritual he adapted from a book on African traditions.

Malawi cried all the time, quieting only when her daddy held her. Bet bounced the child a little too roughly after checking her diaper, feeding her, and singing to no avail, finally plopping her into the crib where she continued to wail. And in the next room, Ghana alternated between running in circles and bouncing on her bed, until Kenya came home from school. Bet hid in the bathroom, listening to Kenya shouting through the locked door, "Mama, what do I do? Mowie won't stop crying. I gave Ghana a cookie. Is that okay? Mama?"

She had never imagined herself as TV's June Cleaver, but struggled to understand her inability to cope. Malcolm, on the other hand, seemed to thrive. Bet resented his relationship with all his daughters. They ran to him, laughed and played with him, loved him. Malawi, in particular, loved him in a way she never loved Bet. He doted on her. Kisses and cuddles all the time. There was nothing she could do that upset him. Nothing she wanted he wouldn't get; all the while, a bitterness settled in Bet's throat that she couldn't, or wouldn't, clear. For so long it choked her and now, the loss of her third child was like a concrete block on her chest, crushing her into silence. What she would give to go back, do it over again and be a better mother. Make the most of each moment.

Malcolm nudged her shoulder and told her it was getting late. "Let's get up and get some breakfast. C'mon, Bet. We should go to Malawi's apartment today. See what needs to be done."

Bet kept her eyes closed. She didn't want to get up. Didn't want to do anything, least of all go through Malawi's belongings.

* * *

Bet sat across from Malcolm at breakfast in the hotel's restaurant, though she wasn't eating. The vegetable omelet and wheat toast Malcolm had ordered sat uneaten on the plate before her. Instead, Bet stared blankly at some distant point to her right.

"Bet," he said, trying to contain his irritation. "Elizabeth!"

She looked at him with that same empty expression she'd held since … since identifying their daughter.

"Elizabeth. Honey. Please eat something. You need to eat."

Her eyes drifted away to where they had been. After a moment she took a sip of tea. Malcolm pressed his lips together and held in anything that would indicate what he was feeling. Something between utter frustration, sadness and impatience. A flash of Malawi, or what had once been Malawi, laying on the table in the hospital morgue stabbed him and he shook it away.

"Okay, look, we need to get her car from the towing company and then get to her apartment and see what needs to be done there. We'll need to figure out what to do about that. All her things." They need to check on the place, he thought, and eventually hire someone to clean and move things out. "We'll need to make funeral arrangements." He rubbed his forehead, stretching the skin toward his temple. "Can you do that, Bet? Can you call the funeral home? I'll handle the car and the apartment, but I need you to handle the funeral. Bet?"

She made no response.

The nurse had given him a plastic bag of items Malawi had when the ambulance brought her in to the hospital: her bloody clothes, a cell phone and keys to her car and apartment. He cringed to think he didn't know her address; she had told him, but he left it to Bet to record such things. She was the keeper of all information on the girls: clothing sizes, addresses, details on their significant others. Phone numbers he had because each girl programmed them into his phone. Bet couldn't remember the street name when he asked for Malawi's address—it was in her smartphone but she was slow to give him the passcode.

"Then we'll need to get to the airport," he said. "I need to get back to work."

Bet glanced at him then, a look of scorn. He wasn't supposed to want to go back to work. But he had to. He'd go mad otherwise.

At the towing company, Malcolm assessed his daughter's car, a 2005 Toyota Camry. Drivable, but not worth repairing. He paid the balance due for towing from the accident site and got a discount for "selling" the car back as scrap—he promised to find the title and get it back to the towing company as soon as possible. He retrieved Malawi's purse, two pairs of dress shoes, a gym bag, a rain jacket and miscellaneous papers from the Camry. His daughter's things. Normally he would think nothing of these items, but now, they were weighted by what her life had been. A life he didn't really know much about. He bundled everything into the gym bag and carefully slid the zipper closed.

In the rental car, he programmed Malawi's address into the GPS and they found the apartment near downtown West Palm Beach with no trouble. It was a quaint garden apartment, the building a muted pink, and Malcolm remembered her on the phone, her excitement palpable through the line.

"I live in a pink house, Daddy. You have to come visit. Promise you will."

"I promise," he had said chuckling, her joy infectious. He had planned to fly down months ago but kept putting it off because of work.

A gecko scurried along the outer wall as he unlocked the front door, which opened into a spacious living room with a compact kitchenette to the left. Bet shuffled in behind him and made a short gasping sound then fell silent. A short hallway ahead of them led to a bedroom and bathroom. Malcolm wandered aimlessly through the space—Malawi's home for just one school year. A few pots and dishes soaked in the sink. Clothes were strewn around the bedroom and the bed was unmade, everything left as if she would walk in at any moment.

Much to his surprise, Bet began to clean up, sorting magazines into a neat pile then tackling the dishes in the sink. She ran water until hot, plugged in the sink and squeezed a generous amount of liquid soap. Her movements were determined and brisk but gradually became slower and slower until she abandoned the dishes and headed to the bedroom. Malcolm followed, afraid of the emotional slide his wife was making to somewhere dark, yet unsure how to stop it. She picked up a blouse from the bed and held it to her face, inhaling deeply. Malcolm stepped back. He didn't want to smell his daughter's scent, knowing that if he did, he would lose all control. Bet picked up a T-shirt and repeated the action, holding both items of clothing to her face. Her sobs came softly and transformed into a deep, dark moan and she fell forward, curling into a ball in the midst of Malawi's unmade bed.

Malcolm placed a hand on her shoulder. "It's okay," he said, thinking it was okay for her to cry, that she didn't need to clean up, they could contact a cleaning service, but she jerked away, scrambling to the other side of the bed and snapped at him: "It's not okay." Kneeling, she clung to the clothing in her hands and yelled, "You have no idea. No idea at all. You go about like nothing has happened. She's dead, Malcolm. Our baby girl is dead and you don't care." Bet threw the T-shirt and the blouse to the floor and rushed past him, through the living room and out the door, back to the safety of the rental car.

Malcolm followed as far as the living room. His shoulders

slumped and he stood hopelessly in the empty apartment trying to accept that his baby girl was never coming back.

* * *

The flight home was a blur. Bet dragged herself up the dark stairs to their bedroom. All she wanted to do was sleep. Malcolm flipped on a light that burned her eyes. He was talking about the funeral arrangements.

"Call Sully in the morning," he said.

Sully of Sullivan's Funeral Home. Sully's wife, Joy, always wore the prettiest suits. But Bet didn't want to call the funeral home and talk about burying her daughter. "I'm not calling them," she screamed, then slammed the bedroom door behind her. Hysteria lived in her throat, in her head and burst out of her mouth at every opportunity.

The door opened instantly, and Malcolm stood, a dark silhouette in the threshold. "I have to get back to work in the morning," he said with that self-important tone. The Honorable Judge Walker, so very important master of his domain, she thought. She almost spit at him.

"How can you just go back to work, as if everything is normal? As if we were just gone for a few days' vacation at the beach?" She glowered at him, but he said nothing. "You are heartless, Malcolm Walker. You always bury yourself in work when things get tough. Not this time! This time it's our daughter."

He narrowed his eyes at her and shook his head, then turned and walked out of the room. Like he always did. Walked away at the slightest hint of discord. He wouldn't stay and talk, face the truth. She screamed after him, "You're a piece of shit, Malcolm Walker. The honorable piece of shit." Who didn't feel anything. Not ever.

They had been having sex when Malawi was dying. Had spent the day celebrating their thirty-seventh anniversary. They had made no special plans, ate breakfast in bed, and later, walked along one of the trails at Great Falls. And in the evening, Malcolm had looked at her with an interest that stirred a flurry of sensation in her chest and stomach. A rush of enthusiasm engulfed her as she crawled across the bed, pausing briefly to be sure she was interpreting his expression correctly—it had been so long. Then she leaned into him and kissed his open mouth. Slow to respond, his hands fumbled beneath her silk nightgown, exploring the lumps and lines of her hips, her waist. Gone were the taut muscles and tight skin of her youth, replaced by the sagging lumps of age. His large hands gripped her back, pulling her closer. She'd almost forgotten the strength of his touch, and the thrill of it. In recent years, their relationship had slumped like a forgotten cushion in a room rarely used. Talking only when needed. Touching as a practical matter. Malcolm's work consuming his days, and most of his nights. Existing, like brother and sister in the same house, the same bed. And for an evening, she thought their world had shifted. And it had. Just not in the direction she had desired.

Bet rushed into the bathroom and made it just in time to vomit into the toilet. Nothing but bile. She settled on the floor and leaned against the bath tub convinced she was dying. "Take me, God. Take me and bring Malawi back." She had taken several over-the-counter sleep aids and had slept for several hours but woke with a dull ache in her shoulder and nausea in her stomach. "Take as needed," the label read. She considered taking all the pills at once, certain that God was punishing her for not being a better mother. Her throat was dry. She dragged herself up to standing and ran cold water into the sink, cupping her hand and lapping from her palm. She had eaten little in the last few days, and whatever she ate came back up. On the flight home, Malcolm had suggested a visit to the doctor, but Bet couldn't get herself motivated to go anywhere.

She felt again the sting of entering Malawi's apartment. Her daughter's flowery fragrance on her clothes and her presence in every room. She had wanted to be strong, to tidy up, gather and organize Malawi's things, perhaps take some items home and tag what should be shipped and what should be thrown away or donated. But then she couldn't do it. She just wanted her daughter back.

In the distance, she heard the house phone ringing; Danita's voice leaving another message about the upcoming fundraiser for the Arts Foundation. Danita had left four messages, asking if Bet had found a location, as if that was of any importance now. Who cared about the Arts Foundation anymore.

She grabbed a washcloth hanging on the shower door. She sniffed it, then smelling nothing sour, rinsed the cloth in warm water, wiped it over her face and staggered back to bed, burying herself entirely under the covers.

All these years being faithful to the church, and now this. And as for Malcolm. She couldn't deal with his "life goes on" philosophy, his almost obsessive need to maintain control. Going about his business as if it were a mere acquaintance who had died. He couldn't just continue on as he always did, not when it was his daughter.

The phone rang again, loud at the side of the bed. Bet curled into a ball and pulled the covers over her ears. She wished she was like him. Like she didn't feel anything, at all.

11

Malcolm gazed at his mother who stood beside her dining table, holding her glasses in her hand although they were strung around her neck. She chewed the inside of her mouth as if contemplating something, preparing to speak, but when she looked at him she simply shook her head. No words. There were no words, he thought. They had shed tears together when he called her with the news, quiet sobs; her soothing words of comfort stopped him from unraveling. Seeing her now, the first morning back from Florida, he imagined himself a child again, running through her house, the home he grew up in, oblivious to the chaos erupting around the world. When the concept of death and destruction didn't yet exist in his mind.

Finally, she said, "How are you holding up?"

He jerked his shoulders.

"Okay," she said, turning toward the kitchen. "Let's get some coffee. Have you had breakfast?"

He didn't want coffee but he'd stay because this wasn't so much for him. It was her way of feeling like she was doing something. Being productive, something to focus on. She had experienced the death of her husband. Ten years ago now. She had been in this emotional space before.

"You have to keep pushing forward," she had said the night his father passed away. They sat vigil in the hospital for two days after his father collapsed from a sudden heart attack. Malcolm had been peeing when his father died. He had been given bypass surgery, but a hidden arterial clot revealed itself and he was gone before Malcolm got back from the bathroom. He had stepped away, took just a few steps down the hall, and was gone less than five minutes. The worst five minutes of his life. Malcolm had cried uncontrollably, yet his mother comforted him as if she hadn't just lost the love of her life. That's what his parents' relationship had been: the love of a lifetime. She said it often. "He's the love of my life." Malcolm admired that about his parents, their absolute dedication to each other. Who's to say if there had been dalliances in the marriage. They had stuck through almost sixty years together remaining, more than anything else, friends.

He watched her now, busying herself in her kitchen. At eighty-two years young, she was majestic. Willowy, straightened short white hair framing a slender face with light brown eyes that almost blended into her eyelids. He wanted to take her hand and wrap his arms around her. Stop her movements. Slow her down. Let her grieve. But he wouldn't. She would shoo him away. "Don't be silly," she'd say and swat at him like a child underfoot. She would make no great display of grieving because what was life without death? Life must go on, she said, or all is lost. So he would face each day with the strength he admired in his mother. He would be strong for his family, because that was his role. He was the father. The man. And he would grieve alone.

* * *

Sitting at his desk, Malcolm read the same sentence several times. A young man—a teenager—had been charged with possession and distribution of cocaine. A young black man. He sighed, removed his glasses and rubbed at the bridge of his nose. Another young black man brought in on drug charges. When will it end?

62

The door to his chambers opened and his friend and colleague Joe Willis stood in the doorway, his face distraught, asking without words, if Malcolm was okay. Malcolm's chest tightened and he nodded, sliding his glasses back onto his face. Joe came forward and Malcolm rose to receive a tight embrace.

"Brother—" The word came as a whisper from Joe's lips. "I just saw it on the news."

"It's on the news?" Malcolm's throat constricted. He leaned against his desk. "National news?"

"Yeah. They're talking about Trayvon Martin and how this is another senseless shooting of an African American. The Black Lives Matter folks are all over it."

Malcolm couldn't speak. He didn't want his daughter to become a headline, didn't want the media intrusion on his family. Cynthia appeared at the door. "Sorry to interrupt, but I'm getting call after call from news outlets asking to talk to you. I've just been telling them you're not available."

"Brother, you need Teddy on this one," Joe said. "You want me to call him?"

Malcolm looked from Joe to Cynthia and back to Joe. "Jesus." Teddy Livingston—the man who had betrayed his friendship by sleeping with Bet—was the last person he wanted in his life right now. "No, I'll call him." But Joe was right. Teddy, Malcolm and Joe had gone to law school at American University together, and despite being an asshole, Teddy was now one of the premier public relations guys in the District. Anybody who was anybody called James "Teddy" Livingston when they had a public crisis. Even if he was an asshole.

"Cynthia, can you get him on the line for me?"

She nodded and closed the door behind her. Malcolm leaned back in his chair. Joe took a seat opposite and waited several moments then said, "You need to take a leave of absence."

"No." Malcolm swallowed a lump in his throat. "No, I'm fine. I'd rather be here. I can't be at home right now."

"How's Bet?"

Malcolm shook his head. "She's …" He could feel himself begin to gasp. Then the phone rang and it was Cynthia. She had Teddy on the line.

"I'll leave you to talk," Joe said, "but let me know if you need anything. I'm waiting to hear back from a friend of mine in Florida who may be willing to take on your case. We'll talk later, okay?"

Malcolm nodded and took a deep breath.

"My man, it's been a long time." Teddy's voice was subdued. "I was thinking about calling you. I saw the news, but I didn't know if you … if …" He fell silent.

Malcolm's throat was closing again. He wanted to shut his eyes and make everything stop. Of all people. Of all situations. That cheating motherfucker would be the one to help Malcolm through this. He took another breath. Time to put the past in the past.

"Looks like I'm gonna need your expertise on this one."

"Look. Stay there and I'll come to you. I got an eleven o'clock, but I'll cancel it. That's no problem. It's best we talk in person."

Malcolm stared at his desk, the papers and folders blurred, and he closed his eyes.

12

Kenya pulled up behind her mother's car in the driveway of her parent's red brick Crestwood home. Her mother wasn't answering the phone. Kenya had called twice this morning with no answer.

The massive chestnut tree stood guard, as it always had, at the driveway's entrance. Two gray squirrels chased each other up the trunk and disappeared into the branches above. The house sat snugly on a quiet cul-de-sac backing up to Rock Creek Park, surrounded by trees and shrubbery. A fairly modest home compared to many in the neighborhood. Years ago it was a haven for upper-class black families. Today it was more diverse. She scanned the house, judging, looking for signs of age. The stone driveway was cracked where it met the road and needed repair, but the rest was in good shape. The white columns on the front porch could use some paint. A family project before winter, she thought. That, and clearing out the garage so her parents could park both cars inside.

Kenya let herself in. Kitty came running and rubbed herself against Kenya's shins. She gave a brief scratch to the cat's head.

"Mama? Mama, you home?" She peeked into the sitting room then walked through the kitchen to the den and through the dining room. The door to her father's office was closed, but the chance her mother was in there was slim to none. She called down to the studio in the basement; still no answer.

As she headed upstairs, panic rushed through her chest and she knocked rapidly on her parents' bedroom door before pushing it open. "Mama?" A lump lay under the bedspread. "Mama, is that you?" The mound made no movement and Kenya settled on the bed next to it, tugging at the covers to reveal her mother's head. Alarmed, Kenya shoved her mother's shoulder.

Bet shrugged her away. "Leave me alone. I'm trying to rest."

The air filled with the hot smell of sweat and the odor of a day or two without washing. Her mother wore a pink, short-sleeved cotton nightgown. Her short hair stuck up in small tufts and her face appeared to have thinned; dark shadows lingered beneath her eyes.

"Mama, please. Let's get you up. Get you washed." Kenya tugged lightly on her mother's arm.

"Go home, Kennie. Leave me alone."

Kenya squeezed her mother's forearm, pleading for her to move. Bet's arm snapped up surprisingly quickly from beneath Kenya's palm and back-handed Kenya's face. Stunned, Kenya jumped up and backed away, fingering the sting in her cheek as her mother curled back under the covers. Nibbling the skin around her nails, she stared at the lump that was her mother. She wasn't sure what she had expected. Solace. Connection. The comfort of her mother, uniting in the loss of Malawi. Sharing memories, and maybe tears. As her romantic notion evaporated, her mother's state of disarray confused her. Mama was always so particular about her appearance. She had weekly hair and nail appointments. Kenya considered calling her father, but decided against bothering him at work. Instead she headed downstairs to the kitchen. Maybe some food would help. A few dishes were piled in the sink and something sticky was on the floor. She found a cloth and wiped it clean, making a note to find out if the weekly housekeeper could schedule an additional visit.

Kenya rummaged through the cabinets searching for something quick and easy to prepare, and pulled a can of chicken soup off the shelf.

She heated it on the stove and found a sleeve of crackers in the pantry, then took the meal up on a tray with a glass of water, a spoon and a cloth napkin.

"Here, Mama, I made you some soup. Chicken." She sat on the edge of the bed, resting the tray on her lap. "You always say that's the most healing soup there is."

Bet refused, pressing her face into the pillow like a child. Kenya closed her eyes and pinched the bridge of her nose. "Please, Mama." Her mother kept her head stuck to the pillow. Placing the tray on the far side of the bed, Kenya sidled closer to her mother. "Maybe we could take a walk outside?" she said. "It's beautiful out. You need to get your blood circulating."

Bet lifted her head, her eyes wide and screamed, "Just. Leave. Me. Alone," pausing between each word as if Kenya didn't understand English. She continued to glare, silently daring her daughter to say another word. A mixture of anger and frustration rose in Kenya's chest, shortening her breath, and for a second she wanted to smack her mother's face. Shocked at her own reaction, Kenya backed away from the bed and rushed out. Downstairs, she stood in the kitchen, hands pressing on the counter, breathing hard, trying to understand what just happened.

In the distance, she heard the house phone ringing. When it stopped, the silence through the home seemed to crush her brain. Her body jerked at the sudden chirping of her cell phone. She searched through her purse but it stopped before she could answer the call. It was Daddy. She called him back.

Cynthia answered saying her father was on the other line. After a brief pause, Cynthia asked, "How are you, my dear?"

This was not the usual "how are you" question. Cynthia was asking, "How are you coping with the death of your sister," but Kenya wasn't ready to talk about it despite knowing Cynthia for more than a dozen years. The woman was practically family—she had worked with Kenya's father since he became an associate judge with the Superior Court.

Attempting a breezy everything-is-fine tone, Kenya said, "I'm good."

Cynthia hmmed, then said, "You let me know if you need anything, okay? Here's your father."

"Sweetheart, listen." He paused and Kenya stood rigid by the kitchen sink. "Things are about to get crazy," he said. "The media are all over your sister's shooting. People are saying it's racially motivated. I've hired Teddy Livingston. You remember him, don't you? Anyway, he's going to help us. I need you to call your mother. Tell her what's happening. She's going to freak out when she sees the news. People may be calling. Don't talk to any reporters. We're going to work on a statement from the family. Get a hold of Ghana and let her know."

He talked fast and Kenya struggled to keep up with what he was saying. The news. Racially motivated. She uh-huhed so he knew she was still there.

"Help your mother. She needs help with the funeral arrangements. I don't know when we'll get her back. Your sister. When they'll send her … her body. I'm waiting for the official autopsy report. But call Sully at Sullivan's Funeral Home. We used him for your grandfather. Sully's great. Just talk to him."

"I'm with Mama now."

"Perfect. Okay, I gotta go. Sweetheart, I'm so sorry to dump this on you. But you're my number one girl. You got this, right?"

"Yes, Daddy. I got this."

She focused on the kitchen cabinets. His number one girl. His first-born. Her face was a shadow reflected in the glass doors, the cups and plates stacked neatly on the two shelves. Ordered and calm, the way she wished life would be. As her father's words sank in, she heard herself say: "Holy shit!"

Kenya kicked into action. She dialed Ghana's number but it went straight to voice-mail. "Sister, please. I need to talk to you. Call me as soon as you get this." She dialed Sidney's number but again got voice-mail. "Sid, I'm going to be late home today. I don't know your schedule, but you need to pick up the kids. I have to— It's Mama. I'll explain later."

Taking two steps at a time, she rushed back up to her mother, calling for her to get up.

"That was Daddy on the phone. We need to get organized." Her mother was again huddled under the covers. As Kenya recounted her father's call, she noticed the tray of food on the floor, toppled over. She imagined her mother spitefully shoving it off the bed with her feet. She suppressed the urge to clean it up. "Mama, please!"

At that, her mother's head popped up like a snapping turtle and her voice slammed into the air, spittle flying from her lips, "Leave me alone, goddammit. Just leave me alone."

Kenya retreated a few steps, feeling the jagged pins of her words piercing her skin. She thought about her father and began again. "You are getting out of this damn bed and taking a shower." She pulled the covers completely off the bed, leaving her mother huddled uncovered on the mattress. Bet hissed once again, ordering Kenya out. The two locked eyes for several tense moments; as a youngster, Kenya could stare the longest without blinking. If her mother wanted to play this game, Kenya would win.

Beaten, Bet slumped onto her side, curled into a ball and began to make loud wailing sounds that Kenya found both heartbreaking and disturbing. She caressed her mother's shoulder with her fingertips. Bet shrugged the hand away, but this time Kenya took a firm hold of her mother's arm and pulled her to a sitting position.

"We're all grieving, Mama. We all feel this, but we can't hide under the covers forever." Bet's face distorted into a frown. "We have to support one another." Gripping both hands, Kenya dragged her mother off the bed and led her to the bathroom. "You're starting to stink."

Bet closed her eyes, scrunching her face as if to cry, but instead inhaled and remained by the sink without Kenya's help. Kenya turned on the faucets, found bath salts and almost emptied the container into the tub. "You'll feel much better." Her mother didn't resist and Kenya took that as a win. She would get the woman into the tub, yet.

* * *

She was glad Dr. Collins had a cancellation and could fit Kenya in for a session this afternoon. She took a seat in the comfy chair opposite Dr. Collins' empty chair; the doctor was at her desk scribbling something in a notebook. Kenya liked this office with its high ceiling and wall of windows. Tall leafy ferns and mini-trees stood in a row along the windows. The carpet was soft and sometimes Kenya sat cross-legged on the floor. Today she wanted the big comfy brown armchair with burnt orange and yellow cushions that made her feel secure. She chose Dr. Collins more than a year ago now, not only because she was a black woman, but because she had a reputation of being blunt and honest. Kenya especially liked that about her. She rocked a short graying afro, but her wardrobe seriously lacked style, and Kenya often found herself wanting to encourage Dr. Collins to wear brighter colors and fitted clothes. Today she wore a gray dress that hung like a sack on the woman's slim body. And her shoes, Kenya thought, were something a nun would wear. Comfortable, perhaps, but god-awful to look at.

Dr. Collins settled in the armchair opposite, sitting upright, legs crossed at the ankles, notepad in her lap, her voice low and soothing. She repeated her condolences. "So how are you today, Kenya?"

Kenya wasn't sure she wanted to talk about her sister. "My mother is losing her mind," she said. "She won't get out of bed. Won't eat. And was just as mean as a bull to me this morning. I was shocked. I mean, all I was trying to do was help her."

"Okay. Tell me what happened."

Her mother was vicious, she said. "Just vicious. I was just trying to help." She shifted her gaze to the carpet. The room was silent for a moment and Kenya could hear the muted noise of cars along Wisconsin Avenue.

"Are you angry at your mother?"

"Well, yes." Kenya looked at Dr. Collins surprised at the question. Of course she was angry at her mother.

"Why?"

"Well ..." Kenya thought for a moment. "Because she wouldn't get out of bed and take a shower. She wouldn't eat. I made soup and she just knocked it off the bed. And I had to clean it up after I washed her

71

like she was a toddler."

"Kenya, she just lost her daughter. You just lost a sister. Tell me what you're feeling about your sister. Do you blame your mother for her death?"

"No, of course not."

"Okay, then why are you angry at your mother?"

"It's like she's giving up. She wouldn't do what I was telling her to do. She can't just give up like that, you know."

"Why does she have to do what you're telling her to do?"

"Because she can't give up. She has to keep on living." She paused. "We all do."

Dr. Collins nodded and Kenya felt like she'd said the right thing. A large truck passed by outside.

"But why?"

Kenya was growing exasperated by the doctor's questions but tried to keep her voice steady. "Why what?"

"Why does she have to keep on living?"

This was a ridiculous question and Kenya almost said so, but instead she said, "Well, of course she … she can't just give up."

"Why not?"

Kenya wrapped her arms across her chest, gripping her elbows. "Because she …" She shifted in her seat, pushing back against the cushion behind her. "She has other daughters. Malawi wasn't the only one. It's like she was the only one. But she wasn't. I'm here, too." Tears filled her eyes, but she didn't want to cry. "That sounds petty."

"No. It's not petty. You're being honest, finally, and that's good." Dr. Collins adjusted her feet and made a note on her notepad. "Okay, take a deep breath and exhale, nice and slow."

Kenya's breath seemed to stutter as she breathed in. She inhaled a second time and fiddled with the hem of her blouse. She noticed a thread that needed to be clipped.

"Now, tell me what you're feeling about Malawi."

"I'm not … I'm not ready to talk about Malawi."

"Why?"

Kenya ran her fingers over the thread knowing that if she pulled at it, another thread could come loose. She wanted to ask for a pair of scissors.

"We don't have to talk about your sister if you're not ready."

Kenya shifted the discussion to Sidney and his efforts to make her comfortable with him again, and her inability to fully forgive him. She talked about the disgust she still felt when he touched her and the angst every time he left for another business trip.

"It takes time." Dr. Collins had said this before, and Kenya had scolded herself more than once, knowing that if she wanted her marriage to work, she had to let go and forgive. Even as she talked about her husband, she was thinking about Malawi. The baby sister she never really knew.

After a long silence, she recounted how her sister had died. "I just feel bad. You know. I wasn't supportive of her. Of Malawi. I mean, it's not like I didn't love her or anything like that, but I could've been a better sister. You know? I could have called and gotten to know her better."

"Do you think that would have made a difference?"

"Sure. We would have been closer." She paused. "Nine years is a long time, I guess, between two people. She and Ghana were closer. They did things together. I should have done things with her."

"And how are things with Ghana?"

"She won't call me back. I've left messages, but ..." Tears threatened again and Kenya pushed them back.

"It's okay to cry, Kenya."

Kenya nodded. "Is it time to go yet?"

"Almost. But I want to come back to your mother for a moment. What do you think will help you with your mother?"

"I was trying to get her to eat, you know. Get her out in the fresh air. But she refused."

"How does that help you?"

"It gives me something to focus on?" Dr. Collins remained quiet. "Makes me feel better if I'm helping her?"

"Okay. Does it?"

"Make me feel better? Yes, I think so."

"Good. And be sure to acknowledge what you're feeling. Give yourself space to grieve. It's an emotional roller coaster and everyone goes through it in their own way. Be open to your own emotions as well as what your mother is experiencing." Dr. Collins tilted her head and smiled without showing teeth.

"I'll try," Kenya said, pushing herself up and out of the comfy chair. She wanted things to be different with her mother. And with Ghana. She always tried to do the right thing, but no one ever appreciated her efforts. Except Daddy. Daddy was always appreciative. Even if Malawi had been his favorite.

13

Ghana moved through the tiny kitchen in Ryan's apartment. She needed movement, rhythm, something to keep her hands busy. She sprinkled flour on the counter and spread the dough over it, stretching it out with the rolling pin. She couldn't just sit and think about her sister. She needed action. She pressed the wooden pin into the soft dough, pushing against the countertop, forwards and back, forwards and back, her mind and body stuck in a rhythm she couldn't stop, until there was nothing but the bare laminate surface between two lumps of dough. Malawi loved pizza. *Loved*. Ghana gathered the dough and tried again to form a pizza round.

The kitchen was small but she liked the coziness of it. She had moved in with Ryan six months ago, after dating for a year; sometimes she was uncertain whether or not she'd done the right thing. She had never dated a white guy before, but something about him just felt right. He had the keenest blue eyes she'd ever seen and dirty blond hair he kept cut short—average in a striking way.

"Was he, like, a quarterback in college?" Malawi had asked, giggling. "He looks like he should have been. You know, that classic all-American guy."

Ghana remembered her sister standing by the refrigerator, leaning on the counter, a wine glass in her hand as Ghana cut a block of cheese into squares. "All-American white guy," Ghana had noted.

"At least you picked a hot one."

Ghana laughed. "You cool with it?"

As she thought back, she wasn't sure why she'd needed Malawi's approval, yet had wanted confirmation that dating someone outside her race was okay. "I think he's awesome," Malawi said, which pleased Ghana.

While still home for the holidays, Malawi had come to their party to celebrate Ghana moving in with Ryan. The evening had been filled with lots of laughing and beer and wine. Ghana had put out some nibbles (cheese and crackers, chips and dip), made a pot of chili, and the tiny apartment had been filled with black, white, and Asian friends. A real United Nations party. Puerto Rico, El Salvador and Japan were in the house. Ryan's best friend Steve was white and Japanese, and his girlfriend was black and Japanese—Ghana loved that their Asian culture had brought them together.

Ryan and Malawi had chatted and giggled together, making Ghana smile, but now air caught in her throat—that evening had been the last time she'd seen her sister in person. Ghana's chest tightened and her breath disappeared. She stopped moving and inhaled slowly, her heart thudding hard in her chest. Just breathe, she thought. She hadn't told Ryan that a white man killed her sister. She covered the dough with marinara sauce and piled on pepperoni, sliced mushrooms and onions.

Ghana first saw Ryan at Walter Reed Medical Center in Bethesda. She'd volunteered to give massages to wounded warriors and he was there visiting his younger brother who'd lost both legs and an arm in Afghanistan. Ghana worked on Jason for almost an hour, though each session was only supposed to be twenty minutes, which didn't seem like enough time for a man who had lost three limbs serving his country. Ryan came to thank her—his brother had raved about how much better he felt. So she started visiting twice a month, and more and more Ryan was there, too. "I have to make sure he doesn't take advantage of you,"

Ryan said with a grin. Jason called him a cock-blocker.

"It's just massage," she told Jason. "I don't provide any 'happy ending' services."

He giggled like a teenager and gave her a mock sad face but said, "Watch my brother. He says he just wants to spend time with me, but I know he's really trying to get with you."

"You think so?" Ghana glanced at Ryan as he slumped in the chair by the bed.

"Hey, I'm right here," Ryan said. "I can hear you."

Jason looked at his brother then back at Ghana. "Just watch him. He's a sneaky bastard."

Several weeks later, as she was leaving the unit, Ryan ran after her. "It's really cool what you do," he said. "You know, helping these guys. My brother jokes but he appreciates it. It makes a difference." He shoved his hands into his jeans pockets. "I should take you to dinner as a thank you." He grinned at her, those blue eyes glinting like they had a secret and would promise to share if she said yes. And she did. A year later, when her landlord decided to sell the house and kicked her out of the basement apartment in Southeast, Ryan asked her to move in with him. She had been sitting on his bed looking at apartments on his laptop. "I don't have much room, but you could crash here for a while, if you want." His eyebrow arched when she looked at him, then he shrugged and looked away. "Just if you want. No biggie."

"Sure." And that was that.

Dating a cop wasn't easy. Carrying a gun belt around all day, working shifts. Ghana was convinced all cops suffered from a lack of sleep. It was no wonder so many lost control. He could be moody sometimes, but she could, too. Sometimes he didn't open up when she knew something was bothering him and she tried not to push. It could be up and down, but that was life, that was relationships.

Ghana checked the time. He should be home around four-thirty, having worked the early shift to cover for a colleague. He didn't expect her to cook dinner, but she often did. Whatever she could do to make his life easier, she tried to do. Besides, she loved to cook.

With the pizza in the oven, she turned on the television and opened her email, but only scanned the list of unopened messages, feeling suddenly overwhelmed. A news channel made noise in the background and then she heard Malawi's name and looked up at the TV. A picture of her sister smiled back at her, her skin glowing, so alive. A selfie she had taken at the beach and posted on Facebook. Tears filled Ghana's eyes. A man Ghana recognized, a friend of her father's, was on the screen saying the family was in mourning and would release a statement soon. "Please keep them in your prayers and demand justice for Malawi Walker."

Justice? Ghana thought for a moment. The shooter had been a white man. The news report said he still hadn't been arrested. Three days had passed since the shooting. She remembered Kenya had called, several times now. But she rang her father first and he answered immediately.

"Did you talk to Kenya?"

"No. I just saw the news."

"Teddy is organizing a news conference at his office for Monday morning. I want you to be there."

"Of course."

"Please, Sweetheart, call your sister."

Ryan came in just as she said goodbye to her father. "Something smells good," he said.

"Shit, the pizza." She ran into the kitchen and turned off the oven, pulling the pan out expecting the pizza to be burned, but the crust was a golden brown and the toppings sizzled delightfully. Ryan kissed the back of her neck then disappeared into the bedroom. He would stay there for a while, separating himself from his day of work and his evening with her. In those first weeks together, she had encroached on his space, eager to be with him; arguments came out of nowhere, until one day he shouted at her, "Fuck, Ghana. Can I just be alone for five fucking minutes?"

They stopped talking for several days while she moped. Then one evening, he snuggled up to her on the couch, gently kissing her mound through her yoga pants before placing his head in her lap.

"Baby, I'm sorry," he said, his voice fading into her thighs. His hand caressed her knee. "I don't know how to explain." She felt his chest expand and contract. "I want to be with you, but sometimes ... sometimes I just need some space." Another breath. "So much shit goes down in a day for me and I need silence. Just for a minute, you know?"

And from then on she let him transition as he needed, not pestering or asking questions he didn't want to answer. Keeping his world of blue confined to a place she didn't go unless invited.

When he finally reappeared in sweatpants and a T-shirt, she was still in the kitchen gazing at the pizza cooling on the stove. "I am starving," he said, then stopped. "Baby?"

"Li'l Sis was shot by some white man who didn't even ask what she wanted." She looked at Ryan who was staring back at her, his face stricken as if she had slapped him. She started to shake, wanting to apologize, afraid of what she had just said out loud: *A white man shot my black sister.* She hadn't been able to talk to him about it, hadn't wanted to acknowledge the significance. *A white man shot my black sister.* Ryan took a step back, his eyes shifting around the room as if searching for something. He started to speak then closed his mouth.

"I don't mean—" she began, but he cut her off.

"Nah, it's cool," he said and shifted around her, not touching, getting the pizza cutter from the drawer and making slices, grabbing a plate from the shelf and taking two slices to the couch. He flipped through channels and ate.

She sat next to him, a foot away and he asked without looking at her, "So you finally ready to tell me what happened, exactly?"

Ghana recounted the story: Her sister had run off the road and sought help at a nearby house where the owner, a white man, shot and killed her. Ryan stopped eating and took her hand. "Baby, I love you, okay. This isn't a black and white thing. He was a fuckin' asshole with a gun and he deserves to be locked up for life. I'd kick his ass no matter what shade of white, brown or yellow he was."

"But the news is saying it was a hate crime."

Ryan frowned and scratched his head, but said nothing. She continued, "The Black Lives Matter people, they're planning a protest march."

"They don't know it was a hate crime. If he just shot without looking, then he didn't know she was black. It makes no sense."

Ghana nodded. "Yeah, but what if he did know? What if he did see who it was and shot her anyway? We only know what he's saying. How do you shoot someone in the chest without seeing their face?"

"Baby, not everything is about race."

She stiffened and moved away from him. He didn't understand. He wasn't black. He didn't get it. Rising, she told him she was going to see her sister. "She's been trying to call me. I should go see her."

Ryan sucked his teeth and reclined into the couch, grabbed the remote and said, "Right."

She considered kissing him but the moment passed and instead grabbed her purse and keys and rushed out.

* * *

Kenya's house was bigger than the one they'd grown up in. Ghana rarely visited her sister and was last here a year ago; she'd almost forgotten what it looked like. There were no fences or sidewalks in this neighborhood, just manicured lawns stretching to the road, tall trees and white mailboxes at the end of every driveway. No sirens, no stop lights, no overflowing trash cans. She surveyed her sister's home: the rolling lawn up to the front door with the cherry blossom tree in the center, the large bay windows on the ground floor and the line of windows watching from the second floor, the two-car garage and the fancy door with the stained-glass paneling. Ghana waited several moments before getting out, feeling self-conscious in her old Honda Civic.

As she locked the car, the front door flew open and Kenya stood open-mouthed. "I've been trying to call you."

Ghana nodded, tears filling her eyes. She cut across the lawn and, in a rush, Kenya's arms were wrapped around her, squeezing tight, her sister's face crushing her cheek. For a moment she couldn't move her body, but simply allowed her sister to squeeze. Slowly, she found her arms and slid them around Kenya, feeling her sister's slim waist and the ribs in her back. So thin, she thought, and pulled her sister closer.

"Oh god, Kennie. I'm so sorry. I'm so, so sorry. I've been such an ass."

Kenya hushed her and continued to hug tighter before gradually loosening and leaning back to look at her.

"Look at you," she said. Her sister's judgment scanned her dreadlocks, her new flower tattoo winding from her shoulder to her neck. Kenya had made it clear she hated tattoos when Ghana came home after her freshman year in college sporting the Chinese letters for "love" on her shoulder. Kenya had said they looked dirty. But today, she simply shook her head and hugged Ghana again overwhelmed by relief at seeing her sister.

"Come in, come in," she said, taking Ghana's hand and pulling her inside, pausing in the foyer where Ghana slipped off her sandals. She stopped by the den where Junior was playing video games and told him to say hello to his Aunt Ghan-Ghan. He lifted his head and smiled keeping his hands on the controller. Ghana could see the irritation fill her sister's eyes, and squeezed her hand. "It's cool. He's a kid. That's what kids do." Kenya rolled her eyes but smiled, then called upstairs to Charlene, who came bouncing down the steps yelling her joy at seeing her aunt.

Ghana tried to swing the girl around, but laughed at her feeble attempt. "You've grown so much!" Charlie stood several inches taller than Ghana remembered. She was a beautiful blend of both her parents, with her mother's poise and her father's cheekbones. Her niece wanted to sit with them, but Kenya sent her back upstairs so she and Ghana could talk first. Charlene's disappointment slumped over her shoulders as she dragged herself back up the staircase.

"She's gorgeous, Kennie!"

"She needs better focus in school, but she's a good girl."

Ghana stopped herself from scolding her sister's criticism. She wasn't here to fight. Kenya gripped her hand too tightly as she led the way into the kitchen. Ghana wiped away tears, overcome with an array of emotions at seeing her sister, at realizing how much she had missed her niece, at the reason that had brought her to Kenya's door. Her sister finally released her hand and offered tea. Ghana nodded.

"Sidney left this morning to meet a client in L.A." Kenya spoke as she filled the kettle and set it back on the plate. "He's traveling more and more these days. I'm kind of glad he's gone right now. I feel like such a mess. It's best he's not here." She took a white teapot from the cupboard and placed it on a colorful tile heat-plate. "I was at Mama's this morning. God, she's a complete mess. You need to call or go see her. And Daddy, have you talked to him?" She pulled two mugs off the rack and put them on the counter next to the teapot. "I've been on the phone with the funeral home and, oh my God, it all just seems so unreal. And have you seen the news? Have you seen what they're saying? One report said she was drunk. These people were talking as if they know us. As if they knew her. And the man who shot her. They haven't arrested him. Can you believe that? The police are saying it was justified. The whole Stand Your Ground thing. It's horrible, Ghan. Just horrible."

Kenya stood by the stove visibly shaking. Ghana rushed over and hushed her sister, holding her close. "I got you," Ghana whispered. "We got this. We'll get through it." A short moan slipped from Kenya's lips and the pair stood in a tight embrace until the kettle's scream separated them. Ghana returned to her seat at the table, wiping her palms across her damp cheeks. Kenya placed a box of tissues on the table between them, taking one to dab her own face.

"You two were so close," Kenya said.

"We were all sisters," said Ghana, grabbing a tissue to wipe her nose.

Kenya closed her eyes. "Yes," she said. "We were all sisters."

14

Malcolm beckoned the bartender to order another round, but Joe shook his head, downing the last of his whiskey sour. "I gotta get home. Liz will get mad if I miss dinner again this week."

Malcolm nodded. "Okay, brother. Thanks for sitting with me." It wasn't his habit to have drinks before going home, but after last night he was reluctant to go home. Bet's anger and her pain had been unbearable. He ordered another drink for himself. He knew she was hurting, lashing out at him simply because he was the one who was there. She wanted him to wallow and be sad with her, only he couldn't. The loss was too profound. He had to keep climbing or he would tumble into an abyss; already he was struggling to scale a wall with no grip—he couldn't stop Bet from falling, as well.

"Judge Walker." Someone called his name and he looked around. A young attorney he'd seen in his courtroom many times was making his way to the bar where Malcolm sat. The man's face was solemn, worried. "Judge Walker, sir, I just want to say—"

Malcolm raised his hand. "It's okay. You don't have to say anything." He offered a wan smile. "I'd rather you didn't."

The young man lifted his chin in acknowledgment. "Can I buy you a drink?"

"No, but thank you." Malcolm looked at him. "I'm going to finish this one and head home."

The man leaned against the bar and said nothing for several moments, then, "I admire you, sir, and support you all the way."

Malcolm shifted in his seat. "Darryl Reeves, right?"

The man nodded. Malcolm knew he was admired by many up-and-coming African American attorneys and he did what he could to coach and guide them, but today he just wanted to quietly drink this last drink and be left alone. "Thank you," he said softly and lifted his glass. The young attorney touched his two fingers to the side of his forehead in salute and wandered away.

Admired. Honored. Respected. Though not at home. At home he was a piece of shit. That's what she'd said. "You're a piece of shit, Malcolm Walker. The honorable piece of shit."

They hadn't been home from the airport five minutes and she'd laid into him. All he'd asked was that she take the lead on the funeral arrangements. He couldn't do that, make arrangements to bury his child. No parent could, but he needed her to stop popping pills and do something constructive. Kenya had called him earlier in the day to say her mother had taken a bath, and beef stir-fry was in a covered pan on the stove. Bless her. He couldn't remember when he'd last eaten. He'd finish this drink, then go home.

"Well, look who it is," said a woman's voice close to his ear.

Malcolm looked up and standing where the young attorney had been was a woman he didn't recognize. Tall, shapely, rouge a little too bright on her brown skin, black hair swept up in a bun on the back of her head. "The Honorable Judge Malcolm T. Walker." She offered him a broad smile revealing large teeth. "You don't remember me?"

Malcolm shook his head, running through in his mind faces from the courthouse. He smiled. "Sorry. No, I don't."

"You dismissed a case against me for prostitution."

At this, Malcolm caught himself glancing at her hips and breasts, and forced his eyes to focus on her face. This woman was no prostitute.

She chuckled. "That was a long time ago. I'm not in that business no more." She settled on the stool next to him. "In fact, it was you who inspired me to do something more with my life."

"Really?"

She nodded. He thought back to when he was a new judge in District Court, presiding over countless petty theft, prostitution and drug possession cases. He still couldn't recall her face. "How did I inspire you?"

She waved at the bartender flashing long red nails. "Made me see the error of my ways," she said, giving another deep throaty chuckle. "The cop who arrested me didn't have enough evidence. I wasn't on the street. Did private escort services. I forget the details now, but what I always remember is you telling me, 'Young lady, you have more to offer this world than your body. Do something more productive with your mind.' I thought about that for days after."

The bartender asked what she wanted and she ordered a Jack Daniels with soda water.

"It's on me," Malcolm said. "And I'll have another."

"No one had ever suggested I had a mind. So, thank you for that."

"You're welcome." She was attractive, he thought, but would be prettier without so much make-up. He wondered if her breasts were real or enhanced. When their drinks arrived he offered a toast. "To new beginnings."

"Sherry, by the way. My name's Sherry Jackson." She downed half her drink. "I saw the news. Don't matter how successful we get, we can't seem to catch a break."

Malcolm watched her take another sip and circle the top of the glass with her forefinger.

"We'll always be a target," she said glancing at him.

He wouldn't talk about his daughter. Not to her. Not to anyone. "What do you do now?" he asked.

"Hmm?"

"What kind of business are you in now?"

"Oh." She grinned at him. "I'm a stenographer. The lady—and it was always a woman when I was in and out of court—she always fascinated me. Sitting there taking notes on everything being said. I took the money I'd saved and went to school. Got a certificate as a court reporter and eventually set up my own business. Always hoped to run into you, but somehow our paths never crossed." She arched her eyebrows. "Until now."

"Congratulations," he said, raising his glass. "I'm proud to have been part of your transformation."

They sat in silence for a moment and then she said, "I had a son who was murdered by a cop."

Malcolm's heartbeat stuttered then lurched into an erratic beat. The urge to run almost overwhelmed him but he remained still, watching the condensation slide down his glass.

"It's hard to talk about, I know," she continued. "For a long time, I just wanted to die. Seemed like no one in the world understood what I was going through. But there are more of us out there than we can count."

She fell silent and his breathing steadied. "What happened?"

Sherry inhaled, her chest rising and falling. "He was smoking weed. Just being a stupid teenager, really. A group of them were hanging out on the street near a park and these two cops came by and started messing with them, lining them up, patting them down." She took a slow sip of her drink. "I wasn't there. His friend told me about it. Why he started to run, who knows, but Tye took off down the street. The cop ran after him and shot him three times in the back. He didn't have no weapons on him and no other drugs. Made no sense. I mean, I know he was doing wrong, but he was fifteen. Did he have to die?"

"They shouldn't run," Malcolm said. "But I know why they do."

"Why's that?"

"It's a survival instinct." She watched him intently now, studying his face and a slight thrill ran through him at her gaze. He cleared his throat. "Since slavery black men have taken their chances at running rather than be killed when they're caught. Justice has rarely been in our favor."

"So as a judge, how do you deal with that?"

"I try to be fair. I have to work within the confines of the law, but I try to be fair, no matter the race or gender. We're all human beings. We all screw up. I try to distinguish those who just screwed up and those who intended to do harm."

"Amen, brother. We need more like you in the courts."

"The system can be tricky."

"But it can be changed."

He smiled. "Not without a lot of fuss."

She leaned close to him and rested her warm hand on his arm. "You're one of the good ones. Your wife is a lucky woman."

He could see flecks of gold in the dark-brown of her eyes, eyes reflecting years of pain and heartache; lines of worry and of laughter. He thought of Bet. She was effective when she wanted to be, sassy and charming, and breathtakingly beautiful. But Malawi's death had squashed her spirit rendering her unrecognizable as the vibrant woman he married. Her face last night, sunken and pale, eyes flooded with rage, had terrified him.

Sherry raised her arm to tuck a stray strand of hair into her bun and pulled a business card from her purse. A sweet fragrance captured his nose. She leaned closer offering him the card, her other hand returning to his arm. He could feel her heat and imagined her skin smooth against him. He imagined kissing her, tasting her burgundy lips, like black cherries, succulent and soft. He could feel himself drawing closer to her.

"If you ever need to talk, call me." Her voice was a whisper next to his ear, her thigh brushed his knee. How easy it would be to turn his head, press his lips against her cheek, slide his hand over her hip. Take her hand and lead her out to his car. Maybe they'd go back to her place. She was looking at him expectantly. He took the card and stuffed it into the inside pocket of his jacket, finished his drink and felt the dizzying effect of the alcohol. He straightened, shifting away from her.

"Thanks," he said, and offered his hand for her to shake. She cupped both her hands around his, her thumb caressing his knuckles. "This was nice," she said. "I hope we can do it again."

"Yeah," he said, retrieving his hand and standing. He paused, afraid that if he moved he would stagger, then he took a backward step away from the bar, turned and managed to make his way to the exit without stumbling. Outside, he couldn't catch his breath in the humid air. Sherry's perfume lingered around him, and for a moment he considered going back inside. But he thought about Teddy being with Bet and how their affair destroyed Teddy's marriage and almost destroyed Malcolm's. If he went back inside to be with Sherry, he would never forgive himself.

He was a better man than Teddy.

He wasn't a religious man, but Malcolm had made a promise before family and friends. A promise for life. To honor and cherish. To covet no other. Till death. Though he had been tempted a few times, he never strayed. Not once, and he was proud of that. He was proud he and Bet had worked through her infidelity and stuck together. He couldn't imagine himself with anyone else.

From what he'd heard, Teddy had succumbed many times, not just with Bet, and continued to flit from one bed to another without any thought about his future. Malcolm didn't want that life. So he drove home, undressed in the bedroom where Bet lay snoring—that soft slightly congested snore that had comforted Malcolm on many nights he couldn't sleep—then settled down in the guest bedroom across the hall.

15

The nights were too long. The clock ticked toward four in the morning and Bet felt like she'd been up for hours. Sitting in the den, she cradled a mug half empty of milk, now a tepid room temperature. She wondered where the notion came from that milk helped people sleep. Or was that just for children? Flooding their little insides with creamy goodness that caused their bodies to fall into a deep slumber. She wanted that. Just to sleep. She'd taken two over-the-counter sedatives before going to bed and an ibuprofen for a headache but woke up in the early hours, and now sat awake with a throbbing in her brain. She hadn't heard Malcolm come home, but knew he was in the guest bedroom. Bastard. If he wanted to sleep in separate beds, so be it. She didn't care.

She remembered when her daddy started sleeping on the couch— there was no guest bedroom in their little house off 13th Street Northwest. Daddy had been a numbers runner for a nightclub owner until he got a promotion and managed the club. He'd been gone a year serving time in jail for what he said were "trumped up charges." His first day out, he and Momma got into an argument about money; there was no honeymoon period, just straight back into it, all loud and cruel. So that night, he slept on the couch. Bet—eight or nine at the time—crept downstairs and snuggled up to him while he slept. A week later, he kissed Bet, soft and sweet on her cheek while she pretended to be sleeping in her bed; he kissed baby William, too, and disappeared into the early morning only to end up in prison a few months later. She never saw him again.

She wondered about Will. If she knew where he was, she'd call him, but they'd lost touch with each other after he showed up drunk at their mother's funeral. She'd been mortified and told him to leave and come back when he was sober. The argument had been loud and embarrassing, but feeling regretful, she'd dialed his number a few days later, only to hear an automated voice saying the number was disconnected. Mutual friends didn't know where he was either. In a way, she was glad. All he'd ever done was borrow money and spend it on drink and gambling.

When she heard Malcolm enter the bathroom around five a.m., she went downstairs to her studio. He wouldn't come down there and she wouldn't have to see him. She listened to him moving through the house, his heavy footsteps on the stairs, crossing the hall into the kitchen, the refrigerator door opening and closing, the front door opening and closing, the car engine starting and fading away as he left for work. She sighed. Finally, he was gone.

She watched the clock until her doctor's office opened. Pushing her fingers into her temples, she waited on hold for several minutes until Dr. Lane came on the line.

"Mrs. Walker? How are you?"

"Oh, Dr. Lane." Bet perked up. "I know I should come in, but can you call in a prescription for something to help me sleep? I'm having such a hard time right now."

"What's going on?"

"Um ..." Bet didn't know what to say. "Well, my daughter ..." She stumbled over her words until the doctor responded.

"Oh, Mrs. Walker, your daughter, of course. I'm so sorry. I saw the news." The line fell silent for a moment. "Yes, I'll call in something for you this morning. But, please come see me as soon as you can." The doctor confirmed the pharmacy's phone number and transferred her back to the reception desk for her to make an in-person appointment, but she hung up before the transfer was made.

She washed quickly in the bathroom sink, wiping her face and underarms, then dressed in casual pants and a blue blouse. She drove slowly to the pharmacy and waited, sitting in the uncomfortable metal chair for almost an hour for her prescription to be ready. The doctor had given her ten pills with orders to take one pill before bedtime.

When she got home, there was a package on the doorstep with a note from her friend Danita. She carried the box inside and opened it in the kitchen to find a selection of bagels and pastries. The note was scribbled on a torn page from a notebook. *Stopped by. My heart is broken for you. Call me. Your phone inbox is full. ~ Danita.* Bet's vision blurred by a sudden flood of tears. Her answering machine was full of messages from friends and neighbors offering condolences and asking how to help. She was grateful, but not ready to talk, not to Danita, or to anyone. She couldn't see how anyone could help.

She took one pill with a small glass of water. She didn't want to visit the doctor, but she'd have to if she wanted more pills. Ten wouldn't be enough.

16

Kenya watched from the sitting room window as her neighbor pulled into the driveway, but instead of idling while Charlene and Junior came inside, Tracy turned off the engine and came to the door with the kids. Kenya opened the front door wide. "Hey, there," she said brightly.

Junior and Charlene offered their customary hugs, as Tracy said, "Do you mind if I stop in for a minute?"

"No, of course not." A twinge of panic ran through Kenya as she hoped the house was clean and in order. She'd known Tracy for several years, but thought of her only as her neighbor who collected the kids one day a week; the redhead with the ruddy pink cheeks, whose daughter had the same complexion. Their girls played violin together in the school orchestra and practiced after school on Thursdays. Occasionally, Kenya and Tracy had coffee or tea, but not much else. All three kids kicked off their shoes at the door and bustled up to the bedrooms.

"Charlie will enjoy having Lilian to play with," she said and led Tracy into the kitchen where she offered to make tea, but Tracy's expression was one of concern and Kenya braced herself for the inevitable. She'd already been flooded with emails and phone calls offering condolences.

"Oh, Kenya. I saw the news. I'm so, so sorry. My God, I just can't imagine. Why didn't you say something?"

Kenya was blinking rapidly and tried to stop. She opened her mouth but didn't say anything. Instead she turned and filled the kettle with water, squeezing her eyes shut for a moment. Finally, she turned to face Tracy and said, "I didn't know what to say."

"Are you all right? Do you need anything?"

Kenya shook her head. This was a private family matter, no reason for Tracy to be involved.

"When I lost my father, I was a wreck, I can tell you." Tracy pulled out a chair at the kitchen table. "I couldn't do a thing."

"I'm sorry. I didn't know." Kenya placed two mugs on the counter and scooped two teaspoons of loose green tea into the ceramic teapot.

"Oh, it's been five years, now, but you never really get over it."

"I suppose not." Kenya leaned on the counter until the kettle boiled then added water to the teapot.

"Was she an alcoholic? My father was."

Kenya almost dropped one of the mugs moving them from the counter to the table. "Excuse me?"

"The news said your sister may have been intoxicated and that's why she crashed."

Kenya stared at her neighbor, again mute. Shame flushed Kenya's cheeks as she remembered wondering if her sister had been under the influence of drugs or alcohol. Only family had the right to ask such questions.

"I just hate to see your family getting mixed up with all of this racial stuff. It must be so ... so embarrassing."

"Embarrassing? No, um ..." Kenya ran her palm over her hair and pinched at the band holding her ponytail feeling her cheeks flush hot. "It's still just so ... so shocking."

"Oh, of course. It must be."

She moved the teapot to the table and settled into the seat opposite Tracy. "What do you mean, all this racial stuff?"

"Oh, you know, all these protesters screaming about racism as if all white people hate African Americans. It's just ridiculous. I mean, look at us." Tracy flapped her hand between her and Kenya. "Look at our children. How can a country that elected an African American man as president be racist?"

An avalanche of emotions she couldn't define overwhelmed Kenya and she said nothing. Unconsciously, she touched the side of the teapot feeling the heat on her fingertips.

Tracy went on. "I just don't understand why every incident that involves people of different races suddenly becomes a hate crime or racial profiling or something absurd. I mean, if someone came to my door in the middle of the night and I felt threatened and defended myself, would that mean I was a racist because the person was a different race?" She shook her head. "Oh, goodness, that really didn't come out right. Your sister wasn't doing anything wrong, but you know what I mean, don't you?" She paused, as if waiting for Kenya to offer reassurance, then continued. "I'm just so sad for you and your parents. How awful for you all."

"Um, Tracy, can we chat another day? I forgot, I need to do something for Sidney before he gets home. He gets back from L.A. tonight."

"Goodness. I'm rambling on." They both stood and Tracy gave Kenya a loose hug. "You call me if you need anything, okay?"

Kenya nodded, certain she wouldn't call Tracy if she needed anything, but said, "We'll have tea again another time."

As they walked through the foyer, Tracy shouted up to her daughter and Kenya suggested letting Lilian stay another hour. The girls' cheers and giggles burst into the air. "I'll walk her home in an hour or so."

She watched Tracy pull out of the driveway and disappear around the corner before closing the front door, then went back to her seat at the kitchen table, poured herself a mug of the tea, and sipped slowly. Tracy had fired so many things at her during that brief conversation that Kenya could barely process it all.

This was what white people really thought. Kenya almost laughed but instead studied her hot tea with a deep frown in her forehead. She should have said something. If she had been quicker with her thoughts, she would have let Tracy know that her sister wasn't drunk—Daddy said the report showed she was under the legal limit—and even if she had been, she didn't deserve to be shot for seeking help. Kenya wasn't sure whether or not the man was a racist, but perhaps if a white woman with long blonde hair had knocked at his door, he would have welcomed her inside. And she wished so much that having a black president had meant there was no more racism, no more hatred of any kind.

17

Seated at a small round table in Jerry's Bar, Ghana felt Cass watching her. The place was dim and crowded and the waiter had just left with their beer orders. Ryan and Allan—Cass' latest boyfriend—were making small talk about baseball.

"Stop staring. I'm fine," Ghana whispered.

Cass tilted her head, leaned closer and said, "You sure? We'll understand if you want to go home."

Ghana pushed Cass away, her palm pressing against her friend's arm. "I'm fine," she said and scraped her chair back. "Just going to the ladies room."

She made her way to the back of the bar and Cass followed close behind. Ghana pushed into the bathroom, which had two stalls, both empty.

"I'm okay. Really, I am," she said before slipping into the nearest stall. She sat on the toilet knowing she didn't need to go. She wanted everything to be like it had been. Hanging out, laughing, talking, knowing her sister was doing the same in Florida, knowing at any moment she could send her a text and get a smiley-face response. Malawi had been gone five days.

"So it's been, what, three or four weeks now, you and Allan?" she asked, wanting to talk about anything else. She heard Cass in the next stall, a rush of pee hitting the bowl and the sudden flush echoing around them. Ghana pulled up her panties and jeans, used her foot to flush and watched the mini-tidal wave swirl and disappear.

"Yep, four weeks," Cass said, grabbing paper towels from the dispenser as if she were collecting enough to wipe up a heavy spill on the floor. She dabbed her hands and dumped the wad into the trash can, then retrieved a black eyeliner pencil from her purse and touched up around her eyes.

"He seems like a good guy," said Ghana. The soap dispenser was empty and she mashed on it a few times getting a sliver of soap. She rubbed it vigorously over her hands and rinsed off with cold water.

"Yeah, I like him a lot. He calls me every day just to hear my voice." She looked at Ghana as if surprised. "Just to hear my voice, he says."

Ghana giggled. "That's sweet."

"Was Ryan like that? Did he call you a lot?" Cass rested her hip against the sink and looked at Ghana.

"Not really. Not at first." She thought for a moment. "He was kind of distant for a while. I could tell he liked me, but he kept me at arm's length at first. Occasionally, he'd send a text, checking in. Then I called him one night, and we sat on the phone for almost three hours. Didn't I tell you this?"

Cass shook her head.

Ghana remembered the call clearly. Having lain in bed for a while unable to sleep, she had decided to see if he would answer her at two in the morning. And he did. They talked about their families, and when he talked about his brother she could hear tears in his voice. He said he felt guilty because he had done four years in the Army and served one tour in Iraq and two tours in Afghanistan, both without incident. His younger brother, who had followed him into service, got sent to Afghanistan where an explosive device hit his vehicle just outside Kabul. He lost both legs—his right, just above the knee—as well as his left arm at the elbow.

The conversation had been raw and intimate. She fell in love with him that night, with his honesty and vulnerability.

"After that we talked every day." She gave Cass a smile. "I didn't tell you that before?" Then she remembered telling the story to Malawi and for a split second she felt lightheaded enough to pass out, but shook away the sensation.

When they returned to the table, their drinks were waiting and, as if he couldn't contain himself any longer, Allan said, "Hey, I'm sorry for your loss."

Ghana felt awkward, unsure how to respond and simply shrugged his comment away. The thought of curling into a ball and never going outside ever again had occurred to her more than once, but Malawi would be horrified if Ghana stopped her life because her sister was no longer in it.

"I don't want anyone mourning my loss," she had said once, while watching on TV hundreds of people gathering to mourn the death of a celebrity. "Make it a party and just, like, keep on keeping on. Think of me with joy, not sadness."

But Ghana couldn't stop the flood of sadness that overwhelmed her in unsuspecting moments. She forced a smile, lifted her bottle and said, "Just keep on keeping on." The others responded by raising their bottles and clinking them together.

"Man, it's scary what's happening out here these days," Allan said. "You know what I think? I think white people are acting out 'cause we had a black president and now they have someone in office they can relate to."

"You think so?" asked Ryan, leaning his elbows on the table.

"Oh, yeah. No question. White folks, especially on the right, they were pissed that a black man won the highest office in the country, and now they're trying to assert themselves once again as dominant. And these cop shootings, man, these guys are out of control."

The table was silent for a moment until Cass said, "Um, Ryan is a cop."

"Oh, dayum, that's right. I forgot. Sorry, man. Here in the District?"

Ryan nodded.

"I mean no disrespect," Allan said, "but seriously. I mean, help me out here. What's with this blue on black crime?"

Ryan swirled the beer in his bottle. "It's not blue on black crime." He looked at Allan. "Just a few cops who are out of fucking control."

"A few?" Allan chuckled and moved his head slowly from side to side. "Again, no disrespect, but every week we're getting news of another cop killing a brother or beating up on a sistah."

Cass put her hand on Allan's arm and said, "Al, c'mon, just leave it." She looked at Ryan and added, "He had a few drinks before we got here."

Ryan shrugged as if to say it's fine.

"No," Allan said, pulling his arm away from Cass. "Let's have an honest conversation about this. As a black man—my parents are from the South, Georgia to be specific—I'm truly confused by what's happening. You're a good man, Ryan, I can see that, and I'm not placing no blame on you, but help me understand."

"You just said it," Ryan said. "White people are acting out because they want to establish control. Isn't that what you said?"

"It's not just black people getting hurt," said Cass. "Hispanic and

Asian folks are dying, too. And not just by the police."

"True. True," said Allan. "But right now, the police are killing a lot of black folks. You can't deny that. I mean take Tamir Rice, what was he, twelve? He had a toy gun and cops shot him down like he's some kinda mobster. I mean, it was a toy gun."

"Some of these toy guns don't look like fucking toys," Ryan said.

"Did they have to shoot him, though?"

"Look, I wasn't there, but what I can tell you is that we live in a society where kids as young as eight or nine are carrying weapons, and when we get called to a situation where there's the threat of a gun, we're on alert. And if a kid is reaching into his pants or coat, we don't know what he's going for."

"So why not shoot his leg instead of killing him?"

"This isn't the fucking movies. Every cop is not a sharp-shooter who can hit a moving target exactly where he wants to. It's easy to second guess after the fact, but in that moment, you fucking react, and sometimes the result is tragic. I'm sorry the boy died, but in that moment, he posed a legitimate threat to the responding officers. He was brandishing what appeared to be a weapon."

"Yeah, okay, blame the victim."

"I'm not blaming the victim. I'm trying to explain the situation from the cops' perspectives. Isn't that what you asked?"

"The *situation* is that black men are assumed to be guilty of something just because they're black. The police profile black men all the time."

Ghana tapped the table with her beer and said, "They wouldn't have shot him if he'd been a white child."

Ryan gave her a look that asked, whose side are you on. She held his stare, silently challenging him to say something else, until he looked away. He was quiet for a moment, then said to Allan, "Tell me something. What is your immediate reaction when a man with a turban and a beard walks into a store and stands by the door with his hands in his pockets just looking around? What do you think?"

Allan sat back in his chair. "I don't think anything."

"Really? You sure about that?"

"Yeah."

"Okay. Well, we got a call one afternoon, few months back, from the manager of this convenience store complaining of suspicious activity by a customer. I get there, and this guy, he's wearing a red turban and has a beard. He's standing outside the store looking at his cell phone. I go inside and talk to the manager. Happens to be a black guy. Tells me the 'Muslim dude' as he calls him has been standing out there for thirty fucking minutes. 'Doing what?' I ask. 'Nothing. Just standing there.' So I go outside and ask the guy if he needs any help. Turns out his car won't start and he's waiting for his brother to come get him. He takes me to his car, and looks like the battery is dead. We chat a bit and his brother finally shows up with a new battery. They fix the car and they're on their way.

"Sure, there's a 'no loitering' sign on the premises, but what was the guy supposed to fucking do?" Ryan took a drink. "And, turns out he's Sikh. Not even Muslim. The manager makes this assumption about the man based on what? Fear. When does anyone know if someone is going to commit a fucking crime or do harm? No one knows for sure. But we respond from a place of fear because the politicians and the media like to create this environment where everybody is afraid of each other. Like you said, white people are afraid because they think that a black president meant black people were taking over, so we have to push back and put them back in their place. Right?"

Allan's face was stony and Ghana was holding her breath. She looked at Cass who stared daggers at Allan, who said, "You wanna put us back in our place, huh?"

As Ryan took another swig of his beer, Ghana placed her hand on his thigh. She wanted him to stop. He glanced at her and winked, as if to say, "I got this."

"Course not," he said. "But, yeah, some people in power, I believe that's the way they think. It's easier to control people when they're afraid. What if the store manager had gone out there and done what I did? What if the guy *had* been a terrorist? Sometimes there's just no way to know for sure. Sometimes we don't know the fucking truth until it's too late. But if we always react from a place of fear, there's no helping any of us. Black, white, or whatever fucking color you are."

Cass asked, "How did you know he was a Sikh?"

"I read." He smiled and tilted the bottle to his lips, downing the rest of his beer. "The Sikh community has been a target since Nine-Eleven and I've responded to a number of calls where their temples have been vandalized or members have been attacked. Just 'cause people think they're terrorists. It's not just black people getting targeted."

"You're a good guy, Ryan," said Cass, raising her beer to him. She glanced at Allan who was looking at the table, as if contemplating something.

"Look, I get it," Ryan said. "Right now there's a focus on cop shootings and everyone is playing the blame game, but there's a fucking bigger issue at play here."

Allan looked up. "What's that?"

"Who's getting the next round?"

Allan broke into a smile. "It's on you, man," he said and laughed.

Ryan pressed Ghana's hand against his thigh, and she smiled, relieved that everyone was laughing. Ryan nodded at Allan. "Sure. I'll get this one," he said and waved over the waiter.

"But what about—" As Allan began again, Cass interrupted him, asking him to stop. "I just want to ask this one thing," he said and looked at Ryan. "What about gun control? How do you feel about that?"

Ryan shrugged. "I don't think we need to revert back to the Wild West with everyone carrying guns, but I believe in the Second Amendment. People should have the right to arm themselves if they want."

Ghana moved her hand away from his thigh, her body stiffening, her heart beat quickening.

Allan said, "So if we're all packing some heat, we can stop all these mass shootings?"

"No—"

Allan chuckled. "Arm all the teachers, huh?"

"That's not what I mean," said Ryan. "Shit, far from it. There should be some fucking controls. But with a license and training, people have the right to own a gun, and use it for protection if they feel they need it."

Ghana glared at him as if she'd never seen him before. Her heart pounded in her throat. "And what if they make a mistake?" she said, her voice shaking. "What if they shoot the wrong person?"

Ryan's eyes widened. "Baby, I didn't mean—" He reached out to her but she jerked her arm away.

"Even with all the training and a license," she said, "what if they still shoot someone just because they're black?"

She stood up and rushed through the bar to the exit. Outside, the evening air was warm and an ambulance—siren wailing, lights flashing—passed by in a blur. She adjusted the strap of her purse on her shoulder and started walking, unsure where to go. Ryan called from behind and in a moment he was there tugging at her arm. She snatched away and continued walking, quicker now, determined.

"Please wait." He gripped her arm tighter and stopped her from moving. She looked at his hand then at his face. He released her and raised both hands, palms toward her. "Baby, I'm sorry."

She could feel the tears coming, a tightness in her throat, an itch in her nose, but she stood motionless looking at the pavement, at his feet.

"I wasn't thinking," he said. "I'm sorry."

She noticed the torn threads on the bottom cuff of his jeans and the scuffed sneakers. He placed his hand on her shoulder and gently tugged her toward him then stepped forward and engulfed her in an embrace, his lips pressing against her forehead. She began to cry, weeping into his chest and he squeezed her closer.

Ryan was gone when she woke up. Her thoughts swarmed around his pro-gun comments last night. They had never talked about gun rights, though she knew he wasn't a member of the NRA. He owned two handguns, one he used at work and a personal one he carried when he was off duty, and he was almost obsessive about securing them safely at home. Once, she'd asked to look at his personal handgun and he responded with a firm, "No." Then he added, more gently, "It's not a toy."

"I know that," she said feeling chided. "I'm just curious."

"Guns are not for casual curiosity," he said.

A week later, he took her to a gun range and let her handle the weapon, which was heavier than she'd expected. Ryan ran through a litany of do's and don'ts that turned to gibberish in her head. He demonstrated how to pull the slide back to look into the chamber, how to load the magazine, and how to position her hands. He stood behind her, helping her get into position. "Widen your stance. Bend your knees. Relax your elbows. Don't grip the gun so tightly." She could feel the sweat on her palms. "The tighter your grip, the more you shake," he said. Outfitted with safety goggles and earplugs, she took a deep breath and tried to relax, yet her body froze into place. With Ryan guiding her, she fired at the paper target and the explosion, the power and potential violence of the gun frightened her. She jerked backwards and almost dropped the gun, the bullet hitting the wall far above the target. Giggling uncontrollably, she gave back the gun and never asked about it again.

To think of Malawi being shot dead with a shotgun made her blood harden and her body heavy and slow. She recalled the explosion of the handgun, the noise—even with earplugs—had echoed in her ears, and now the image of two bullets shattering her sister's body ricocheted through her mind.

After Monday, Ghana had taken the rest of the week off from the spa—she'd had no energy to give to the physical effort of massage, instead spending her days reading, watching the news, and thinking about Malawi. She dumped a load of clothes in the washer, then turned on the news channel while she slumped on the couch and ate a bowl of muesli. She soon turned off the television in disgust; reports of fighting in the Middle East, more race-related protests around the country, and a brutal attack in the District on a young gay man all turned her stomach. She was sick of all the hatred.

As she filled the drier with freshly washed clothes, she thought about her mother. They were far from close, but under the circumstances, perhaps a visit was in order. Kenya had set a tough act to follow—graduating top of her class, following Dad into law, marrying a successful businessman, and having two adorable kids. Ghana never wanted to fit into a box the way Kenya did, and Mama always resented that she followed her own path and spoke her mind.

She hadn't seen her mother since Christmas—the dreaded annual family gathering with the expectation that everyone arrived on the afternoon of Christmas Eve, helped in the kitchen to prepare a feast, attended the evening church service on Christmas Day—mandatory when the girls were younger—and joined in the candle ritual on the first day of Kwanzaa. When they were small, the family honored each of the seven principles before dinner every night for the seven days.

"This is so dumb," she told her mother one year when she was around nine or ten, while cleaning the candleholder. "Nobody celebrates Kwanzaa. It's a made-up holiday."

"Ghana Caroline, you will do as you're told," Mama said, stabbing the air with her finger just above Ghana's nose. "This is important to your father, and you will celebrate like everyone else in this family."

"None of my friends celebrate it."

"We don't do things because your friends do them. We Walkers follow our own path in this world."

Her mother never seemed to see the irony in her words, but Ghana took the opportunity to repeat the line back to her mother on several occasions throughout her teens.

Once she and Kenya moved out, Kwanzaa became a condensed event—they mostly acknowledged the seven principles on the day after Christmas. When Kenya married Sidney, Ghana was envious that her sister had an excuse to spend some of the time with her in-laws. Ghana wished she could have simply skipped the whole thing every year. Between her mother and Kenya's criticisms, those three days were unbearable, yet she kept going. It was family, after all. What was worse: hearing the criticisms about her life choices, or the moaning from her mother if she didn't participate? Last year, she'd shown up a day late, on Christmas morning, much to the chagrin of her mother who'd kept commenting on how a family tradition should be honored and not ignored. In retrospect, Ghana was grateful for attending; it had been the last holiday with Malawi.

On that Christmas Day, they'd stood in their parents' foyer, hugging and hugging, despite having talked almost every day after Malawi had moved to Palm Beach. Malawi hadn't mentioned the married man and Ghana hadn't asked, not wanting to dig up feelings her sister may have been trying to let go. But she'd seemed happy, saying she had settled into Florida life and had made new friends, which had cheered Ghana.

That had been the last time the family had seen Malawi. The thought took Ghana's breath away. She stood in the narrow hall, listening to the chug of the drier as the clothes tumbled around inside the machine, neatly hidden away behind metal closet doors. Yes, she would surprise her mother with a visit. It was time.

Ghana cut through the Columbia Heights neighborhood in Northwest to 16th Street, and from there Crestwood was a straight shot. Though she lived closer now after moving in with Ryan, she still didn't visit. Kenya had called her childish when Ghana said their mother disliked her. And though it seemed wrong to admit it, somewhere deep inside, she didn't like her mother, either. It was better to keep her distance. When she dropped out of college, Mama complained about all the wasted money.

"I'll get a job and pay you back," Ghana had said, knowing she hadn't really meant it but was trying to get her mother to stop ranting on. Her father had said money wasn't the issue. His concern had been her future. Ghana had masked her shame in sarcasm and bravado, and her mother wouldn't let it go; the argument raged on for months.

"You're just embarrassed that a daughter of yours didn't get a fancy college degree. Whatever will you tell your friends?"

Her mother had slapped her face causing her brown cheek to flush a deep apple red. Ghana packed a suitcase that night and slept on her friend's couch in a one-bedroom apartment on Chillum Road until she'd found a job as a bartender in Adams Morgan. With her first paycheck, she moved into a two-bedroom apartment with another friend in Laurel, but that was too far out. When she moved into a tiny basement apartment in Anacostia, her mother—as was reported to her by Malawi—had been terrified, as if she'd moved to Afghanistan.

That year at the annual holiday gathering, Mama had raised the issue and Ghana tried to explain that it was a beautiful part of the city no one seemed to care about. "All anyone talks about is the crime," she'd said.

"The crime there is outrageous," asserted her mother, though

Ghana suspected her mother's knowledge was from a few news headlines, and she'd refused to engage in any further discussion. Her mother hadn't been any happier when she announced she was moving in with Ryan.

"Who is this man, anyway? I haven't even met him."

Ghana had rolled her eyes. During the summer, she had been returning a book to her father and Ryan had driven, so she'd invited him in. Mostly to meet her father, who smiled broadly and shook Ryan's hand.

"Yes, you met him once," Ghana told her mother. "I brought him over and you said he seemed nice."

"I did?" Her mother had waved her hand in the air in her classic dismissive style. "Well, he obviously didn't make much of an impression."

But it hadn't mattered what her mother said because her father liked him. He'd told her later that he liked a man with a strong handshake, which Ryan had. "Says a lot about a man," he said. And that was all the approval she'd needed.

She pulled into the driveway and marveled at the chestnut standing at the entrance. Memories came of the many times she had climbed its branches and flung the nuts at her sisters, giggling hysterically as Kenya ran inside screaming her injury to the neighborhood. She sauntered up the brick walkway thinking of the years she and her sisters had run around the yard and through the trees behind the house, playing, arguing, teasing one another. Her father had named them the three musketeers. Such good days, she thought, and an unexpected pang of longing grabbed her, desperate to pull her back to when all three girls ran careless across the lawn. Her father was right. It was time to take care of each other.

Although she had a key, out of respect, she knocked at the door. Several minutes passed with no response so she let herself in, opening the door slowly and calling through the house. "Mama. It's me, Ghana. Where are you?" She closed the door behind her and waited a few moments.

Her mother appeared at the top of the stairs wearing a bathrobe and slippers, despite it being well past noon. "Mama? You doing okay?" She stood at the bottom of the stairs, waiting for her mother to come down, but her mother appeared hesitant.

"Why are you here?" she said, her sharp tone piercing Ghana's chest.

"Just coming to see you." Her voice was cold now, wary. "That's all. Thought I'd surprise you."

"Shouldn't you be at work?"

Ghana swallowed a lump in her throat. If she turned now and left, she wouldn't have to endure her mother, she wouldn't experience this gripping pain in her heart. But instead she remained glued to the bottom step looking up, a child again. She wondered why her mother couldn't simply be glad to see her, but instead of revealing her thoughts, said: "You need anything?"

"No." Bet descended, taking one step at a time as if she was about to fall over.

"You alright?"

"I'm fine. Christ! Why does everyone want to know how I am?" She reached the bottom and passed Ghana without a word or gesture of welcome and headed into the kitchen. "Have you talked to Kenya?"

Ghana followed and leaned on the island counter. "Not today."

"She calls me every day, you know." Bet appeared to be

halfheartedly searching for something. "She came by the other day. Dropped off some food for me and your father. I thought that was sweet of her."

Ghana tried to ignore the dig and watched her mother looking around the kitchen. She grabbed the kettle and filled it with water. She appeared smaller since Ghana last saw her; eyes sunken and dark, hair brittle and dull, gray advancing up from the roots.

"You talk to Kennie every day?"

"Well, I'm usually resting, but she leaves a message. It's nice to know someone is thinking of me."

A heaviness descended upon Ghana. She watched her mother shuffle from one cabinet to another, aimlessly searching for nothing in particular as if orienting herself to a new home. Eventually, she opened a crockery jar and pulled out a teabag. "I was just going to have some tea, then go back up and lay down."

Ghana noticed her mother place one teacup and saucer on the counter, and rummaged through her thoughts for what to say. She wanted to talk about Malawi, but was afraid of how her mother would respond. At the sink, her mother stared through the window with her back to Ghana.

"Okay, well, I see you're busy. Just thought I'd stop by." Ghana straightened and turned to leave, but her mother called her back.

"Why did you come here?"

"Really?" Ghana swiveled around to face her mother. "At a time like this, you think I wouldn't want to see you?"

"Took you long enough. It's been almost a week."

Her mother's words were like a smack across her cheek. Yes, she should have come sooner, but she was here now. "Really? This is how it is?"

"Oh, Lord, Ghana." Her mother covered her own face with her palm. "I can't do this with you."

"Do what? Have a fucking conversation."

"Good God, Ghana. Who curses at their mother like that?"

"And you wonder why I didn't come sooner."

"My God."

"I lost someone too, Mama." Her voice had steadily been getting louder until she realized she was shouting, but couldn't stop herself. "I lost a sister, and you're not the only one who feels the loss."

Her mother placed her hands over her ears, shaking her head from side to side. "I won't listen to this."

"You're not the only one in mourning."

"Leave me alone. I won't listen to this." Her mother padded out of the kitchen as quickly as her slippers would allow. "Just leave me alone."

Ghana followed her into the hallway. "I thought I'd come here to talk and reconnect with you, but fuck it. You don't want me here anyway."

Her mother stopped at the bottom of the staircase and turned to Ghana. "You're ungrateful. You always were. Just so ungrateful."

"Ungrateful? Can you hear yourself? Do you even hear anything you ever say to me?"

"Get out." Her mother waved her hands as if shooing away a stray animal and ascended the stairs.

Heat charged through Ghana's neck into her face and she began to shake. "Don't worry. I'm leaving and I'm never coming back."

Ghana slammed the front door behind her hoping something would shatter inside the house. She began to cry and struggled to put the car into reverse and back out of the driveway.

18

Kenya sat alone in a conference room in Uncle Teddy's office. The room was cozy with a round table that sat eight and a side table with bottles of water, glass tumblers and a box of tissues. Teddy Livingston wasn't really an uncle, but he was such a close friend of her father's that she grew up calling him Uncle Teddy.

She touched the pearls in her ears and the gold heart-shaped pendant at her neck, a gift from her father on her eighteenth birthday. She hoped he'd notice the pendant, that it comforted him in some way. Kenya had spent much of the weekend considering a suitable outfit for this news conference. She hoped she'd struck the right tone and wondered if she should have called her mother to see what she would be wearing. Sidney had said nothing to her when she left this morning. But then, she hadn't said much to him since he got back from L.A. She was in this weird emotional space right now and couldn't figure out her feelings. She just needed time. That's what Dr. Collins said.

She didn't like the spotlight being on her family; they should grieve in private. Growing up, they—the girls—weren't supposed to talk about their life, about Daddy, because of his work as a judge. Mama had said people didn't need to know their business.

Kenya studied a piece of art on the wall, modern and colorful, shapes and shades that meant nothing to her. She smoothed her navy skirt and adjusted her jacket, wondering if a suit was too formal. She tried to picture her family standing before cameras. Her in her suit, Ghana wearing God-knows-what with her hair askew and tattoos showing, and then their parents. They would be formal, too. Daddy in a suit and

Mama in a nice conservative dress. She should have gone to the house to help her mother get ready—to make sure she came. Kenya inhaled and counted the bottles of water. There were five bottles and six glasses.

When the door opened, her head snapped up and her mother walked in, her face stern and pale, eyes red and sunken. Kenya rushed to her side and took her arm to guide her to one of the chairs.

"I'm not a child," her mother barked, jerking her arm away.

Bitch, Kenya thought, letting her mother seat herself. She wanted to scream in her face, "I was just trying to help you," but instead she turned to her father, who wrapped his arm around her shoulders and kissed her cheek. She held on to him, unable to let go, as if her limbs would melt away without him.

He kissed her forehead and pulled away. "I'm so glad you're here," he whispered.

"Thank you, Daddy," she said, lightly touching the pendant.

"Thank *you*, Sweetheart. You look beautiful. Grab me a bottle of water."

Her chest warmed with pride as she opened a bottle and set it on the table in front of him before taking a seat. Teddy rushed in holding several sheets of white paper. Kenya admired his Armani suit and burgundy tie, and noticed a diamond in his ear. The man gave her father a firm handshake, then bent down and kissed her cheek causing her to blush. "Thanks for coming," he said, straightening up. He was her father's age with a goatee almost completely white, yet he had an energy that seemed much younger. He had a strong presence and authority that Kenya found attractive. He talked about the press conference, which would take place in the reception area. When he caught her staring at him, she shifted her gaze to her mother, who seemed to be studying the grain of the conference table. Kenya took a breath and leaned forward, touching her mother's hand. "You doing okay?"

Bet pulled her hand away, folding her arms into her lap and again Kenya felt a stab in her chest. The door opened and Ghana strode in, transformed from a beatnik hippie chick to a professional businesswoman. Her hair was scooped up and pinned in a neat pile on her head. She wore a short-sleeved white blouse and a plain brown skirt that fell to her ankles, and a burgundy linen jacket was slung over her forearm. Kenya stood up while her father gave Ghana a tight hug and kissed her temple. As with Kenya, Teddy kissed Ghana on the cheek and whispered what Kenya guessed were welcoming words. Ghana smiled and nodded. When he shifted away, Ghana opened her arms as if to present herself to her sister. Kenya took her hands and they giggled and admired each other.

"You look amazing," Kenya said.

"Well, figured if I'm going to be on TV, I should try to look like I fit into this family." Almost as if choreographed, they both turned to their mother, who made no acknowledgment that anyone else was in the room. Ghana's smile disappeared and she whispered, "Make no mistake, I'm here to support Dad." Something happened, Kenya thought, but Teddy asked everyone to sit down before she could ask. Her father remained standing, his hands fidgeting, knuckles cracking.

"I just want to review what's going to happen," Teddy said. "It will be brief. Malcolm will read a statement, but we're not taking any questions. The goal is to show the family is united, and that Malawi was a model citizen, an amazing teacher who didn't deserve to die. Sound good?" He looked at the three women at the table. "I really appreciate you all coming. It's important the family is seen supporting one another. Malcolm, especially, needs your support."

Kenya glanced at her mother, who was giving Teddy a hard stare.

"This is not about Malcolm," Bet said, her voice a sharp hiss.

"Mama—"

Bet's voice got louder. "This is not about Malcolm. It's about my little girl."

Teddy and Malcolm exchanged a glance. Her father said, "Elizabeth, this is not the time, nor the place. You want to get loud and shout at me, do that at home. Not here."

She pushed the chair back and stood, pressing the forefinger of her right hand into the table. "This is about my baby girl. Not you."

Malcolm stepped forward, but Teddy intervened. "Bet," he said, gently. Moving to her side, he leaned in between Bet and Kenya and placed his hand on her shoulder. Bet shrugged him away, cutting her eyes at him before shifting her gaze back to the table. He adjusted his tie then continued. "Of course it's not about your husband, but you have to understand as a Superior Court judge, he could become a target, and we want to avoid that. Okay? We all know this is about Malawi, and that's made clear in the statement. You all need to be seen supporting each other. I don't care what happens behind closed doors. Okay?"

Bet narrowed a stare at him that, when they were little, would force the girls into silence. Ghana leaned her left arm on the table, gripping her chin with forefinger and thumb, eyeing her mother with disgust. Kenya tried to imagine what Malawi would say if she were here. She cleared her throat ready to encourage her mother to be calm, but Bet sat back down, folded her arms across her chest and stared at the table like a reprimanded child.

Teddy blew air through rounded lips, checked his watch, and asked if everyone was ready. Malcolm slid his palm under Bet's elbow and helped her back up, and to Kenya's surprise she let him hold her as they followed Teddy down the hall toward the reception area. Kenya let her sister go ahead, then followed in behind.

A lectern was set up at the end of the hallway, and beyond it, Kenya could see several photographers and hear the click-click of their cameras, already snapping pictures. Several reporters stood with notepads in hand, calm, patient, waiting for the announcement. The family took its place behind Teddy who made some initial remarks. His voice was firm, almost stern, though Kenya couldn't retain any of what he said. She looked at the faces gazing back at her and her family and felt queasy. Teddy said Malawi's name and Mama, who was just in front of Kenya, began to shudder, her shoulders jerking. Kenya realized her mother was silently crying. Cameras flashed, capturing this moment of anguish, and Kenya wanted to grab her mother and run back down the hall to the conference room. *We're a private family, not a reality show.* Instinctively, she placed a hand on her mother's shoulder and hoped she wouldn't shrug her away. Malcolm extended his hand and clasped her mother's fingers. Teddy moved to the left and Malcolm stepped forward, releasing Bet. Kenya leaned in and filled the gap by grabbing her mother's hand; she could feel her shaking. She heard only a few words but knew what was being said because she'd read the statement last night when Teddy emailed it to everyone. When Malcolm stopped talking, a ruckus of questions arose but Teddy raised his hand. "Please respect the Walkers' grief at this time," he said. "They are not taking questions today. Thank you. I'll be back in a moment to answer your questions."

Malcolm grabbed Bet's hand and the group hurried up the hall, back to the safety of the conference room. Bet almost collapsed and Kenya dragged a chair closer to the door so her mother could sit down. "Ghana get some water," said Kenya, gesturing to the side table. Ghana offered a slow blink in response, her lips pursed. "Please, Ghana." Painfully slowly, her sister poured water into a tumbler and passed it to Kenya.

"Here, Mama, drink." Bet took a short sip but the glass was unsteady in her hand. Her face was wet with tears and Kenya pulled several tissues from the box. Bet blew her nose and rested her head on the table.

"Okay," said Teddy. "You folks wait while I finish up and get these guys out of here. There's a back way out, in case anyone is hanging around."

"Why don't you want us to say anything?" asked Ghana.

"I just want the message to be clear and consistent. Sometimes these guys get you on your own and they can twist your words. There's already some rumblings that Malawi was drunk, that she brought this on herself, just dumb shit like that, and I want to make sure they can't create a story out of some innocent comment. Make sense?"

Ghana nodded but seemed skeptical. Or maybe just annoyed by her mother.

"I want to make sure we get an arrest," he added. "And nothing should distract from that right now."

* * *

Kenya arrived home just as Sidney was coming down the stairs.

"Not going into the office?" she asked.

"Surprise," he said with a chuckle. He approached her slowly, almost cautiously, and kissed her cheek, sliding his hand around her waist. Her limbs stiffened.

"C'mon, Kennie," he said, taking a step back from her. "When are you going to give me a break?"

"I just lost my sister, okay. I'm not in the mood."

"You think I'm trying to have sex with you because I want a hug and a kiss? Seriously?"

She tried to pass him to go upstairs, but he caught her arm. "I said I'm sorry. Goddammit. I want my wife back. That's all." He squeezed her arm. "Babe, I'm trying to be the man you married, but I can't do it if you keep pushing me away."

She took a deep breath and forced herself to relax. "I'm just—I'm just confused right now. I don't know what I'm feeling about anything."

He opened his arms and asked, "Can I hold you?"

When she nodded slightly, he came close, wrapping his arms around her waist, his hands pressing into her back. He held her for several moments, the side of his chin resting against her temple, and she felt the tension begin to slip away. He started to sway, his hips moving right to left and she let her body move with him. His right hand slid up and cradled her neck, the back of her head. He's going to mess up my hair, she thought, but kept silent, forcing herself to relax.

"Remember when we used to dance all night long, letting the music move us?"

She smiled thinking about those days before the kids were born, when they were young and struggling to pay the bills, yet happier than she could ever remember being. They would sit up at night with all the lights out, a couple of candles on the coffee table and listen to cassette tapes that Sidney had compiled with all his favorite jams. They'd jump around, twisting and swaying to the fast ones, then press together like they were now to the slow ones, moving their bodies in time to the music. Nineties music—Junior calls it old-school. Kenya chuckled and Sidney squeezed tighter, pressing his thighs against hers. She had enjoyed his touch once. Perhaps she could again.

"I love you, Kennie," he whispered. "I don't ever want to hurt you again. Please believe me."

She returned his squeeze and was ready to let him back in.

19

Malcolm survived another day in court, struggling to be fully present. Several times the attorneys had to repeat themselves because he'd lost his focus. He had seen their looks of concern and irritation—the unspoken words: "Don't fuck up my case, Judge." Joe had suggested he take time off, but Malcolm wouldn't know what to do with himself if he wasn't at work. He didn't want to be at home with Bet, listening to her moaning, her accusations, her rejection. He didn't want to be in his own head, yet couldn't get out of it.

He sat alone at the bar in the same place he had been every night for the past week, drinking one bourbon-on-the-rocks after another, thinking about Sherry, both hoping and worrying she would show up, afraid of what he might do with her if he let himself. With each drink, the ice hadn't had a chance to melt before he was done with it. He swiveled his glass, watching the cubes swirl around the bottom. He figured he shouldn't drive, and gulped down a glass of water before heading out, hoping it would help. As he walked to his car, his body was a little out of sync with his mind and he leaned on the car door for a moment trying to get his balance before getting behind the wheel. Though not certain, he didn't believe he'd had more than on previous nights. Besides, he'd made this drive so many times for so many years, he could probably do it with his eyes closed. He'd be fine.

He took it slow, staying at or just below the speed limit, making sure to slow down at every yellow light and not accelerate too quickly. Still, as he made a left turn onto Florida he heard the familiar woop-woop of the siren and saw the blue lights flashing behind him. He pulled over, got his paperwork ready, rolled down his window and waited. Despite his job title, despite the number of times he'd been stopped without incident, each time he still felt panic. Too many stories of black men being harassed, being killed for the slightest infraction, for simply being black. He inhaled and told himself to stay calm.

The officer was white, not someone Malcolm recognized. He was stern, asking for license and registration. Malcolm had everything ready and handed them over, careful not to make a sudden move. Keep it slow. Keep it smooth. Breathe. Malcolm placed his hands on the wheel where the officer could see them. He read the name plate: Banks.

The officer scanned the driver's license and asked, "Where you headed, tonight, sir?"

"Just on my way home."

"And where are you coming from?"

Malcolm's heart lurched. Jesus, keep it together, he thought. Watch your tone. Don't say anything stupid. "Worked late," he said. Normally by now he would ask why he'd been stopped, but he knew he was in the wrong and wanted to comply; he wasn't going to trigger the officer if he could help it. The officer likely knew he was over the limit. He could probably smell the alcohol.

"That's a pretty long day, sir. You know it's almost midnight."

"Yeah. Yeah, it's been a long day." A long week, he thought.

"You didn't stop in for a drink on the way home by any chance, did you?"

Malcolm's hands started shaking. "I, uh— I had a drink or two with dinner."

Officer Banks narrowed his eyes at him. "One drink or two, sir?

Which is it?" Young and focused, suspicious, but not aggressive. Malcolm took a chance, hoping this young officer wasn't out to prove himself to be a badass.

"Officer, I'm Judge Malcolm Walker, with the Superior Court. I've had more than I should. It's not in my nature to over drink, but I'm taking it slow. It's been a tough week. I don't want any problems. I'm being careful."

"You crossed the white line into the other lane several times, sir."

"I'll be careful. I don't have far to go to get home."

"One moment please." Officer Banks returned to his patrol car and Malcolm's entire body started to shake while he waited for what felt like an eternity. Finally he saw Officer Banks get out of his vehicle and walk back. This was when things could go horribly wrong. He could ask Malcolm to get out of the vehicle, pat him down, get angry if Malcolm said the wrong thing, feel threatened if he moved too quickly. He'd seen countless cases where a black or Hispanic man had been beaten almost unrecognizable because the officer had interpreted the man's actions as threatening. Malcolm was well aware of his height, of his black skin. Aware of the threat he posed by simply being there. A big black man. White women crossing the street, moving their seat on the bus, squeezing their purse just a little closer to their bodies. Dismissing the intelligence behind his eyes, under his skin. Assuming violence lay in his fists. Though sometimes, just sometimes he wanted to explode, to rage, to batter and punch. But he didn't. Instead, he used his head, he took a breath, he swallowed, smiled, nodded, shrank as much as he could to say, "I'm not a threat."

Officer Banks held out Malcolm's paperwork. "Judge Walker," he said. "I'm deeply sorry for your loss." Malcolm's eyes filled with tears and his chest almost caved in. The officer continued, "With respect, I'm going to follow you home, sir. I want to make sure you get there safely. Take it slow. I'll be right behind you."

Malcolm took his information and dropped it on the passenger seat. He closed his eyes for a moment and pushed back this overwhelming wave of emotion. Gratitude. That's what this was, he thought. He looked at the young officer. "You're a good man. Thank you." He took a deep breath, pushing back potential tears. "Thank you."

20

Charlene played with her broccoli, moving it around her plate with her fork. Kenya told her to eat up.

"Why are we going to Florida?" the girl asked.

"We're going to participate in a march. A march for justice."

"For Aunt Mowie?"

"It's like Trayvon Martin," Junior said. "Black folks are getting gunned down just for being black."

Kenya's chest tightened. This wasn't something she wanted her son to think. "Well, it's not as simple as that, really," she said, but she wasn't certain how to explain the complexity of race.

"Who's Trayvon Martin?" Charlene looked from her brother to her mother.

"A teenager who was shot down because he was black," Junior said with authority.

"It's complicated," Kenya said. "He was in the wrong place at the wrong time."

Junior gave her a look she didn't understand—contempt or bewilderment. "That's not right," he said. "Mr. Pierce, our sociology teacher, says he was killed because he was black."

Kenya took a deep breath. She hadn't given her children "the talk." Always putting it off, waiting for Sidney to be there to lead the discussion; hoping for a better time, as if there would ever be a better time to talk about what it means to be black in America. The topic made her uncomfortable, almost like talking about sex—it would change them; they wouldn't be her babies anymore.

"Trayvon Martin was walking home," said Kenya. "That's all, and a man shot him because he thought he was dangerous."

"Why was he dangerous?" asked Charlene.

"He *wasn't* dangerous," Junior said, his voice rising, hands spreading out, punctuating his words. "That's the point. He was just walking home, but he had a hoodie on and the man *thought* he was dangerous. But he wasn't. The *man* was dangerous, not Trayvon."

"We don't know the whole situation." She remembered the news reports and the confusion of what happened. Wondering why a Hispanic man would shoot a teenager walking through the neighborhood. Thinking there had to be a reasonable explanation.

"Seriously, Mom?" Junior stared at her aghast and she felt rebuked.

"Well, yes, you're right," she conceded. "He was just walking through a neighborhood. Kind of like ours, really, except they had a security guard. A neighborhood watch guy, I think, who confronted the boy and they got into a fight, started to argue, and the guy said he felt threatened. And he fired his gun. And—" A sudden pain swelled in her chest, a tightness constricting her breath. Malawi wasn't coming back. She inhaled filling her lungs as if she wouldn't get the chance again and looked at Charlene. "You have to be careful. There's a lot of crazy people out there. Dangerous people with guns."

"Like the man who killed Aunt Mowie," Charlene said.

"Yeah," said Junior. "Some white man shot her because she was black." He folded his arms and leaned back in his chair. "But marching won't do nothing. It's a waste of time."

"Won't do anything." Kenya waited for him to repeat the sentence correctly but instead he gulped his milk. She didn't push it and instead asked, "Why do you say that?"

"Because people marched for Trayvon, but it didn't change nothing. People marched in Ferguson for Michael Brown. People protested in Baltimore for Freddie Gray. They've been protesting all across the country. What's changed?"

Flustered at her son's maturity and knowledge of the nationwide protests, Kenya stumbled over her words. She wasn't sure marching would make any difference this time either, but Ghana said it was important to be there. Show family unity.

"It's a way to show the people in charge, the politicians, that we want something done," Kenya said. "That laws should change so people with guns can't just shoot an unarmed person just because they feel like it."

Charlene's face still looked puzzled. "So why did the man shoot Aunt Mowie? Was it really just because she was black?"

"Yeah, that's exactly why," Junior said firmly, pushing his chair back from the table.

Kenya looked at her daughter. "She just needed help with her car and went to the man's house. He says he thought she was an intruder and that's why he fired the gun." She wanted to leave her daughter with some hope and said, "It could have been an accident."

Junior tilted his head to the side, his mouth slanted as if silently saying, "You know that's bullshit." She could try to hide behind the notion that people who get shot have somehow brought it on themselves because of their attitude or their lifestyle, but truth was, black people have been dying for decades simply because of their skin color, and all that had changed was the technology to capture it on video. There had been no reason to shoot Malawi. There had been no reason to shoot Trayvon, or any of the countless others, but it was easier to blame the victim and stay safe in a bubble of "it can't happen to me because I'm good, I'm better." She wanted to believe there was a reason beyond skin color. That America had moved forward since the sixties, but it hadn't. Not really. Her sister's murder was proof beyond a doubt. Nausea twined its way to her throat knowing she had blamed her sister, because of alcohol or drugs, because of bad choices. But now the slime of reality was thick on her skin.

Kenya wanted to protect her children, wanted them to feel good about the world, to believe the color of their skin wouldn't limit their opportunities in life. She didn't want them to fear being shot just because they were black. But they could be. Her twelve-year-old son already knew it, and now, so did her nine-year-old daughter. She couldn't keep her children swaddled anymore. Kenya swallowed a dry lump.

"Honestly, yes, it was probably because she was a black stranger at his door, and he was afraid."

Charlene's crumpled expression wrecked Kenya. Junior nodded as if satisfied his mother had finally spoken the truth.

"May I be excused?" he asked. She nodded and watched him lope out, heading to his room.

Charlene listlessly poked the broccoli with her fork. Kenya caressed her cheek. "Being black is …" She hesitated. "Be proud. Be smart. Be all the things you want to be. There are evil, horrible people out there, but that's not the whole world. There is good out there, too."

Her daughter continued to frown at her plate.

"You're excused if you've had enough," said Kenya, feeling

defeated. Charlene responded with a quiet thank you and meandered into the den to watch cartoons before bedtime.

21

"This whole Black Lives Matter movement is fucked up," Ryan said. He was lying in bed, propped up on a pillow, scrolling through the news feed on his phone. "I don't mean any disrespect, but damn, doesn't everyone matter?"

"You're missing the point." Ghana rolled out of bed, picked up her T-shirt from the floor and slipped it over her head covering her bare chest, then looked around for her panties, finding them by the bathroom door. The orgasmic afterglow was now a doused flame. "You don't get it. We're not saying—"

"*We're* not saying? Who's we?"

She tilted her head and looked at him. He stared back at her. "Black people."

Ryan heaved a sigh. "I thought we weren't going to do this." He got out of bed on the other side and faced her, his nakedness in full view. "I thought we weren't going to take sides like that. What happened to 'we're all one, we're all human beings,' blah, blah, fuckin' blah?" He bent over, his head disappearing for a moment as he found his jeans and slid them on. No underwear. This usually gave Ghana a thrill. She loved that he often went commando, and when she got the chance would slip her finger between the buttons of his jeans when she was close to him, but right now she dismissed the thought and let loose a groan.

"I can't help it that I'm black."

"And I can't help it that I'm white, but you're acting like it's all my fault."

"Well, maybe it is." She was daring him now, pushing his

buttons, wanting to see how he'd respond, this white cop who served a predominantly black community.

In the eighteen months since they'd met, they had never had an honest discussion about race. They'd acknowledged their different backgrounds—he grew up in the Maryland suburbs, went to a mixed public school and always had black friends; she grew up in an affluent section of the District and went to a mostly white private school—but despite his exposure and acceptance of non-white communities, he didn't fully understand what it meant to be black in America. A minority, even with money, faced perceptions and judgments white people didn't.

"Not you personally," she said, "but cops. Cops act like black people are evil unless proven, without a doubt, that we're not."

"Oh, Jesus fuck, Ghana, are you kidding me?" He slapped his hand to his forehead. "It wasn't a cop who killed your sister."

"Maybe not, but they help create an environment that supports people like that asshole who *did* shoot my sister." She knew her voice was loud. Her heart raced and her pulse throbbed in her temples like a hand tapping a stretched drum. "They make it okay for white people to harass and fear black people. To burn black churches. To shoot young men walking through a wealthy neighborhood and murder a young wo—" Her breath escaped her and she stood unable to say anything more, anger throttling her throat. Malawi had only been twenty-seven.

Quietly, Ryan said, "I'm not the enemy, Ghana."

She wanted to smash something, and said, "You sure about that?" He was quiet and she said again, louder, fury running through her blood. "Are you sure?"

"C'mon, Ghana, that's not fair."

She knew he wasn't the enemy, yet was ready to explode, to batter him with all the firepower she had surging inside her. She screamed at him, "Life's not fair."

"For who?" he yelled back. "For the African American girl who thinks she's so connected to the people, but grew up in a wealthy neighborhood with a father who's a judge and a mother who stays at home and paints flowers all day?"

She stared at him, heaving. "You're an asshole."

He almost spat at her. "You know what? Fuck you. Fuck you and your Black Lives Fucking Matter campaign." He stormed out of the room, his arms in the air, stretching a T-shirt over his head. She heard the front door open and slam closed.

The room settled into a quiet calm, the air shifting, allowing her to breathe. On the bed in her T-shirt and panties, she was shaking, shocked at her outburst. He wasn't the enemy, she thought. But someone was to blame: The political monsters who thrive off the fear and hatred within us all. Police departments across the country. The white man who held a shotgun to her sister's chest. All of them. She wiped her palms across her wet cheeks. But it was so much bigger than all of them.

Ghana slid on a pair of yoga pants, tied her hair back and settled at her computer, trying to focus on a client's design project, but the chaotic emotions continued to swirl inside her.

"He's a cutie," Malawi said the first time she met Ryan. He had been working the evening shift and stopped by Ghana's place to say hello. They had been dating just a couple months, then. Malawi made a "wow" face behind his back so only Ghana could see. "Something about a man in uniform," she said after he left, and giggled. Ghana had to agree.

"I'm not sure I could be with a white guy, though," Malawi said, "but you sure picked a hottie."

"A man's a man," Ghana said. "Doesn't matter what color."

"Nuh uh," said her little sis. "Brothers be like 'girl, we getting it on' and white boys be like ''scuse me miss, can we have sex?' They all proper and shit."

"Girl, you're crazy. That is so not true."

"Okay, then tell me about Ryan. Your first time. What was it like?"

Ghana adored her sister but wasn't about to share. Not about Ryan. Other men, maybe, but for the first time, what she shared with him was something she couldn't talk about with others. What she shared with him was sacred. Malawi, on the other hand, talked about men like they were purses: this one was nice and big, that one was too small, this one had no depth, that one lasted forever.

"My first time with Ryan is my business, not yours," Ghana had said, feeling heat in her cheeks. "But I will say this, he's the first man who can make my toes curl just by looking at me."

"What?" Malawi had been incredulous. "A white boy?"

"Yeah, a white boy."

Then her sister had gotten serious. "Aren't you afraid, though, that he's only with you 'cause of your skin color? You know, like the whole jungle fever thing?"

"Girl, what do you know about jungle fever?"

"Enough to know to stay away from white boys."

Her sister's words had given Ghana pause. She wondered if Ryan was just interested in the exotic, rebelling against his parents. She'd never asked him, afraid perhaps of what he would say. But when he invited her to dinner with his parents, they welcomed her. His mother awkwardly asked about her hair—does she do it herself, does she get it trimmed, was it all her own hair? Perhaps Ghana's expression caused the woman's cheeks to flush a bright red. "I'm so sorry. I don't know anything about, what do you call them, braids?"

"No, no. It's fine." Ghana wanted to put the woman at ease realizing there was no malice in her questions, just simple curiosity, an attempt to connect. So she explained her hair was a style called dreadlocks. "Some black women do have what we call extensions, you know, fake hair that gets sewn into their own. Mine is all natural. It's taken a number of years to get this long, but I visit a friend who twists it for me to keep it from getting matted."

"I swear," the woman had said. "All women, no matter their race, have issues with their hair. Mine's starting to fall out and by the time I'm seventy, I'll be bald as an eagle. Maybe you could help me pick out a wig?"

They laughed then and Ghana felt accepted, knowing she could be herself with Ryan's mother. If he was rebelling, it hadn't worked. Although, she wasn't so sure about his father, who seemed to keep a slight distance. "He likes you," Ryan said with a wry smile. "He's just wary of women who get tattoos." Ghana didn't let it worry her. If Ryan's mother liked her, that's what counted.

Now, though, she wondered if the divide between them was simply too wide. This blond, blue-eyed man, who wore a uniform with a badge and carried a gun. He belonged to a community that too often inflicted pain and degradation on her people. Across the country, black men and women were dying at the hands of police and vigilantes. The numbers grew every day. It was frightening. And now her sister. Another statistic. Murdered by a white man who said he was afraid. Afraid! Ghana blew snot into a tissue, folded it over and wiped her nose.

Ryan wasn't evil, she knew that. He wouldn't kill someone because of the color of their skin. Still, maybe it was time to walk away, sever her connection to a populace that believed black people didn't matter.

22

Bet tidied around her studio wondering if she was ready to paint again. The prescription had been working, gifting her each night with heavy sleep like a newborn; she felt human again. She skimmed through her sketches of Malawi. Pencil drawings of her daughter seated on the couch. She'd been developing into such a beautiful woman, so smart and thoughtful. "Dear God, why did you take her?"

The sudden burst of noise from the phone shocked her and she froze, listening to it ring, as if any movement would give away to the caller that she was home. When it stopped, she exhaled and gathered stray paint brushes, setting them together in a box.

Malcolm wanted her to go with him to Florida for this stupid protest march, but a knot had lodged in her chest at the thought of going back there. The march was in Malawi's name; Teddy said the family should be there.

Teddy Livingston. Cocky son-of-a-bitch. Bowing to Malcolm and being overly loyal as if he hadn't once planned to steal his wife. She wondered if guilt had him acting as Malcolm's champion. What would have happened had she left Malcolm for him? This thought plagued her at times when she wasn't happy, though deep down, she loved Malcolm and thanked God he'd forgiven her. Thanked God he'd stayed.

A sliver of light reached through the basement window, just touching the long wooden workbench. The floorboards creaked as she shifted her weight and surveyed her workspace—the stacks of paintings (some she'd completed, some she'd abandoned halfway through), the art supplies that could fill a store, and the old oak drafting table she'd found in an antique store in Virginia. The room needed dusting.

Her father poked his way into her mind. He had resurrected himself, for reasons she hadn't yet figured out. As a child, she had stuffed him into a dark box inside her mind and told the world he'd died when she was eight. Truth was, he had died in prison when she was seventeen. From a lung infection, according to a letter her mother received. Good riddance. But here he was now, in her thoughts. Seated on a high stool, she closed her eyes and saw him reach for her, cuddling and kissing her cheek, his rich laugh reverberating through her chest. How could she not have seen it then. Or perhaps she had, but wouldn't admit how much Teddy reminded her of her father. That same "I got a secret" smile and wink.

In many ways, Teddy was more handsome than Malcolm, roguish yet sweet and tender when he wanted to be, just like her father. Three, no four times they had shared a bed over two months. There's no telling what would have happened had they not been caught, if his wife hadn't hired a private detective who took pictures.

"I adore you, Bet," Teddy had whispered, nuzzling her neck in the darkness of a hotel room. Yes, yes, I adore you too: She'd kept the thought to herself, but it had surfaced each time they were together, and frightened her. "Come away with me," he'd urged. "We can go to Europe and start over." But she hadn't wanted to go to Europe. She hadn't wanted to leave Malcolm. Not really. She loved her husband, which didn't explain Teddy's allure. Just a fling, an indulgence of her desire, she reasoned. Though it had been more than that. Teddy had made her feel free, free of motherhood and from being the responsible judge's wife. As tedious as her married life felt sometimes, Malcolm was safe, steady, reliable. There was comfort in that. Years after the affair, Teddy would look at her when their paths crossed at an official function, a look of longing. The one who got away, he'd said. But that would only be true if she had ever been his.

She opened her eyes and looked around the room, searching for what to do next. Dust motes hung as if caught in the stream of light from the window. She didn't want to return to Florida. Didn't want to be anywhere near the place of her daughter's murder. But she'd go. For Malcolm's sake.

And for Teddy.

Flipping through an old notepad, she found drawings of all three girls when they were youngsters. Beautiful girls, all three. Each one a slightly different shade of brown, but all with the same dark chocolate eyes of their father. She stared at a recent sketch of Malawi on the couch then looked at the couch as if her daughter was sitting there now.

"Can you hear me, Sweet Pea?" She walked over and settled into the cushions imagining Malawi lounging there, eyes down, focused on her smart phone, fingers tapping out messages to who knows who. "I miss you. Miss you a lot. I never really told you." Her words disappeared instantly into the stagnant air. Bet rested one hand on top of the other. "Figured you knew. What mother doesn't love her children? I hope you knew, but I should've told you."

She fell silent, her thoughts spinning through the years. Malcolm loved his girls with a gentleness Bet could never muster. Surely she could have been a better mother. To all of them. She winced at the memory of her anger at their chattering, their giggling and screaming at one another, such racket shattering her focus and disturbing her work. Fuming, she'd watch them run from her, escaping, huddling in Kenya's room, humming and singing as if to drown her out. Their singing irritating her all the more, as if they cared nothing for her sanity. And now, thinking back, she didn't understand why she'd been so angry at them. They were simply being children.

She sank farther back into the cushions hugging the notebook of pictures to her chest. "I'm so sorry," she said. "So, so sorry."

The doorbell startled her and she gripped the notebook tighter, holding her breath, waiting for the person at the door to go away. The bell rang again and when she heard rapid knocking, she decided to answer. Maybe it was Danita with more food. She laid the book on the couch and, wiping her palms across her face, took her time going up the stairs, still hoping the visitor would leave. She peeked through the glass and saw the outline of a tall, thin woman. She closed her eyes. Good God, not Caroline.

"Elizabeth? Elizabeth? Open the door!" Her mother-in-law's voice shouted from the other side.

Reluctantly, Bet opened and peered out. Caroline held two newspapers in her hand. "These were on the lawn." The woman pushed through and strutted inside.

"What's going on?" she said and stared at Bet with those sharp, bird-like eyes that never missed a thing.

Bet feigned a smile and said, "Well, hello Caroline. So good to see you. What brings you here?"

Malcolm's mother walked through the foyer to the kitchen and sat at the table. Bet obediently followed behind. Her mother-in-law was dressed in white slacks, a floral blouse and white sneakers. Her silver hair was trimmed neatly around her face and gold earrings dangled from her pierced ears. She looked in her late sixties instead of early eighties.

"Would you like some coffee or tea? I think I have some lemonade in the fridge."

"You look better than I expected." Caroline chewed on the inside of her cheek, a habit that annoyed Bet for reasons she didn't know. "Malcolm says you're not doing so well."

"Does he now?" Bet pulled out the carton of lemonade and shook it vigorously before pouring. She sat the tall glass on a coaster in front of her mother-in-law and took a seat opposite her. Caroline waited for a response and wouldn't move until she got one, a stubbornness Bet had both admired and despised over the years.

After their first meeting, Bet was certain Caroline hated her. Malcolm reassured her that his mother always was "a tad cold" toward any woman he dated, though he said he had only introduced her to two previous girlfriends. "She's just protective," he explained. The woman's protectiveness had never wavered in the forty years Bet had known her.

"I've lost a child, Caroline. How do you think I am?"

Caroline said nothing for several moments, taking a short sip of her lemonade and wrinkling her nose slightly as she returned the glass to the coaster. "I lost two children before I had Malcolm. A girl in childbirth and a boy who died at two weeks old from a problem with his heart. I know what it's like to lose a child. I know what it's like to lose my parents, to lose a sister, and I know what it's like to lose a husband. You may have forgotten, but Malawi was also my granddaughter, and I feel this loss as much as you do. So don't act like you're the only one in the world who is suffering."

Bet's cheeks flushed hot. "You don't have the right to come into my house and talk to me this way."

"No?" Caroline took another sip of lemonade, this time without the frown. "Malcolm may be your husband, but he's still my son and I worry about both of you. Yes, both of you. What happens to you, happens to my son. What you feel, he feels. You are both in pain. I understand that, but this moping around the house, acting like you're the only one in the world who has suffered a loss, is a complete waste of time. Get it together, Elizabeth, or you will lose more than your daughter."

Bet raised her eyebrows. "Is that some kind of threat?"

Caroline laughed. "I have no reason to threaten you. What happens is your doing. Not mine. I'm just here to let you know you are on a slippery path, and if you're not careful you're going to fall over the cliff." She stood up, smoothed her blouse and walked back to the foyer.

Bet remained in the kitchen, seething at the audacity of that woman, angry that after all these years Caroline Walker could still get under her skin.

And she'd wasted an entire glass of lemonade.

23

Kenya rummaged in her purse for a tissue and pressed it firmly on her forefinger, trying to stop the bleeding, trying to be discrete. Chewing the skin until it bled was a habit she had never understood, and struggled to stop. She folded over the tissue and dabbed the clean side on her temple. The temperature was hotter than she'd expected, and she knew the back of her dress was soaked with perspiration. She looked around hoping no one was paying attention to her despite sitting on a stage before a mass of people. She hoped she still appeared cute and stylish.

Signs bobbed and swayed above the crowd: "Justice for Malawi" … "Make an Arrest" … "Black Lives Matter" … "Black Women Matter" …. Something about that last one stung. Until now, she hadn't seen any headlines about black women being killed by cops or vigilantes. She was sure her sister wasn't the first and wondered if the news media didn't consider the deaths of black women as newsworthy enough. Black women did matter. They were mothers and daughters and sisters. And wives. She thought of Sidney, always expecting her to take care of everything at home, always taking her for granted. He had promised to be here today, but an important meeting had come up in New York. That was what happened when married to a man who ran an international events business. It made for a comfortable life, but he was never home, which gave him plenty of opportunity to stray. Two times that she knew of, but her gut said there'd been many more. She loved and hated him. The two emotions collided, bashing each other and jockeying for the forefront of her mind. She wanted to love him, to put his transgressions behind her. That was how her mother put it. "It's a transgression. Something men do.

You can't blame them for it."

"Has Daddy cheated on you?"

"Oh, heavens no." Her mother had laughed as if it was unthinkable, but he was still a man.

Junior kicked his feet against the legs of the metal chair and Charlene leaned heavily on Kenya's arm. She should have left them at home, but when Sidney said, "no" to them attending the rally and then up and left for New York, she decided he didn't get to dictate what she did with the kids.

Ghana had stressed the event would be a teachable moment. "The children need to know," Ghana said, her hands gesturing wildly. "They need to understand what kind of a world we live in, the horrors they face. Malawi is part of something bigger. This is a movement. We're on the cusp of change and if we don't engage the young people, then all hope is lost."

Her sister's enthusiasm had inspired Kenya, swooping her up in the moment with the notion that the event would teach her children something about race and unity, something she hadn't figured out how to teach them herself. Now sitting on a stage in front of all these emotional people, Kenya began to nibble another finger. She eyed her sister standing by the lectern, next to a woman (whose name Kenya had forgotten) speaking into a microphone. Television cameras were lined up along the front of the stage, filming every move made by anyone at the mic. Her father sat on the other side of Junior, calm, stoic. Her mother, next to him in dark glasses hiding dark circles around her eyes, and a straw hat with a small brim shading her face. Kenya looked back at her sister, dressed in a long skirt and a tank top, her jacket slung on the back of the seat next to Charlene. Such a hippie chick. But Kenya was glad it was her sister addressing the audience and not herself.

Ghana was graceful as she stepped to the microphone, and this surprised Kenya. Her sister was eloquent, strong, passionate. All the things Kenya wished to be. Ghana was free. Free to be anything she wanted. In high school and college, Kenya panicked whenever she got a B; the fact that Ghana never got her bachelor's degree dumbfounded Kenya, who would never have gotten away with not graduating. But then, look at her life. She got paid by the hour and probably had no health insurance. There was no security in that kind of a life.

Junior patted her forearm. "Mom, when will the speeches be over? I want to march."

"I don't know, Honey. Sit up. It won't be long. Look at your Aunt Ghan-Ghan. Isn't she beautiful?"

Junior shrugged. Ghana was beautiful, Kenya thought. She wished she were more like Ghana.

Speeches and more speeches, then everyone would march to the courthouse to demand the arrest of Jeffrey Davies, who apparently hadn't been seen since the shooting. Ghana said a group had been camping outside his house with signs, and the police had come to make them leave him alone. Because they were across the street and not on his property, the police couldn't legally get them to move. Ghana found this amusing, but Kenya thought it was pathetic.

"Too many of us are dying," Ghana said, her voice echoing through the speakers into the air. "My sister will not die in vain. We must demand change."

The crowd burst into applause, and Kenya nudged her daughter to a sitting position and clapped her hands with a sudden burst of energy. The balled-up bloody tissue fell to her feet and a breeze shifted it toward the edge of the stage causing Kenya to panic. She watched it teeter like a red-spotted carnation afraid of it being blown into the audience. Then her father stood up drawing her back into the moment and she looked at Ghana, who glanced back, perhaps seeking reassurance or checking to make sure everyone was still awake, and Kenya stood up to applaud, forgetting the tissue. Her sister was a superstar.

* * *

They marched slowly; this was Kenya's first protest march. Some linked arms, making her feel awkward. She avoided linking arms by walking between Charlene and Junior. This wasn't the march in Selma across the Pettus Bridge, after all, yet a weight settled in her stomach. A woman approached. Older, perhaps her mother's age, wearing a bright green blouse and black pants. Arms outstretched, she took Kenya's hands forcing Kenya to stop walking. The crowd nudged past.

"I lost my brother," the woman said. Her small eyes were full of tears yet to fall. "He was shot by the police. They just don't care about us. Just don't care."

Kenya wasn't sure how to respond. "I'm so sorry," she said, squeezing the woman's hands. She didn't understand why so many African Americans were being shot. And why Malawi? Ghana was right, this was bigger than the Walker family. Bigger than their loss and their pain.

The woman said, "You're not alone," then pulled away, and Kenya gripped Junior and Charlene's hands. As the crowd swallowed the woman, Kenya tightened her hold on her children and spied Ghana's hair up ahead.

* * *

After the march, the Walker family sat in the hotel restaurant. No one said a word. Mama, Daddy, Ghana, Kenya, Charlene and Junior. Four glum faces staring at nothing in particular, while the children played games on their Nintendos. A young man with black straight hair and brown skin sat at a table by the window; Hispanic, Kenya thought. He stood as another man approached. A white man with curly brown hair. They embraced, kissing lightly on the lips and Kenya looked away, frowning. When she glanced back the pair were leaning into each other, hands clasped across the table. She checked to make sure her children weren't seeing them. Two men kissing in public, that was just nasty. Two grown men acting like girls. They need to keep their perversion behind closed doors where no one could see.

Kenya shifted her gaze to her sister and cleared her throat. "You were fantastic," she said. "You looked amazing talking to the crowd. They really responded to you."

Ghana's face brightened, though she didn't smile. Energized, yet solemn and thoughtful. She nodded but said nothing. Her phone buzzed and Ghana gazed at it for a moment then turned it off. Her eyes drifted to something in the distance, and Kenya wanted to bring her attention back, to ask her what was wrong, but she wasn't sure how. Kenya guessed it was something not related to the march or to their little sister. Suddenly protective, she reached out, touching Ghana's arm. Ghana shifted her arm away but offered a small grin, turning to Charlene to ask if she'd enjoyed the march. The girl shrugged.

"I thought it was cool," chimed in Junior, without looking up from his game.

"This was an important day, you know," Ghana said, leaning down to be close to her niece. Charlene looked blankly at her aunt, who rested her hand on the girl's head for a moment, then leaned back in her chair and gave a heavy sigh. Ghana looked at their mother then at Kenya and back at their mother, as if to say, "Are you seeing what I'm seeing?" Mama sat with her sunglasses on, slouched in her chair not eating. Their father stared at the table as if defeated.

"You okay, Daddy?" Kenya asked. He smiled and nodded.

"Just tired," he said. "I'll be glad to get to bed tonight."

Kenya would rather be flying back with them on the six o'clock flight. Instead she and Ghana were staying to organize Malawi's things at her apartment for shipment back to their parents' house. An activity she didn't relish, but it was better than hiring strangers to rummage through their sister's possessions. She glanced back at the two homosexuals sitting by the window—young, in the prime of their lives. They should be with pretty young women. Two men in love; it was perverted. Then it occurred to Kenya that she hadn't known if Malawi had been in love, that she'd never met any of her sister's boyfriends or heard her talk of them. Ghana likely knew all about them. Sadness leaned into Kenya's chest, and she tried to push it away with a deep sigh. The two men erupted into laughter. Why would anyone choose to be gay, she thought.

24

The sisters spent the morning cleaning Malawi's apartment, washing dishes and packing them in boxes, pulling clothes out of closets and stuffing them into large plastic bags for charity, discarding spoiled food and toiletries, and tagging furniture to be donated.

Surrounded by shoes, Kenya sat on the floor of Malawi's bedroom, while Ghana pulled underwear and T-shirts from the chest of drawers. Charlene, seated on the couch in the living room, searched through several boxes filled with fashion jewelry with the direction from her mother to keep whatever she wanted. Outside, Kenya could hear Junior on the porch exclaiming a victory or loss with whatever electronic game he was playing—she'd given him specific instructions not to leave the porch. Periodically, he ran in announcing a gecko or lizard sighting, but for the most part, stayed rooted to the lounge chair playing his Nintendo.

Ghana had said little most of the morning. She pressed a colorful shirt to her chest and said, "Two weeks today."

Kenya nodded, unable to summon any words. Then, "I wish I had known her better. I'm here in her space, yet it feels alien to me."

The furniture, the pictures on the walls, none of it reminded her of Malawi. Then Ghana talked about shopping trips and stores where they'd bought this dress or that T-shirt. Kenya listened, thinking how much more alike they all were than she'd realized. All of them, in many ways, more like Mama than she cared to admit.

"Did you and Mama get into it?" she asked.

Ghana remained quiet, shaking out a blouse and re-folding it for the charity pile. She jerked her shoulders and harumphed. "I went to see her last week at the house. She's such a bitch sometimes. I swear she hates me."

"Don't say that. That's just Mama. She's … she's …" Kenya couldn't think of how to describe their mother.

"See, you can't even defend her. What about self-centered? Dramatic?"

Kenya started to smile and added, "Martyr."

"Cold."

They both laughed. "We have her genes," said Kenya.

"Maybe you do. I have Dad's through and through."

"No. Malawi was like Daddy."

"Yeah, she was."

Kenya wiped dust off a pair of flats, then tried to squeeze them on her foot; a size too small. She couldn't remember the last time she and Ghana had spent time alone and was unsure what else to talk about. Ghana held an olive green skirt against her and moved around as if considering keeping it for herself. "That suits you," Kenya said.

"Doesn't seem right keeping her clothes. Feels weird, like we should keep everything in case she comes back. You know, like she's not really gone forever."

A thickness filled Kenya's throat, but she managed to say, "Yeah."

Her sister settled on the bed and looked out the window. Kenya dumped another pair of shoes into the donations bag.

Ghana said, "Things are a bit awkward with Ryan right now."

"What do you mean awkward?"

"He feels like I'm against him because I'm supporting the Black Lives Matter movement."

"Really? Why?"

Ghana stopped and turned to her as if she'd said something stupid.

"What?" said Kenya. "What did I say?"

Her sister gave a slow blink. "He's a cop."

Kenya instantly felt dumb. Perhaps she'd forgotten, or maybe she had never known what he did for a living. She struggled to picture his face and wondered if they'd ever met. It took a moment, but gradually a memory surfaced of meeting Ryan last year at the fourth-of-July cookout. Ghana didn't seem like his type. A clean cut, Caucasian man with a focused look about him; the total opposite of her sister. She'd never thought they were a good match. The whole opposites attract thing just didn't seem legitimate. And yet, they'd been together a while now.

"The Black Lives organizers have been pretty focused on some of the shootings and abuses by cops across the country," said Ghana. "And because I'm supporting them, he feels like I'm against him."

"Are you?"

As before, Ghana flashed Kenya a puzzled expression. "What do you mean, 'Am I?'"

"Are you against him? Like you said, he is a cop."

"Of course I'm not against him."

Kenya knew she'd hit a nerve in her sister, and pushed deeper. "Then why does he think you are?"

She couldn't hold Ghana's irritated expression, and returned to assessing shoes to go in either the donation bag or the trash bag. Finally she looked up, and said, "I'm just curious. I mean, why would he think you're against him if you're not? What have you said or done to make him feel that way?"

"Why do you always blame me?" Ghana said. "I haven't done anything."

Kenya paused before responding. She wanted to talk, to share, but she'd never been good at making conversation—it became either an interrogation or an indictment, according to Sidney. "I'm not blaming you, and I'm not trying to upset you. I'm just asking." Trying to be a caring sister.

"I'm not upset." Ghana stuffed a pile of underwear into a bag for trash, then said, "I'm not against him. But, some cops *are* racist."

"Are you worried he's racist?"

"What are you, playing therapist now?" Ghana snapped a T-shirt in the air and folded it roughly. "Of course not. He wouldn't be with me if he was racist."

Kenya stretched her legs out, feeling her knees start to ache. "Yeah, but I mean, some guys, you just don't know how they really feel until something like this comes up." She gestured with a shoe in her hand. "You never really know a person until there's some kind of crisis. That's when you really get to know someone."

"This isn't a crisis."

"No? Okay." Kenya tied a knot in the plastic bag with the shoes to be thrown out with the trash and added it to the pile of bags at the front door, then she opened the coat closet in the hallway. It was true, she thought, crises show a person's true colors. Sidney didn't think cheating on her was a crisis, but it had been a huge one that cracked their foundation, and even though he kept trying to plaster over it, Kenya could feel the fissure. You never really knew a person.

"Oh, my god," her sister yelled from the bedroom and Kenya rushed back there.

"Look at this!" Ghana held a yellow blanket. "Remember this?"

She shook the material and displayed it in the air, a yellow baby blanket trimmed with satin and a large teddy bear covering one quarter of it. The edges were frayed; loose threads and small holes made the bear appear sad, but the fabric was still soft, though worn thin. The blanket first belonged to Kenya and had been passed down from sister to sister, becoming a security blanket for Malawi, who refused to go anywhere without it.

"I can't believe she still has it," Kenya said, reaching out to touch the satin with her fingertips.

"And that she brought it with her to Florida." Ghana pressed it to her face. "How adorable is that?"

Kenya leaned in and smelled a sweet fragrance clinging to the fabric, Malawi's perfume. She shifted closer and her head touched Ghana's. They began to sway, their bodies bending ever so slightly left to right, left to right, a rhythm bringing comfort. Kenya wrapped her arms around her sister, feeling the warmth of her body, the firm muscles in her back, the solidity of her sister in her arms. Alive. Kenya squeezed tighter and tighter.

* * *

With the few coats sorted, most of them in the charity bag, Kenya pulled down a suitcase from the closet shelf. The case was heavy. Kenya dumped it on the floor and tugged the zipper open, finding a plastic bag and a shoe box filled with notepads, cards and letters. The contents appeared so personal that Kenya hesitated to look through them. She spied Christmas cards from Mama and Daddy and people Kenya didn't recognize. Then the handwriting on one of the envelopes seemed familiar and Kenya looked closer—her husband's. Why would Sidney have written something to Malawi? Kenya couldn't think of any reason; she was in charge of sending holiday and birthday cards—there was no occasion she could remember when Sidney would have written a card to someone other than to her. Kenya even bought and wrote the cards for his parents. She pondered what would have prompted him to write a card to her baby sister. After some thought, she opened the envelope and inside was a Valentine's Day card with a silhouette of a couple in an embrace and the words, "You Are Special to Me" on the front. A card similar to one he had given Kenya. Her heart leaped into her throat. A Valentine's Day card from Sidney to Malawi. She stared at the front for several moments then slowly opened it. Sidney's signature was at the bottom, his wild scrawling S-i-d. She wanted to pinch herself, to wake up, but she knew she wasn't dreaming. She read the printed words, expressing love and desire. Her breakfast gurgled in her stomach and threatened to inch up to her throat while all the blood in her head seemed to drain to her feet. She searched the box for an explanation, something to confirm this was a joke. Instead she found a hotel receipt from late January with Sidney's name on it, and Malawi's and Sidney's initials scribbled in the corner inside a heart drawn in blue ink, all in Malawi's handwriting. Kenya's stomach lurched and she tasted food in her throat. This couldn't be real.

She thought back to Christmas when she'd caught Malawi and

Sidney alone, talking quietly in the kitchen. Their close proximity to one another had made Kenya uncomfortable but she dismissed her thought as paranoia. Looking at the card and the receipt, she wondered if the other woman had been her sister. Was Malawi the AfricanQueen?

Kenya rushed to the bathroom and vomited into the sink, chunks of eggs and bacon covering the porcelain, a sour taste lingering on her tongue.

"Sis? Sis?" Ghana's hand pressed on her lower back and Kenya felt dizzy. "What's going on?"

"Just let me sit for a minute," Kenya said and lowered herself to the floor, leaning back on the bathtub.

"Are you pregnant?"

Kenya couldn't respond but shook her head. She could see her husband with Malawi and she wanted to puke again. She could see him crying when she told him Malawi had been killed. He had shed tears for her. My God!

"I just want to be by myself for a minute, okay? I'm fine. I just need a minute. Maybe the eggs were off from breakfast."

Ghana was reluctant to go and Kenya waved her away, insisting she was fine. Her stomach churned and she crawled to the toilet bowl, vomiting more chunks that splashed into the water.

* * *

Entering the house through the garage, Kenya fussed with the kids, getting them to help with the luggage. Sidney's car was there but she wasn't sure if he was in the house. He may have been on the road.

He usually took a limousine service to the airport when he traveled. She couldn't keep up with his schedule anymore and they'd become lax about telling each other what they were doing. She and the kids were home late because of a delay with the plane and though there was no school in the morning, she wanted the kids ready for bed as soon as possible. Junior did have to get up for summer camp. They groaned but followed her command to get upstairs and wash up.

On her way to her bedroom, she passed the office and Sidney was at his desk, earphones plugged into his ears on a video-conference call. He looked over and waved. Glaring at him, she fought the urge to smash his face into the computer screen.

She took her bag into her room and unpacked, emptying the bag of dirty clothes into the laundry hamper then placing the clean items back into their respective drawer or closet. She did the same with her children's clothes and as she walked back to her room, Sidney came out of the office.

"Hey," he said cheerfully. "Did you have a good time?"

"It wasn't a vacation," she said and nudged past him into their bedroom. He followed behind.

"Yeah, I just meant … well, you know. How was the march? I saw some of it on the news. Ghana was great."

"You going to befriend her online, too?"

He was silent for a moment, then said, "Oooookaaay. You all right?"

"Oh, yeah. I'm good. Peachy."

"Okay, just give it to me." He offered a loud exhalation. "Obviously you're not peachy. What is it? What did I do now?"

Kenya turned to face him. Shaking, her fury was palpable, consuming everything inside her. "You're a piece of shit and I hate you." He stepped back as if she'd slapped him, but said nothing. "I never should have married you. Mama was so mad when I got pregnant. Said if I didn't get married as soon as possible, I'd be stuck. It was the right thing to do, only because she knew you had a wealthy family and a strong bank account. She said you would give me a comfortable life, but what kind of a life is this?" She felt breathless but continued on. "It's broken and painful and now in pieces because of your selfishness, because you thought sleeping with my sister was okay." She stood, heaving, trying to get breath. "You piece of shit. I hate you."

She could almost see the blood drain from his face. "What are you talking about?"

"Don't act like you don't know." She grabbed her backpack, her movements violent, and pulled out the card she found in Malawi's apartment. She waved it in his face. "Remember this?" Then she pulled out the hotel receipt. "And this?"

"She was my sister!" She screamed so loud her throat immediately began to ache.

He was breathing hard but said nothing. She stepped forward and punched his chest, once, twice, and almost reflexively he slapped her back, his hand striking her cheek. Kenya stumbled backward and glared at him, though not shocked. This was not the first argument that had ended with a punch or a slap between them. She would pummel him with punches until he smacked her back, and that stopped her.

As her hand rose, he said, "Don't hit me again."

Spent, she flopped on the bed. Quietly now she said, "She was my sister. She was young and silly and vulnerable, and you took advantage of her."

He closed his eyes, covered his face with his hands and sat on the chaise longue at the end of the bed. "We had ended it. It was over."

"That doesn't make it okay." She collected the receipt that had fallen on the floor and laid it on the bed next to her. "You were with her in January, right after she'd been home for the holidays. In December you said the affair was over. But it wasn't." She could feel the hysteria resurfacing and tried to push it back with a deep breath. "You were sleeping with my ... my sister."

"Kenya." He reached out to her but his hands hung in the air.

"For how long?"

"Please. I've been so afraid you would find out. I don't want it to destroy us. Please, listen to me. I was serious when I said I want to begin again. You and me. I don't want to be with anyone else. That was for real."

"I can't. I just can't. You have to leave. You can't be here. You have to leave." The words seemed to get stuck like a needle on a record and she couldn't stop repeating herself.

"Kenya. Please."

She shook her head fiercely, like a little girl refusing to eat her dinner, determined to get what she wanted. "You have to go now. Maybe we can talk later, but you have to go. Now."

"What do you mean, go?"

"Just go." She screamed at him, "Get out!"

Sidney backed away from her and stared until she screamed again. She could see him flinch. He turned and without another word, left her. She heard him talking to Junior and Charlene. No doubt they'd heard the argument and Kenya felt sick. This wasn't the home life she wanted for them. She and Sidney were supposed to be the perfect couple. Happy together. Respectful of one another. Committed for life. But their love was unraveling like an old knitted sweater and there was nothing she could do but let it come undone.

25

The news of Jeffrey Davies' arrest was on every morning news channel.

Finally.

Malcolm turned off the radio and showed his ID to the parking attendant. The attorney Joe had found had come through. Now to make sure Davies went away for good. Malcolm was sure Florida still had the death penalty. He successfully navigated to his space in the lot under the courthouse. He remembered getting an email from the Palm Beach prosecutor late yesterday afternoon. Malawi's body would be released for burial. He'd asked Cynthia to help coordinate the shipment of the body.

The body.

He hated to think of his baby girl that way.

From the parking garage, he took the elevator up. Normally, he would take the stairs, but he was tired and out of sync with everything around him. He had wakened with a killer hangover, something he hadn't experienced in a number of years. A Bloody Mary for breakfast had become a questionable habit, but it helped him feel better. Took away that dull achy feeling and helped him focus. He stumbled upon exiting the elevator and hoped no one saw him. He kept his head down and walked across the marble expanse to his office on the west side. He spotted several attorneys glancing his way, odd expressions on their faces, but he focused on placing one foot in front of the other.

Just before he made a left to get to his office someone stopped him. "Judge Walker, are you okay?"

Malcolm turned and saw the young attorney, Darryl Reeves, frowning at him.

"I'm fine." He stumbled back a step then steadied himself. "I'm fine," he said again.

"Sir, I think maybe … perhaps we should …" Reeves reached out and gripped Malcolm's arm and Malcolm jerked away.

"What do you think you're doing?"

"Sir, I just think it might be best …" He reached again, grabbing Malcolm's elbow as if trying to move him aside.

"Get off me." Malcolm felt unsteady. He just wanted to get to his office without a scene, but a surge of anger at the impertinence of this young man swooped through his chest and when Reeves reached out again, Malcolm balled his fist and punched the attorney in his nose. Reeves fell back, stumbling into the wall, his nose bloody. Shocked at what he'd done, Malcolm tried to apologize, but Reeves backed away holding his nose. Then Joe was at Malcolm's side, steadying him, gripping his shoulders.

"C'mon, Brother. I got you. C'mon."

"I didn't mean …" Malcolm tried to speak but couldn't seem to form the right words. He looked at Joe who was apologizing to Reeves. "I got him," he said and Malcolm tried again to speak, but Joe continued addressing the young man. "Go put some ice on that. I'll take care of him."

Malcolm couldn't seem to make sense of what was happening and let Joe lead him to his chambers. Cynthia's face expressed shock and she stood up as soon as they came in. Again, Joe spoke for him and Malcolm surrendered to his friend's guidance. "Get some water and some strong ass coffee," Joe said to Cynthia.

Malcolm dropped onto the couch in his private office and

immediately Joe was peering into his face. "I'm fine," Malcolm said, swatting his friend away.

Joe laughed, a nervous concerned laugh. "Brother, you are not fine. Where the hell did you sleep last night?"

Malcolm closed his eyes and tried to remember. He'd been at home, hadn't he? But the evening was vague. He remembered waking at home this morning, pouring a drink, vodka and tomato juice. Bet was sleeping. Bet was always sleeping.

"Brother, drink some water." Joe handed Malcolm a bottle. "We got some coffee coming."

"I didn't mean to hit him," Malcolm said thinking about Darryl Reeves. He took several gulps from the bottle. "Christ, I don't know what happened."

Cynthia came in and presented him with a large paper cup of coffee. The bottle of water started to slide out of his hand and he gripped it before it spilled. Joe took the bottle from him and warned him not to spill the coffee.

"Though it wouldn't really matter if you spill it on yourself. I'm not sure what that is."

Malcolm sipped the coffee and looked down at himself. His pants were wrinkled and there was a stain just above his knee. Tomato juice, he thought.

"You need to take a leave of absence."

"I'll be okay." He'd have some coffee and get himself together.

"That's not a suggestion, Brother. I'll talk to Reeves and let's hope he'll be understanding of your situation. You can't continue working. Take some time off."

Malcolm started to argue, but Joe's expression, a mixture of sympathy and irritation, told him to be quiet and accept his fate. He'd fucked up. He'd have to accept the consequences.

Joe dropped him at home, and he immediately showered feeling unclear on when he'd last bathed. He dried off and dressed in a loose shirt and sweatpants. Bet was likely still sleeping. He didn't check on her. As he surveyed the contents of the refrigerator, unsure what exactly he was seeking, Teddy called his cell phone and asked what the hell had happened at court this morning.

"How do you know about that?"

"There's a fucking video of you staggering through the courthouse and then taking a swing at someone. Jesus Christ, Malcolm, what the fuck were you thinking?"

"A video?"

"Yes. A video. You know that little app on everyone's phones these days? Didn't we talk about this?"

Malcolm ran his fingers across his forehead. What had Teddy said? Don't do anything to attract attention. He hadn't done it on purpose.

"My phone has been buzzing all morning," Teddy said. "Listen to me, Malcolm. No talking to anyone. You hear me? Nobody."

"Right."

Malcolm couldn't fathom why someone had recorded his encounter with Reeves. He'd apologize to the young man, of course, but the memory of what had happened already was a blur in his mind. He poured himself another Bloody Mary and turned on the news. The last thing he'd wanted was for Malawi's death to become a headline. And now he'd just made it worse.

26

By mid-morning Kenya unplugged the house phone. It'd been ringing repeatedly for hours. The first few times she answered only to hear a voice she didn't recognize ask if her father was an alcoholic. Another caller asked if alcoholism ran in the family. She wouldn't answer any more calls.

Kenya skipped her morning run, feeling nauseous, her stomach in knots, her head pounding, but she got Junior off to summer camp and called Grandma, explaining that she didn't feel so well and asked if Charlene could spend the day there. Fortunately, the kids were subdued and hadn't asked about their father. She couldn't talk about him.

She swept and mopped the kitchen floor, then vacuumed the sitting room. When all the cleaning was done, she stood in the hall listening to the silence until her cell phone rang. It was Ghana.

"Have you talked to Dad?" her sister asked.

Kenya said, "No," fearing something had happened.

"He's all over the news," Ghana said, her voice panicked. "He was drunk and punched someone. It's been caught on video. They've been showing it on the news. The national news. Have you talked to him? I called but he didn't answer the phone. Do you think we should go over there?"

Kenya took a moment to consider what her sister was saying. She'd never seen her father drunk. He drank wine occasionally, bourbon during the holidays, but there was never a time she could ever remember him being drunk.

"Get online and look," Ghana was saying. "I called Uncle Teddy

173

and left a message for him to call me back. We have to get this taken down."

"Who did this?"

"I have no idea. But I swear, if I ever find out, I will kick the shit out of them."

Kenya was confident Ghana would do such a thing. She had seen her sister angry, seen her punch and kick a boy in middle school who'd called her a bad name. The boy had teased Ghana about her large chest. He had tried to touch her there, and Ghana responded by kicking the boy in his private parts. When he was on the ground, she kicked him again, shouting at him to never touch her there ever again. And he never did. But their father, he was not a violent man.

Kenya pulled open her laptop and typed her father's name and the word "drunk" into the search engine. The video popped up as the first selection, and Kenya clicked on it. "I'm looking at it now," she said into the speaker. The image was grainy but she could see the back of her father staggering through the courthouse. Another man stopped him and seemed to be trying to escort him out of the hallway. After a brief interaction, her father swung at the man and hit him in the face. The man staggered back against the wall and just a moment later another man showed up. Kenya recognized Joe Willis, another judge at the courthouse and a good friend of her father's. The video stopped.

"Oh. My. God," she said.

"Exactly," said Ghana. "Look, let's go over to the house. It will be better if we go together, don't you think?"

"Sure," said Kenya, still seeing the image of her father punching the young man.

* * *

Ghana parked on the street and walked by her sister's Mercedes, already in the driveway behind her parents' cars. Chaos was oozing from the house. The front door was ajar and the voices inside were loud and angry; her mother's voice shaking the walls. Ghana closed the door behind her and found her mother, father, and Kenya in the kitchen.

"You never listen." Bet poked the air with pointed fingers. "You never listen to anyone. People calling here asking personal questions, all because you don't have any control."

Her father stood by the refrigerator, his mouth pursed in a tense line, watching her mother with a loathing Ghana had never seen before, and it frightened her. Kenya was positioned close to her mother, her hands outstretched but not touching, her face begging for peace. "Mama, please stop. Please, Mama. Please stop." Kenya repeated these words like a quiet mantra their mother didn't seem to hear.

"I'm tired of all of you," Bet said, sweeping her hand in a wide circle.

Ghana was dumbfounded. This was not her family, she thought. They didn't fight like this. She couldn't remember her parents fighting, storming through the house shouting at one another. No, it never happened that way. Yet it did. She just didn't want to remember. These disputes were never real brawls. Instead a tense silence filled the house and Daddy would disappear while Mama began raging. The girls would listen, silently, while their mother thundered through the house, screaming insults at their father who was nowhere around to hear. Or worse, she directed her anger at them, frustrated they were making too much noise, complaining she couldn't work, couldn't focus. They cowered from their mother's fury. Her hostility.

"Just be quiet," Mama would scream. Ghana, small, in Kenya's room, arms around Malawi while their mother raged on like thunder they hoped would eventually pass. Kenya, humming, trying to distract them with a song. A song their father used to sing to them. Trying to remember the words and throwing out a word or two—*when I wake up in the morning love*—until Ghana would remember a line—*and something is heavy on my mind*—and they would all sing, *Then I look at you, and the world's alright with me.* Quietly, while their mother whirled and roared. Their tiny voices tuning out the disturbance, pretending everything was fine. *A lovely daaaaaaayyy…*

"No one understands," Mama would scream. "No one. I can't do all this by myself. I just can't do it."

Do what? Ghana was never clear on what her mother was so upset about. Being a mother to three girls? Being a wife to an important judge? Her mother, the artist. It was just who she was, they reasoned. Who she had always been. Dramatic. Emotional. Uncontrolled.

"This is all your fault," she was screaming now, her face scrunched, her eyes almost closed, her fingers pointing toward her husband. "You did this. She wanted to get away from you. You ruined her. Treated her like she was the only child in the world, and it turned her against us."

"Enough!"

Ghana was startled by her father's voice, booming, strong, filling the kitchen, freezing her mother by the dishwasher. Everyone stared at him.

"I am done." His chest seemed to expand as he heaved in a breath.

"Done with you blaming me. This is not my fault. I am done." He didn't acknowledge his daughters, simply turned and pushed past his wife. The air continued to swirl and Ghana felt dizzy. Her mother was motionless, focused on the spot where her husband had been, as if in shock.

"Mama," Kenya said, moving gingerly closer, palms up, head cocked. "Mama, come sit down." Ghana pulled a chair from the dining table and waited for her mother to move, but Bet continued to stand, now searching the floor as if she'd dropped an earring.

"Please, come sit." Kenya patted the chair.

A drink was in order, Ghana thought, but instead of liquor, she put on the kettle for tea. Something to relax her mother. Bet finally moved, dropping heavily into the chair, like a rock dropped from up high. Kenya quickly pulled out another chair, dragging it close to her mother, squeezing Bet's forearm. She looked at Ghana, but Ghana didn't know what to say or do. So she shrugged, feeling exhausted and took a seat on the other side of the table. Kenya reached across and squeezed her fingers; Ghana squeezed back. Everything was crumbling. Her family. The world. Everything.

"What do we do, Kennie?" she said.

Kenya started to hum. Ghana immediately recognized the old song and sang a few words, "When the day that lies ahead of me, seems impossible to face." She stopped, terror filling her chest. Malawi wasn't with them. Just two musketeers. But she cleared her throat and began again, singing the words she remembered, "When someone else instead of me, always seems to know the way." Kenya joined and they sang together, "Then I look at you, and the world's alright with me." Her mother's head fell forward and she slumped to her right, leaning into

Kenya who stretched her arm over her mother's shoulders. They would get through this, Ghana thought. They would get through it. She kept singing and Kenya kept singing.

"And I know it's gonna be, a lovely day …"

27

Malcolm stared at the casket, mahogany with a glossy finish and brass fixtures. Beautiful workmanship. Kenya chose well. After a few moments studying the wood grain, his gaze drifted to the colorful stained-glass windows of the church. His wife's church, with the Reverend Willoughby in the pulpit talking about his daughter as if she were dead. Outside the sun was shining. He closed his eyes, the bright windows leaving an image on his eyelids.

But she was dead.

His mother shifted next to him and her fingers patted and squeezed his hand; for a moment he wanted to push her away. He didn't need her sympathy. He needed to get up and walk out and keep walking until he could make the whole world disappear, go back in time, tell Malawi to stay in D.C. And maybe she would still be alive. But he was stuck now on this wooden seat between his slumped wife and his mother, whose back was as stiff as the pew. He was stuck in this ceremony to say goodbye to Malawi, this funeral service, this private hell. His close friends were here, seated behind him, including Joe and Teddy. Cousins, too, he barely knew. All here to remember, as if he could possibly forget his baby girl.

Reverend Willoughby said, "let us pray," and Malcolm leaned his head in his hands, each elbow resting on each knee. Malcolm wasn't a man of prayer. He considered himself a man of action. Action, he could control. Prayer, he couldn't. Praying had never done anything to help him. It didn't save his father. It didn't help the criminals in his courtroom or any of the thousands of children who died every year from disease and violence despite the desperate prayers of their parents. God has a plan for everyone's life, Bet used to say. So what was His plan now?

Soon Malcolm would be called up to speak about Malawi, to tell the world how wonderful she was, how sweet and kind and sassy, how much she'd be missed. That wasn't quantifiable, he thought. He should have prepared remarks to stop himself from rambling, but he couldn't hold a particular thought long enough to write it down.

His mother nudged him to stand and pointed at the hymnal, sharing it with him as if he was going to sing along. Her voice was low but firm as she sang a song only vaguely familiar to Malcolm. Bet, on his right, groaned along, the book drooping in her hands. Kenya's voice rose strong and beautiful. She was on the other side of Bet, towering above her mother.

A large wooden crucifix hung behind the pulpit. So how does taking Malawi figure into your big fancy plan, Christ Jesus? Tell me that. A plan. That was what Malcolm needed. He needed a plan, though to do what exactly, he wasn't sure.

* * *

The minister was overly dramatic, Ghana thought. But he was playing to the emotion of the greater community, not so much to the Walker family. Not to say the Walkers were not heartbroken. Of course they were. But not like that. Not dripping with this thick sentiment of sadness the Reverend Willoughby was slathering over the people from the District of Columbia, as well as friends and family members, distant and close. This service was a show for the cameras and reporters who sat dotted throughout the church.

The Walkers had gathered this morning for a private moment with Malawi. Their father had hugged Ghana for so long she felt lightheaded when he let her go. She held Kenya close for a long time, too, feeling this deep loss in their trinity. She even embraced her mother, whose shrunken body seemed to flop like a rag doll, unable or unwilling to hold itself up, leaning heavily on her husband to get through each moment of the day.

Ghana was empty of any more emotion. Her subconscious had said goodbye during the night, in a dream; that dream of them sitting by the ocean, but this time Malawi ran down the beach, laughing, and dove into the water, disappearing in a large blue wave that rose up like the mouth of a whale and swallowed her whole. Standing on the beach waving goodbye, Ghana awoke slow and heavy and sobbed. Through her tears, she thanked her little sister for all the happy moments they had shared.

Seated at the other end of the pew, her father looked depleted in a way her mother didn't. Mama had been drained for so long it was almost normal for her to look thin and frail. But her father appeared downtrodden and stunned, smaller than he had ever looked to Ghana. Teddy and Joe sat behind him, protecting him from the poking and prodding of the world. He's been exalted and vilified in the television talk shows and opinion columns. His court decisions have been analyzed as if his work as a judge could offer insight into why his youngest daughter had broken down on the side of the road and sought help at a nearby house only to be murdered by a fearful Floridian who shot first and asked no questions.

Ryan's solidity next to her, their fingers entwined, gave her comfort, yet there was a chasm between them she wasn't sure she could close. He would never understand who she was. She carried a burden in her genetic coding, the burden of dark skin, the double-whammy of being black and a woman. The assumption that she would steal, that her hair was dirty, that she was lazy and sexually promiscuous. That she had no right to speak her mind. That her life was worth less than a white life just because she was black. That she didn't really matter. Something was deeply wrong with a world where a white man saw a black woman at his door and shot to kill. An act of kindness would have cost him nothing—to ask what she needed, to make a simple phone call for a tow-truck.

After meeting Ryan, she had studied the Loving case, amazed and thrilled by it; amazed that two people could be jailed just because a black woman had married a white man; amazed that her relationship with Ryan had only become legal in Virginia around fifty years ago. Thrilled that two people had refused to be defined by a state law. Thrilled that love had conquered the pettiness of a nation. And yet. Here we were again pitting black against white, white against black.

Ryan squeezed her fingers. She wanted to be strong and embody the strength of Mildred Loving. Wanted to stay with a white man who carried a gun to work, who for many, represented oppression and extreme violence, sometimes death. She just wasn't sure she could.

Dad had always been the one she sought for advice about men. Mama was dismissive in her responses, the stay-at-home mom who was too busy painting to talk to her kids. But Dad, the important judge, always had time, even just a moment to listen and respond. Gently he would say, "I only have a moment. What do you need?" At a young age Ghana recognized that her father had once been a boy and could help her understand boys, though at thirty-one, she still found them confusing.

"What do you think of Ryan?" she had asked her father after he met him.

"Seems like a good man. Respectful."

"What about him being white?"

Her father chuckled. "Do you like him?"

She hesitated. "I think I love him."

"But do you *like* him? Can you sit in a car with him driving from here to San Francisco and back and still want to be with him afterward?"

Ghana laughed then, saying, "Sure I could," but thought about such a drive for days, months after. They probably could survive that kind of time together. When it was just the two of them, life seemed simple and easy. But the world had a way of intruding, poking into their lives, shaking things up and creating chaos. It wasn't being in the car together, it was what they encountered on the road and how the world influenced their thoughts and actions. Finding a way to navigate the rocks and potholes, that was the challenge.

Everyone stood as the pallbearers gathered around the casket and carried it down the aisle to the hearse waiting outside. Her parents followed first, then Kenya and the kids—Sidney wasn't here—and then Ghana and Ryan and each pew thereafter. She was pleased to see Cass here, though she was by herself near the back. Her friend blew a kiss and Ghana beckoned for her to come with them, but Cass refused, not wanting to intrude. Outside, the family climbed into a limousine and Ghana stared at the carpeted floor thinking about Malawi diving into the ocean.

The ride to the graveside felt longer than twenty minutes; no one said a word, the only noise was Mama quietly sobbing.

* * *

The sun was bright, yet the air was cool in the cemetery. A field of headstones spread out across a rolling hill and Kenya felt the chill of grief that stuck to the grass, the trees, and the stones all around them, a grief she didn't feel.

Malawi was being buried next to their grandfather. The Honorable William G. Walker. Hundreds of people had come out for his funeral. Junior had just turned two and Sidney had carried him in his arms up the hill to the grave site. She looked at her son now, wearing a black suit and tie, looking much older than twelve, looking much like his father. She prayed he didn't become the asshole his father was.

All day, staring at the casket, Kenya had wanted to rip it open, pull her sister out and scream at her, "What the hell were you thinking? He's my husband." She wanted to hear Malawi explain how it happened. Did he seduce her? Did she approach him first? When? Kenya was fighting the hatred boiling in her stomach for her sister, for her husband. It was wrong for her to hate her dead sister, gunned down for seeking help. Practically a martyr in the black community. But she did hate her. She'd slept with her husband behind her back. Wore sexy underwear and sent him messages knowing he was married to her sister. And him. He eagerly went along with the affair knowing how wrong they both were.

As family and friends placed flowers on the casket, Kenya wanted to spit on it. Instead she walked away, taking Charlene's hand in her own and linking arms with her son. Her life was unraveling, all the threads coming undone and she couldn't stop it, couldn't keep the fabric tidy and neat, not anymore. Her children must be her focus now, yet she feared what the world held for them. Junior, not yet a teenager, would grow to be a black man in a world killing young black men, killing their spirits, their hearts, their ideas. Their lives. Charlene, still so innocent. So many black women were lonely, struggling to be strong in a world that didn't hold them in its heart. She didn't want her children to be confused by what the world told them. By the messages in the media and what teachers would try to make them think. They were strong and beautiful and they could think for themselves. That's what she wanted them to know. She wanted them to read and learn and understand who they were. She wanted them to be unafraid, to succeed, to thrive.

She stumbled on the gravel path heading back to the car. Stopped moving and closed her eyes, clinging tighter to her children.

A white man shot her sister. Shot her in the chest, and Kenya didn't know how do deal with that truth. How to make peace with the fact that she'd never get to confront her. To hear Malawi's side of the story. To ever make peace. She didn't know how to move forward and raise two strong and loving children in a world that allowed this murderer to go free.

"Mom, you okay?" Junior's voice seeped into her thoughts.

She reassured him that she was fine and hugged him close. "It's just a sad day." She kissed the top of his head. "Just a very sad day."

28

For the third time this week Ghana talked to a woman who had lost a loved one. This woman, her name was Brenda, had lost her son when he was shot by a stray bullet in Columbia Heights. He'd been three months shy of his sixteenth birthday.

"He was walking home from school when shots were fired from a passing car," she said. "We don't know what the target was, but my boy went down, and the police still haven't found the shooter. That was five months ago."

"I'm so sorry," Ghana said, knowing these were helpless words that did nothing to change what was wrong. She was becoming a better listener. All they wanted, really, was someone to talk to, someone who understood what they were feeling.

The first time someone called her, Ghana had panicked realizing her information was available for anyone to find—the woman had tried to contact Bet, but instead found Ghana's name and number online. She thought the call would last only a moment, but instead it was almost ninety minutes. The woman had lost her sister to a shooting; the sister had been a drug addict. "Didn't mean she deserved to die."

"Of course not."

"She was high and got into a fight with a police officer," the woman said. "The details are unclear, but they shot her. She didn't have no weapon. They say she was resisting arrest. And they shot her."

Ghana couldn't find any words. There was nothing she could do, but she asked anyway. "What do you need?"

"Just wanted to talk to you. To let you know, you and your family ain't alone."

The gesture made Ghana cry. A complete stranger had reached out to her to let her know she wasn't alone. Then two days later another call came and this woman said her husband had been choked to death by a white man in Philadelphia. The men had gotten into a fight over a parking space. A parking space!

When Cass called, inviting her to happy hour, Ghana admitted she could do with a drink.

Arriving early, she settled into a booth at Jerry's bar, ordering two light beers. A small group, laughing and talking loudly, were spread out across several tables pulled together in the center of the place. Ghana suspected they were co-workers from a nearby office; the group was mixed: men, women, black, white, Latino, Asian, all enjoying drinks and appetizers. What a world it would be if this reflected every community. People accepting one another at face value, working and socializing together, appreciating what each one offered.

"Tough day?" Cass said as she slid into the seat opposite.

Ghana rolled her eyes. "There's too much death."

"What? What's happened now?"

"No, nothing new." Ghana told her about the women who'd called, about their pain and heartache and sense of loss at having no outlet to express their hurt. Cass tilted her head and offered a sympathetic expression. "So they call you to talk?"

"Yeah. I feel so inadequate. It's like they have no one else. Yet at the same time, I completely understand. You can't relate to anyone unless they've gone through it themselves."

When Ghana had called Cass to tell her about Malawi's death, Ghana had cried on the phone with her for an hour. She knew Cass would understand because she'd lost a brother to cancer. But after talking with these women who were strangers, and yet not strangers, Ghana realized there was a deeper connection of loss because the loved one had died, not from some disease inside their body, but from a malicious disease outside of themselves. Destroyed by a violence and hatred that was eating at the core of society. And that was a different pain. A different feeling of loss, of no control; while death may be the result of a physical disease, death should not be the result of being black or Asian or Latino or Muslim or Christian, or anything that sets a person apart from another group of people.

"Aren't there groups to help, you know, support groups?" Cass asked. "Professionals they can call?"

"Not really. I did some research and there are plenty of grief support groups and counseling but nothing for this kind of loss, where a family member is killed, you know …" She stumbled over the word. "… murdered." After a moment she said, "Who would have thought more than twenty years after Rodney King, the country is still fighting about race?"

"Girl, this country's always been fighting about race."

Ghana's mood slumped at the thought, fearing what the future held for the nation. For herself. Maybe different races shouldn't mix. Maybe people from different cultures should have remained in their respective sections of the world and not gone exploring, had not transported millions like chattel across continents to become enslaved.

She watched the bar fill with men in suits and women in heels, looking for happiness for an hour before they head home. Loud laughter erupted from the mixed group in the middle of the bar, and she watched them gesturing and laughing. She wanted to believe this group did represent most of America.

"So what's the deal with you and Ryan?" Cass asked.

Ghana released a sigh and shrugged, uninterested in talking about her relationship. "I don't know." Cass nudged for information, prodding until Ghana responded. "I still love him, but this whole race thing, and the gun thing, just has me feeling weird about it all."

Her friend nodded and sipped her beer.

"I mean the color of his skin had nothing to do with anything for me. That's not what I saw when I met him, but I guess I just didn't think it all through."

"What's there to think about? You either love him and think he's worth the effort, or you don't." Cass swirled the last of her beer in the bottom of the bottle. "My parents, they've been together since the mid-seventies. They met and married in Philly, but still, they experienced some shit for being a mixed couple. My mom would tell me about folks asking her if she was babysitting. A white woman couldn't have two dark-skinned babies. Just crazy shit like that." She shook her head. "But my parents stayed true to their own belief that they were meant to be together. They've argued, and my dad even cheated on my mom at one point—though I don't think he knows I know that." She chuckled and asked if Ghana wanted another beer. Ghana nodded and Cass waved over the waiter.

"Yeah, my mom found out and jacked him up," she continued. "Told him he either got his act together or he'd never see his kids again. He chose his kids. At the time, me and Kwame were little, like babies, but as far as I know, Dad's been faithful ever since." She sighed. "What I'm saying is, they didn't let other people influence what was between them. They got looks, but still, they held hands and walked with God, as my mom says."

The waiter brought fresh drinks and Cass took a sip. "You need to focus on what's between you two," she said, "and stop thinking about what other people are doing and saying."

Ghana considered this for a moment, then said, "What worries me is, can I trust that he really loves *me* and not this exotic image that white men sometimes have about black women? You know?"

"Girl, yes, I know. But you have to search your heart for that. You either trust that he loves you for you, or you don't. And if you don't trust him, then you don't need to be with him."

"You make it sound so simple." Ghana wanted to trust him. Wanted to trust that he loved her and not her skin color, yet she was afraid to ask him outright.

As if reading her mind, Cass asked, "Why don't you talk to him about it. Ask him if your race was a factor in why he's with you."

"I can't ask him that."

"Why not?"

"Because if that's not the case, he'll be insulted."

"Well, how would you feel if he thought you were with him because he's white?"

Ghana paused, unsure how to respond. "But that's not the case."

"Sure, we know that, but he doesn't."

Before Ghana could answer, Allan surprised them both and came into the booth next to Cass, kissing her repeatedly on her face. Cass giggled and asked if he wanted a drink. Ghana decided to head home and gave Cass a hug, thanking her for listening.

She took her time walking down the block, the bright sun still hot in the sky, the street filled with people rushing home after work. She thought about Ryan, about Malawi, about the women she'd talked to, about their loss. So many women looking for a connection with someone who understood. She could create a support group. She could do it with Kenya's help. An organization that would honor Malawi. Ghana increased her pace, suddenly eager to get home and research how to start such a group.

29

Malcolm didn't like having nothing to do. He used to play chess on the computer, but these days he couldn't focus on it. He'd buried his little girl last week and each morning since, he'd awakened feeling gutted, expecting to see his insides splayed out on the bed. Flashes of Malawi waking up in a coffin, screaming that she was still alive stopped him from sleeping. He headed downstairs, another entire day ahead of him with no appointments, no cases to review, nothing. His breakfast was two Bloody Marys and a bowl of cornflakes. He would walk, he thought. Through the neighborhood or take a drive to the C&O Canal. Maybe later.

He slumped into his armchair and turned on the television searching for something mindless. He paused at "Judge Judy" and laughed. If only it were that easy. CNN was reporting a bombing in Afghanistan. The Weather Channel warned the country to prepare for hurricane season. The History Channel was analyzing the shooting of JFK. He stopped at The Discovery Channel and watched a spider spinning an intricate web, the narrator's voice soft as if not to disturb this creator at work. After a while, he continued flipping through channels and stopped when he heard Malawi's name. A talk show discussing the arrest of Jeffrey Davies. That motherfucker! Arrested but immediately released on bail. At home as if Davies had violated a traffic law instead of committing murder, while his baby girl was rotting in the ground. Malcolm was convinced the son-of-a-bitch wouldn't be convicted. He deserved the death penalty. Malcolm would give him the death penalty. In fact, he should kill him himself. The thought floated around his mind and then hung like a leaf caught on a web. He should kill him himself. Malcolm imagined stabbing the man in his chest multiple times, blood spurting everywhere, then he shook the image away, only for it to return with Davies screaming for his life while Malcolm pushed the knife deeper and deeper into his flesh. He could almost feel the muscle and bone. But, no, in reality he wouldn't kill the man that way. It was too intimate, too messy. He'd rather shoot him, blast him backwards into hell with a shotgun just like he did to Malawi.

He heard Bet's soft tread on the stairs. He sank lower into the cushions, hoping she'd stay away from him. They hadn't touched each other in weeks, but she poked him with her criticisms, her accusations. He heard her go into the kitchen and fill the kettle with water, then she came into the den and hovered near the settee, likely watching him from across the room, though he wouldn't look up.

"Are you just going to sit there all day?"

Malcolm said nothing in response. She spent most of her time drugged with sleeping pills and had no right to judge him for watching TV.

She walked over to the window. "I feel that draft coming through these sliding doors," she said. "Needs caulk, I think. You said you'd do this months ago."

Malcolm didn't want to move, but he knew she wanted him to look, to confirm she was right, get the caulk and fix it now because this was the focus of her attention, and so, it should be his, too. She'd complained about this draft last winter and no, he hadn't fixed it then. And he wouldn't now. Not now. Besides, there was no breeze, no wind outside. The weather was still and humid.

Her breath inhaled sharply, but she didn't push for a fight. "It's not so bad now with the warm weather," she said. "But when it gets cold it's going to be bad. We should fix it soon."

"We," she said, but she meant him. With a sigh he got up and walked to where she stood, crouched down to inspect the seal along the bottom of the sliding glass door. "I'm thinking I might go to Florida. Just take a few days away." The words tumbled out of him before he even realized this was what he'd been thinking.

"Florida? Why in the hell would you go there?"

"Go to the beach, maybe?" But it wasn't the beach he was interested in.

"I never want to go back there."

"I'm not asking you to come," he said more sharply than intended and glanced at her stricken face. He looked back at the floor. "I just want to be alone for a while. Maybe work on my golf swing."

"You hate golf."

A frown creased his forehead and he ran his fingers along the rubbery seal. "I'll get someone to take a look at it. Looks like it might need more than just caulk." He stood up and left her in the den with the television talk show rambling in the background.

30

Ghana could see there was something off about her sister. She was unsteady but not in a drunk way, more of an absent-minded way. Unfocused. And that wasn't like Kenya. She watched her sister slather teriyaki glaze on two chicken breasts, her hair pulled back in a severe ponytail, her casual shirt and jeans crisply laundered, her face crumpling as if the action was painful. Then the brush spontaneously slipped out of Kenya's hand and bounced off the counter onto the floor leaving a trail of teriyaki sauce along the marble. Kenya stared unbelieving at her hand and Ghana stifled a laugh.

"Sis, let me do it." She bent down and retrieved the brush and dumped it in the sink.

"That was weird," said Kenya, a puzzled smile tugging her lips as she stood helplessly at the counter.

"Don't worry about it. It's been happening to me too. Sit." Ghana pointed at the stools on the other side of the breakfast bar then poured a glass of the pinot noir she'd brought. "Have some wine."

She used a spoon to finish glazing the chicken then placed the tray in the oven to bake, marveling at the expansive clean kitchen with stainless steel at every turn. Kenya had called earlier in the afternoon inviting Ghana over for dinner, but something in her sister's voice had put Ghana on alert. "We have to do better," Kenya had said. "Be better sisters to one another." Yes, but Ghana suspected something more, something beyond the loss of Malawi and being better sisters. When she arrived, Kenya welcomed her with red puffy eyes. Ghana couldn't remember the last time she'd seen her sister cry—not even at the funeral. This wasn't the bossy, in-charge sister Ghana knew so well, which was unnerving.

She began slicing tomatoes for the salad while Kenya settled on a stool. Since Kenya had yet to open up, Ghana nudged her now, softly. "What's going on?"

Kenya's forehead wrinkled as she tightened her grip on her glass of wine. Her voice flat, she said, "Sidney has moved into an apartment in Georgetown. The kids are visiting with him for the weekend. We would be having our seventh annual Fourth of July cookout this weekend, and I've had three people call today asking if it's on." Her sister finally looked up and jerked her shoulders. "I said he was out of town."

Ghana released a half grunt, half groan. She'd never considered the premature end of her sister's perfect marriage with her two perfect kids and perfect house. Though in reality, it wasn't perfect. Kenya had let it slip a few Christmases ago that Sidney had been unfaithful, but was confident they would recover and, as far as Ghana could tell, they had.

But he'd done it again. "Cheated with … with another woman." Kenya closed her eyes for a moment. "It's over this time. For real."

Ghana dumped the tomatoes on top of the lettuce already in a bowl and paused to look at her sister. "Are you considering a divorce?"

"Yes."

Everything stopped, just for a second, until Ghana drew in a long breath. She had still been in high school when Kenya started dating Sidney. The two of them not being together seemed implausible—like her little sister being dead. Life had become distorted, she thought. Maybe they were living in a parallel universe and eventually everything would sort itself. She wished everything would go back to normal. But this *was* the new normal. She realized she'd been holding the knife in the air and placed it by the bowl, then surveyed the shiny kitchen.

"Will you keep the house?" Instantly, the question seemed absurd and she immediately felt guilty for thinking about such a material thing when her sister's heart was likely in pieces. "That's probably the last thing on your mind."

Kenya raised her glass of wine, holding it above her head. "Hell, yes, I'm keeping the house. I'm taking that asshole for all he's got."

Ghana chuckled, feeling her body relax. She moved around the bar and straddled the stool next to Kenya. They clinked glasses and toasted to new-found freedom.

"He's definitely going to pay," Kenya said, but her voice broke. Ghana grabbed her hand.

"You're strong. And I'm here for you. We'll get through this."

Kenya didn't reveal the woman's name. "Just a woman," she said too quickly. Ghana figured it was likely someone Kenya knew.

"The affair lasted longer than he admitted," she said. "I found things, receipts, cards, stuff that proved it went on awhile. I'm done with the lies." Wiping her nose with the back of her hand, Kenya sniffed and made a slight shaking gesture with her head, a cat shaking off a sneeze.

"Thanks for cooking," she said. "You're better at it than me."

"Just baked chicken with salad."

Cold air blew vigorously through the vents but the wine made Ghana's face warm. Returning to the bowl of lettuce and tomatoes, she added grated carrots, sunflower seeds and cranberries. She grabbed a block of cheese from the refrigerator and grated part of it into the bowl, wondering why Sidney would risk his family for a piece of ass.

Kenya changed the subject. "How are things with you and Ryan?"

Ghana shrugged. Switching from her sister's likely divorce to her own impending break-up didn't seem like a good idea, but she considered how to respond. "Ryan and I are ... well, we're in a bad place."

"I never thought you two were a good idea."

"Don't start." She wasn't in the mood for her sister's judgment, but Kenya talked on about opposites not lasting longer than the initial attraction, that police officers have a reputation—domineering, aggressive. "They're known to cheat, too."

Ghana raised her hand, palm facing Kenya. "Stop! Just stop. You're not doing this to me. We're not doing this."

Startled into silence, Kenya sat open-mouthed, blinking in that annoying way she did when she didn't know what to do. But Ghana needed a moment. She wasn't going to make her sister feel better. But then Kenya spoke, softly, apologetically. "Ghan-Ghan, you're right. I'm being petty. I don't even know him."

She reached for Ghana's arm. "I know I haven't been there for you in recent years, but let's do better. Okay? Daddy says we should take care of each other. Especially now."

Ghana considered her sister's words. Especially now. Now there were only two of them. She patted her sister's hand, took a gulp of wine and opened the oven door to check the chicken. A blast of heat hit her face. Using two large oven gloves, she set the pan on the range.

"Thing is," she said, "I'm not sure how I feel about him." She studied the meat as if waiting for it to move. "I thought I was so in love, but now, I'm not sure."

"Is it still the race thing?" Kenya leaned on the counter, watching Ghana.

"Yeah." She placed the salad bowl and a vinaigrette dressing on the kitchen dining table then returned to the chicken. "He just doesn't seem to understand how I feel about these shootings that are happening and the protests." She reached into the cupboard for plates. "He dismisses the whole Black Lives Matter movement and is in the 'everyone matters' camp."

"But everyone *does* matter."

Ghana almost dropped the plates and looked at her sister. "You're kidding, right?"

"No. I'm not." Kenya wore her stern face, the one she got when she was about to climb on her horse. "I mean, I get it, I get this movement is saying more focus should be on black lives and how society isn't respecting us as much as white lives. But what bothers me is the black-on-black crime no one seems to be talking about. I mean, isn't that something we, as a people, should be addressing?" She lifted her wine glass but didn't drink then put it back on the counter. "We get all up in arms because white cops are abusing and killing black people, but we don't seem to care that we're killing our own people in much larger numbers."

"But it goes deeper than that," Ghana said, stumbling through her thoughts to respond. "Our people have struggled economically. And when you start with nothing, you've got nothing to lose. So you act out."

"Act out? Is that what's happening?" Kenya snorted. "Black people are acting out like children who don't get what they want?"

"No, not like children," Ghana said. "Like human beings who have been oppressed for so long they feel they have no recourse. No way to get their needs met. So they resort to violence, toward each other, to anyone in their way. It may not be right, but economic inequality goes back to slavery."

"Oh, Christ, really? Oh, poor little black people, we can't get it together because we were once slaves? That's ridiculous."

Ghana could feel her own irritation and frustration in her breathlessness. She wasn't explaining well. She wanted to stress the hopelessness in many depressed communities, the idea that a predominantly white environment had created subtle inequalities that often went unnoticed. "It's not ridiculous," she said. "Not if the system is set up for you to fail."

"Yeah, fail like our family? What a bunch of losers we are, who can't get ahead."

Ghana scraped a chicken breast onto a plate for herself and one for her sister. Kenya took both plates and set them on the table, sat down, and with bowed head, silently said grace before dumping a mound of lettuce on her plate. She covered the leaves with dressing then cut into the chicken. Ghana brought the wine and sat down.

"You always do this," she said, spooning salad onto her plate.

Kenya swallowed a mouthful of lettuce and gazed out the window above the sink. "Do what? What do I always do?"

"You turn everything into an argument."

"No I don't."

Ghana looked at the ceiling as if searching for some celestial help. "I don't even know how we got here. I was trying to talk about Ryan and … and we said we wouldn't fight … and I can't even talk to you without you disagreeing with everything I say. This happens every time."

Slow and steady like a cow chewing grass, Kenya ground her food. Finally she wiped her mouth with a cloth napkin and made eye contact. "You're right. I'm sorry."

They ate in silence until Ghana's irritation subsided. She said, "Well, it's good to know you actually have some passion in you."

Kenya swatted at her and Ghana dodged her hand.

"You make a good point about the violence within the black community," Ghana said. "I have no idea where to start with that, but at least there's a movement happening across the country that's acknowledging our people are dying unnecessarily. That's worth supporting, don't you think?"

"Sure. Of course it is."

This was the moment, she thought, to bring her sister in on her plan to create a support group. Excitement built as she talked about the good they could do in reaching out to women and families who had lost a family member from a shooting. She talked about the women seeking support, wanting a shoulder to lean on, about the research showing only a few such groups across the country, with not one in the D.C. region.

"And you came up with this because of Malawi?" Kenya asked.

"A way to honor her." Ghana could tell from Kenya's expression that she wasn't sold on the idea. "You should listen to the women I've talked to," she added. "Hear their stories. There's definitely a need. I've even thought of a name: Sisters of the Slain."

Kenya screwed up her nose. "That sounds morbid."

"But it's the truth. Plus, I've already thought of a logo. I want you to help me organize the group."

Kenya shook her head. "I wouldn't be any good."

"You can be the legal counsel, and you'd be fantastic." Kenya made a face that said you've got to be kidding and Ghana chuckled, then got serious. "There are a *lot* of women out there in need of support. I had no idea. Mostly they just want someone to talk to, and I figured we could create a group that would support one another. We can figure out what they need, what other resources are out there for them, maybe provide legal resources. Dad would know folks who we could refer. You know, that sort of thing. What do you think?"

"Maybe." Kenya thought for a moment. "What about 'Malawi's Sisters' as a name?"

A thrill rose in Ghana's chest at having her sister on board. "That's a great name. It honors her and recognizes all the women as sisters. Perfect!"

Kenya suggested talking to their father before making any concrete decisions, and Ghana agreed. "Have you talked to him?"

Kenya said she hadn't. "He's gone to Florida. I've no idea why."

"What about Mama? Have you talked to her?"

With a shake of her head, Kenya said, "I'm worried about her. I call every day but she doesn't answer the phone."

31

In line at the pharmacy, a tall woman stood too close behind Bet, smelling of some strong fragrance that irritated Bet's nose, and every time Bet inched forward to create more space between them, the woman moved closer. She could feel the woman's breath on the back of her head. The man ahead of her was called to the counter. Not long now. She needed a refill on the prescription sleeping pills. Less than three weeks had passed and already she'd gone through her thirty-day supply, but she was certain she had one refill. Malcolm would caution her that she was going through the pills too fast, but he wasn't here. And she didn't miss him. Not one bit. He never listened to her, tuned her out and walked away, and that didn't solve anything. So he'd gone off to Florida of all places. To find himself? Take a break? Grieve in private? What kind of a man wouldn't grieve with his wife, wouldn't share in the pain she was feeling. He said he was heartbroken, but Bet didn't see it.

When she got to the counter, the young clerk searched the rows of prescriptions waiting to be collected but came back empty handed. "There's nothing for you," he said.

"Oh, but I called it in on the automatic refill line. Here." She handed over the empty bottle. She had only been half listening but thought she'd pressed all the right buttons to refill her prescription.

The man consulted with a stern-looking woman behind a glass window and returned. "I'm sorry, we can't refill for another seven days."

"But I need it now," Bet said, desperation rising in her throat, though she tried to sound composed. "I just really need it now."

"I'm sorry. We can't refill it. You'll have to come back."

She wandered away from the counter and loitered helplessly in the aisle near to tears. "What am I going to do?" She was whining but couldn't stop herself; like beads falling from a broken necklace her words spilled out of her mouth. "What am I going to do? I really need these pills."

Just one pill had given her the best sleep she'd had in weeks. A few days later, she found that having just one additional pill in the afternoon made her feel more relaxed. She pulled out her cell phone and called her doctor, waiting on hold for five minutes while she wandered through the store looking at vitamin supplements and bandages for joint sprains. When her doctor finally came on the line, she explained that Bet would have to wait until the time passed. "It's not me. It's the insurance companies," said Dr. Lane.

Bet paced up and down the aisle murmuring to herself. A young white man approached and asked what was wrong. Without looking at him she moaned about her plight. "I just really need my pills. I'm going through a tough time right now and I can't sleep. The pills have made such a difference."

He moved close to her and whispered, "I might be able to help you with that." She stepped away and scrutinized him. Young, twenty-something, not too tall, creamy white skin, black spiky hair, and a stocky build. He could supply her with as many pills as she wanted, he said.

"What do you mean?"

"Well, if you're interested I know someone, and whatever you need I can get it for you. You interested?"

A small voice inside her head said she shouldn't trust this man; accepting his offer would be a mistake, never mind illegal, but she squashed that voice and nodded vigorously.

"How much?" she asked, but he covered his lips with his forefinger and beckoned her to follow him. He led her to his car in the parking lot and produced a bag of pills from a box in the trunk. A shock ran through her as she viewed his supply.

"What are you looking for?"

Shaking, she showed him her prescription bottle and he found a bag with thousands of pills that matched what she had. Excitement and fear trilled in her chest. "How much?"

He leaned close to her ear and said a dollar a pill for the first twenty if she was willing to play.

"Play?"

He grinned revealing small child-like teeth that Bet found adorable. He was so young and yet old for his age. He slid the back of his hand across her breast. "You're an attractive woman. I like curves and you got plenty."

Bet shoved his hand away but giggled. "I'm old enough to be your mother."

"I like a mature woman." He leaned into her and kissed her cheek, soft and slow, lingering against her skin creating a stir of goose bumps down her neck. He shook the bag. "Forty for this bag or half price if we get to play."

It'd been weeks since she and Malcolm had been intimate. She tried to imagine this boy, with his minty breath and fake New York accent, having sex with her. It would be like prostitution, but she considered it. Twenty dollars. She had that much in her purse. No random cash withdrawal to alert suspicion from Malcolm. Before she could stop herself, she nodded.

In her bedroom, excitement swelled between her legs. The boy—he said his nickname was Tripp—was so young Bet blushed at the thought of him touching her body. Without his shirt, his skin stretched across his bones, revealing small muscles in his shoulders and arms. He ran his hands up her thighs, took hold of her panties—large, practical, unsexy cotton panties—pulled them ever so slowly down past her toes and flicked them to the ground. He grabbed her ankles and pulled her across the bed sprawling her naked, except for her bra, on her back. She emitted a nervous giggle, feeling like a teenager having sex for the first time in her parents' bed. Her forearm rested across her breasts as if attempting a semblance of modesty. He separated her legs, sliding his hands up her inner thighs until the tips of his fingers were pushing against that private place only Malcolm had touched in forever.

Suddenly she remembered the night Malcolm proposed on the living room floor of his tiny apartment on Newark Street in Northwest. He still had a year left at the Washington College of Law. They'd ordered Chinese and after consuming a bottle of wine made love on the couch with Heatwave crooning in the background. Naked, Malcolm got on his knees and proposed.

"Marry me, Elizabeth Ellis. Marry me right now."

She giggled when he twisted tinfoil to make two rings, but then he asked again with such a serious expression that she stopped smiling too, took a deep breath and responded with an equally serious, "Absolutely yes, Malcolm Walker." She joined him on the floor, facing him, both on their knees, hands clasped together, vowing to love and honor each other forever. *Always and forever.* He slipped the tinfoil ring onto her finger and she slid his tinfoil ring onto his finger.

With the boy on top of her, she shuddered, eyes at the ceiling, afraid of what was happening, thinking she should tell him to stop, he should go, yet craving the excitement, wanting him to consume her. She considered stroking his hair, but instead reached for the bedspread. When she heard the crackle of a condom wrapper, her body went rigid and she wanted to say "stop," but in a second he entered her, pushing deep and painful. She scrunched her eyes closed. His body and hips pumped into her, hard and rhythmic, out of sync with what her body was used to, smaller than Malcolm, not so gentle. When he came, he yelled as if he'd been stabbed, then flopped down at her side, eyes closed. After a while of silence, a loud snore escaped his lips and Bet stared at him in disbelief. She turned away from him and saw the bag of pills on the nightstand. Dear God, what had she done?

32

After vacuuming, folding laundry and heating up a meal of leftovers, Kenya considered taking a bath, but instead settled on the couch to watch a TV movie, but couldn't focus on it. She eyed her phone as if it would ring any moment now. She wanted Sidney to call, yet didn't. Loved him, yet hated him. She felt the same about her baby sister, blobs of love and hate shifting within her like a lava lamp. The agony of not being able to talk to her, to find out why. Simply why. "Why would you do that to me?" She said the words out loud as if her sister might hear and respond.

Sipping a glass of Cabernet, she was thankful to have the house to herself. Both Junior and Charlene were sleeping over with friends: Junior with Timothy Krane and Charlene at Christine Nichols' house with Kesha. Kenya needed time alone to process a life without her husband.

She had met Sidney during her first year of law school at Howard. He tapped her right shoulder while she stood in line at the campus cafeteria, and when she turned, of course, she saw no one; he stood chuckling on her left side. She spun around and he gave her his hand. "Sidney Dubois. Pleasure to meet you."

His wide smile, dark skin and gentle eyes softened her chagrin. They stood shaking hands until the woman behind him complained they were holding up the line. He assailed her with questions—what was her name, her major, where did she grow up—then shared that he was studying for his MBA. He liked that they were both D.C. natives. Unable to sit with her for lunch—no explanation given—he wrote her phone number on the back of his hand and promised to call. But she didn't hear from him for several weeks until he came running across the Yard shouting an apology. "I got caught in the rain and your number got smudged. Been hoping to see you again." She wasn't sure she believed him, but liked the way he looked at her with an expression of sheer delight. They met that evening at a local cafe where he talked about music and made corny jokes she found funny despite herself. The next day he gave her a card he'd made out of notepaper, a cream-colored page folded in half then quartered with a sketch of flowers and geometric shapes done in colored ink. Inside were lines from Luther Vandross' "Because It's Really Love." She frowned at him, feeling heat flush from her neck to her face. It was far too soon for such sentimental expressions, she thought, but when he kissed her hot cheek, all she could do was grin at him like a fool.

Thinking of him now living in an apartment in Georgetown, away from her, was confusing and uncomfortable, so she watched her phone willing him to call. Even though she knew, all they'd do was argue and insult one another.

She'd gotten pregnant with Sidney Junior in her last year of school, and instead of listening to her friends—"think about your career"—she had the baby and still graduated on time. Her mother almost had an aneurysm when she found out about the pregnancy. "You never get pregnant before you have a ring on your finger," she admonished. "If he doesn't marry you, you'll be stuck. Stuck!" Her mother had said the words as if Kenya would be working in a factory for the rest of her life with no chance to ever do anything else. But there was no question whether or not they would marry; they were in love. Her mother almost jumped in the air when she realized Sidney was the son of Reginald Dubois of the Dubois Hotel Corporation.

In retrospect, her mother unwittingly had been right. Kenya was stuck. Had been stuck for years. And now, betrayed in such a profound way she could barely comprehend what had happened. She couldn't fathom why a woman would sleep with her sister's husband. Kenya had sat in stunned silence for most of today's therapy session. There was nothing to say. Yes, she was angry. Yes, she felt confused about the death of her sister and the affair. It was the kind of situation where you wished the woman dead, but the guilt inside Kenya was overwhelming. And she worried about her children. Bouncing between parents on alternating weekends and one night a week—she knew families going through that. That was no kind of childhood.

When the phone rang just past midnight she jolted upright, realizing she'd fallen asleep. A woman identified herself as a police officer and said she was at Cabin John Park with her son.

In a state of panic and confusion, Kenya gathered herself and drove to the park as quickly as she could. When she arrived, Timothy Krane's father was standing beside a petite uniformed police officer, likely the one who called. A second officer stood by one of the police cars on the other side of the parking lot with a young man, hands cuffed behind his back. Unable to see her son anywhere, she approached the officer and Mr. Krane, who was pacing and grumbling.

The officer asked, "You're Mrs. Dubois?"

Kenya nodded. "Where's my son?"

"He's in the patrol car, Ma'am. I'm Officer Slater. We talked on the phone. He and a group of teenagers were smoking weed and loitering in the park after hours." The officer excused herself and talked to a voice on the other end of her radio. Kenya looked at Krane with disbelief.

"What's going on?" she said again, struggling to take in what the officer had just said.

"Your son is a bad influence," said Krane, pointing his index finger at her. "I've called my lawyer."

Called his lawyer. A bad influence. Kenya was more confused. She didn't know the man well and had mostly interacted with his wife, Cindy, but she'd always liked their son, Timothy. He was in the same grade as Junior.

"What do you mean, a bad influence?"

"He and his friends were smoking weed and got my boy arrested."

"My son was not smoking weed. Why would you even say that?"

"Oh. Well …" Krane kept shaking his head and poking the air with his finger. "You clearly don't know your son. They were hanging out with his friends. These older boys who had drugs on them."

The lights in the parking lot were dim but she could see a picnic table at the edge of the trees. It was a pretty park during the day, but sinister in the dark. She peered through the windows of the police cars, but couldn't make out who was in them. The male officer helped put the teenager into the car.

Krane's phone rang and he turned away to answer it. She dialed her father's number but there was no answer. She wanted to call her mother, but knew it would only create more stress; her mother would be of no help. Instead she called Sidney, but he didn't answer either.

Officer Slater came back and said the boys would be released with a warning.

"Was my son actually smoking weed?" Kenya asked, feeling her eyes blinking repeatedly.

"I'm not sure, Ma'am, but he was with a group of boys, and two of the older teens were in possession of narcotics and marijuana." Kenya's mouth fell open and she covered it with her palm. "Those two have been arrested and charged with possession. Mr. Krane indicated that his son was having a sleepover at your house, is that correct?"

"No, that's not true." Kenya closed her eyes for a moment, trying to stop the rapid blinking. "I dropped my son off at Timothy's house myself earlier this evening. Junior was sleeping there. That's what Junior told me." She hadn't gone to the door with him. Had simply pulled into the driveway, kissed his cheek and left. She hadn't even waited until he was inside like she usually did.

The officer pulled out a notebook and made a few notes. She was a small woman, but sturdy. Not a woman Kenya would mess with. She looked at the two police cars, trying to see inside them. "Who are these older boys?"

"They are underage, so I can't reveal their names to you. Perhaps your son knows them?"

Kenya's arms and shoulders were rigid, an ache beginning to pulse in her neck. She needed to sit down but waited helplessly for her son to be released from the confines of the patrol car. After several long moments, Junior and Timothy came walking over, their heads low like dogs who'd been caught stealing from the kitchen table. Krane grabbed his son by the arm and dragged him toward his car, but paused, looked back at Kenya and said, "I don't want your son anywhere near my boy, you got that?"

She said nothing, simply glared at him, then turned to Junior who kept his eyes on his friend, watching him get shoved into his father's car. As she drove home, she called Sidney again, this time he answered.

"You need to get over to the house, right now. Your son almost got arrested." She gave him no time to respond and hung up.

At home, she sat at the kitchen table silently fuming while Junior slouched in the chair opposite, kicking the leg of the table. When Sidney finally wandered in, he glared at Kenya. "Okay, what's this all about?" He looked from Kenya to Junior and back and leaned his arm on the breakfast bar.

"Talk," Kenya said to her son.

Junior kept his eyes toward the floor, saying nothing until Kenya banged her fist on the table. Startled, he began to talk. "We weren't doing nothing wrong."

"Obviously you were—" Kenya was cut short by Sidney who raised his hand.

"Explain what happened," he said.

The boy took a deep breath. "We were thinking about running away." Kenya gasped but with a look from Sidney said nothing more. "We went to the park to figure out where we were going to go first. These older boys were there and they started talking to us. They seemed real cool. I knew one of them 'cause his sister goes to my school. They were the ones smoking the weed. Not me and Timmy. We were just hanging out, talking to them. They were making jokes and being funny. We were having fun till the cops showed up."

"Having fun?" Kenya was horrified.

"We should've let the cops take you to jail," Sidney said flatly. "Maybe you would have learned something." He checked his wristwatch.

"I'm not driving back at this hour. I'll sleep in the guest bedroom."

"That's it? That's all you have to say?"

"Kenya, it's almost two o'clock in the morning, and I'm tired. What he did was stupid, but I believe him. Nothing I say will change the situation. Now, if you want to sit up lecturing him, you go right ahead." He looked at his son. "I will, however, talk to you tomorrow."

"See, this is the problem." Kenya leaned back trying to control her anger. "You just walk away like nothing's your fault. Maybe if you had been more present in his life he wouldn't have been thinking about running away."

"Seriously, Kennie? I'm the problem?" He came closer to her. "You don't think your insane fixation on controlling everything around you, making sure everything is in its place, everyone is buttoned up all nice and pretty. You don't think that may have driven him insane? 'Cause it did me."

Fury imploded in her chest; Kenya could barely breathe. She rose to her feet and snapped at her son to go to his room. Junior scampered out and bounded up the staircase. She turned to Sidney and lifted her hand to slap him but he grabbed her arm.

"Don't," he said.

"Or what?"

"Or you will never see me again."

"You think that bothers me?" Kenya laughed, a chuckle verging on hysteria and snatched her arm away from him. "You can look for divorce papers as soon as I can get them prepared because I'm done with you. You have done nothing but bring me down and given little to your children. I have proof that you cheated on me, not once, but twice.

217

And all that money you got stashed away in the Cayman Islands, I will get half."

"Don't count on it. On second thought, I will drive back tonight."

She felt the scrape of the keys along the marble countertop as if they had grazed her back and closed her eyes as he walked out.

"Good riddance," she said to the air.

33

Ghana laid in bed listening to the sirens wailing and fading. Each rise of a horn sent a chill through her. Ryan was on the streets and each wail could be for him. Despite herself, she kept checking the clock, promising that if he wasn't home by midnight, she'd call his cell phone. This was what she said every night he was working, although he was usually home well before midnight. The rhetoric in the media that there was a war against police officers was fear mongering, she was certain of this, but that didn't mean he wasn't in danger. Anything could happen on the streets. He wore a vest. A vest, he said, like it was a casual piece of clothing. But Ghana reminded herself that it was a bullet-proof vest. Every day, he wore a *bullet-proof* vest. She wondered how wearing armor every day to work affected a person's psyche.

She jerked awake. Another dream of standing on the beach looking for Malawi, but this time Ryan was in the water being tossed by the waves and a dark figure—possibly Malawi—was pointing at him; when Ghana realized he was drowning, she woke up. He lay next to her now. He must have snuck in while she slept.

"Baby?" she said and turned over to face him.

He was on his back, hands clasped behind his head, staring at a streak of light from the streetlamps cutting across the ceiling.

"Yes," he responded, terse and distant. She slid her left hand over his stomach and felt a T-shirt. He was wearing shorts, too. He never wore clothes in bed. Feeling rebuked, she pulled her hand away. He was still mad at her, for all the arguments, for going to Florida without telling him, for disappearing last weekend to her sister's house and not coming home until the next day. They had spoken little in the last few days. She rolled onto her back, ready to turn away and try to sleep, in the same bed but separated. Then she changed her mind and reached out for him again, pushing her hand under his shirt, feeling the hair around his navel, sliding down to where the hair grew thick and smooth. He didn't move. He would make her work for it, and she would because she was sorry. She pulled his shorts down to his knees then used her foot to push them farther down to his ankles and past his feet. She climbed up, straddled him, pushing his T-shirt up so she could kiss the hair on his belly. His body shifted and she felt him harden, then his hands slid around her waist gripping her hips. She flattened her body against him, her mouth seeking his tongue and as he bit her lower lip, he pushed into her, taking her breath away. Every time, that same sweet capture of air from her mouth.

With her hand behind his head she clung to him, never wanting to let go. In a breath, he flipped her over and was on top pushing deeper. Don't leave me, she thought. He was looking at her, his mouth open, eyes focused on her face. His baby blues watching her. Blue eyes, dirty blond hair and for a moment she felt panic. Was it *his* looks she loved, his classic all-American good looks, a hidden desire to have what society had claimed to be the epitome of handsome? Had she fallen for that? No. No, no, no. That wasn't it. Yes, he was fine, but his heart was what had captured hers. His values. His beliefs. His laugh and sense of humor. His indifference to race. Yes. His acceptance of different cultures. Sure, he liked her skin tone, but he also loved her laugh, her views, her cooking. Their love was not about race.

He was slowing down, his eyes glazed and a grunt, deep, guttural escaped him making her toes curl. That noise she loved, so visceral and raw. His release, her satisfaction. Then he was still, his weight on her, his cheek against hers, his slowing breath tickling her ear. He kissed her temple, her cheek, her nose and looked at her, his eyes—those baby blues—full of laughter.

34

Charlene hadn't argued against being escorted into Studio Theatre for the drama camp, but Kenya could tell from the way she walked a few steps ahead that her daughter would have preferred to be dropped off on the street like everyone else. Kenya just wanted to make sure Charlie got to the right place, that she was in safe hands. Though standing in the entrance, watching her daughter give her name to the camp counselor— who was checking attendees on a clipboard and directing kids upstairs— Kenya felt superfluous. Charlene gave a small wave and disappeared into the folds of the theater. Her daughter's request to attend the two-week drama camp had surprised Kenya, but she thought it would be a great experience. Maybe get her out of her shell a little.

Kenya smiled at the counselor and slowly returned to her car, parked illegally on 14th Street. Fortunately, no ticket. She drove home knowing Junior was there and tried to calm her thoughts about his almost-arrest. Traffic stalled on River Road and she moved forward slowly before coming to a standstill on a slight incline. Must be an accident, she thought. She would talk to her son, but she must contain her anger. "They won't talk to you if you shout and get angry all the time," her therapist said. She wished Sidney hadn't screwed things up and was home so they could talk to Junior together, as a team.

The car behind bumped into her. She groaned, put the car in park and got out ready to get insurance information and hoping for a straightforward encounter. The other driver exited from a beat-up Honda Accord, and Kenya's shoulders tightened as the young man strolled to the slight gap between their cars. He had cornrows tight across his head, faint tattoos on his brown muscular arms, and his jeans hung low on his hips showing checkered boxer shorts. She took a step back as he approached, her arms stiffening at her sides. She imagined a gun stuffed into his waistband, illegal drugs hidden in his glove compartment, and waited for him to insult her and denigrate her wealth. He scowled as he inspected his bumper then faced her, squinting in the sunshine.

"Ma'am, you okay?" He waited a moment for a response then crouched down and ran his palm over the back end of her Mercedes. "This a nice ride right here," he said straightening. "Don't look like no damage though."

Kenya looked at her car. He was right, not a scratch.

"You aiight?" He squinted at her and she stuttered a yes. "You rolled right back on me." He chuckled revealing a flash of yellow teeth. "Thought you was trying to get outta the lane. This traffic's a bitch."

"I rolled back?"

"Yeah." He cocked his head. "You sure you aiight?"

She was blinking at him and he was eyeing her, probably wondering if she was crazy, and she wondered if she was out of her mind. Traffic began moving again and the honk of a car jolted her. "Um, yeah … I'm good. Thanks. Sorry." She scrambled back into her car and moved forward. There was nothing to be afraid of, yet she *was* afraid. Shame sprang up from her stomach and caught in her throat. She hadn't even asked if there was any damage to his car. She swallowed a lump and turned up the A/C.

Fear. Fear is driving us all mad.

* * *

Junior was still in bed when she got home, so she enticed him downstairs with the promise of pancakes with fresh blueberries and syrup. When he was settled at the breakfast bar, she watched this burgeoning man-child, dark like his father, his height almost casting a shadow over her and she pictured him a few years from now, taller, bulkier, walking down a street, maybe wearing a hoodie, maybe with a tattoo, stopping to help a woman on the side of the road. She wondered what the woman would think of him, what she would see. A threat or someone offering help?

When he rested the fork on the empty plate and gulped his milk, she asked why he wanted to run away. He stopped swallowing but the glass remained at his lips then he continued gulping as if she hadn't spoken.

"Junior, please. I just want to understand what happened."

He put the glass on the counter and wiped his mouth with the back of his hand. "Are you and Dad getting a divorce?"

"Is that what this is about?"

"Are you?"

She ran her fingers across her forehead. This wasn't how she wanted to tell him, to tell her children. She and Sidney were supposed to sit down with them both and explain that … that what? That because their father was an asshole the family would be split up.

"Yes, I think so."

Junior nudged his plate. "Why?"

Kenya stumbled. She hadn't prepared what to say. "Sometimes … sometimes men and women can't always get along. It doesn't mean we don't love you. That won't change. We will always be your loving parents. We will always be here for you, no matter what."

Junior wasn't looking at her. His eyes were directed at the counter, his brow furrowed more than any child's should be. Kenya wanted to take away his hurt and squirmed in her seat not knowing what else to say. "Running away won't make anything better."

"It would for Timmy."

"What do you mean?"

Junior hesitated before responding. "He likes boys. And his dad says he's, uh, an a—an abomination. Did I get that right?"

Kenya's fingers found her mouth and her breath came sharp and fast. "That's awful." Though having met the boy's father, it didn't surprise her.

"We thought it was best to just run away so we could be together and—"

Kenya put her hand out, not quite touching his arm. "So you could be together?"

"Yes." He was giving her that look as if she was stupid.

She felt her eyelids blinking. "You like boys, too?"

He looked away from her and said, softly, "Yeah."

Anxiety rushed through her chest and she wanted to stop him, block the path he was on and turn him around, send him back and rethink his direction. He couldn't be a homosexual. She would have known. He never played with dolls or liked pink things or wore girls' clothes. He was always … normal. She moved her teeth from one finger to another, tugging at the skin around her nails. She'd find someone to help her, to make him see right. Boys shouldn't like other boys.

Quietly, Junior asked, "Do you think I'm an abomination?"

She stopped nibbling, motionless, silent for several seconds then said the word "no," but she believed homosexuality was a perversion. The grooves in his frown deepened and Kenya almost fell off her seat to wrap her arms around him. "Oh, Junior." He felt the same. Smelled the same. Her son couldn't be an abomination. God wouldn't do that. Not to her. Not to her son. Silently, she prayed it was a phase. That he'd wake up tomorrow and realize that liking boys was wrong.

35

The violent images on the television screen horrified Bet. Cops in riot gear pushing back crowds of young black and brown bodies demanding justice. She watched as if compelled to. Curled on the settee in the den with her back to the kitchen, she smelled something hot and spicy wafting through the air. Charlene was on the floor with headphones covering her ears, watching a movie on her tablet, and Bet was glad she wasn't looking at the TV. More protests were erupting around the country. Another young man shot by a police officer. A black teenager. A white officer. Armored tanks dispatched to control the mobs. Police barricades looking like they should be on a street in Baghdad. A queasiness caught in her throat.

Kenya fussed around the kitchen making dinner, some sort of pasta dish. Junior was outside on the patio sulking about something. And Ghana would be here soon. Her girls were worried because she was alone while Malcolm was off "finding himself." Her cell phone rang, a cheery melody she had no idea how to change. She recognized Tripp's number and quickly declined the call then fumbled with the phone to turn off the ringer. She didn't need more pills; it had only been a week. Looking over her shoulder as if Kenya was about to appear behind her at any moment, she texted back that her daughters were visiting. She hit send then laid the phone on the coffee table, face down, afraid she'd be found out. The memory of him touching and kissing her flashed through her thoughts like a lighthouse that started working after she'd crashed on the rocks. She wouldn't sleep with him again. She just couldn't do it again.

Bet jumped as Kenya came up behind her saying, "This is unbelievable."

"What?"

Kenya pointed at the television. "Another shooting. All these protests. It's unbelievable." Kenya took the remote and turned up the volume. The Reverend Curtis Bishop, the New York City pastor who'd been demanding justice and leading marches across the nation was, once again, charging police departments all over the country with racism. "This must stop," he said, looking directly into the camera.

"I don't want to watch it," Bet said sharply. "We shouldn't have it on around the children."

"Oh." Kenya paused then said, "Of course." And changed the channel to a talk show. "So when is Daddy coming back? Why did he go to Florida?"

"Jesus Christ, Kennie, how the hell should I know?"

Her daughter looked as if she would cry and Bet closed her eyes. She wasn't going to talk about Malcolm. She didn't know who he was anymore. Kenya returned to the stove and Bet heard Ghana call through the house as she came in the front door. Kenya yelled back that they were in the kitchen, and Charlene jumped up shouting "hooray."

All this yelling. Bet could do without it.

Ghana lifted her niece off the floor and spun her around, then settled next to Bet and presented a bouquet of colorful flowers. Pink carnations, yellow and purple gerbera daisies and orange roses. Bet was taken aback. "How pretty," she said and sniffed at the blooms. Charlene ooohed, leaning in to smell the fragrance just as her grandmother had done. Bet held the bouquet as if she didn't know what to do with it and Ghana smiled. "Mama, I want things to be better between us. Dad always says we have to take care of each other, and, well, I need to make a bigger effort."

Bet acknowledged her daughter's words with a nod, but wasn't sure how to respond. She knew she was as much to blame as her daughter and needed to be a better mother, too. And she would. Soon.

"Here," Ghana said taking the bouquet from Bet and returning to the kitchen. "Let's find a vase."

Bet got up and lingered in the archway between the den and the kitchen watching her daughters. Ghana was rummaging under the sink while Kenya nudged her out of the way so she could drain vegetables. They argued and laughed with each other and for a moment Bet felt like everything was normal. Malawi should be here. She should be a part of this. And Malcolm, he should be here, too. Bastard.

"Did you see the news," Ghana said, placing the flowers on the fireplace mantel. She switched the TV to a news channel. "If these were white people flooding the streets, rampaging after a ball game defeat, the news would be calling them revelers or hoodlums. But black folks are called looters and thugs. It's such a—"

"Turn it off," Bet shouted. She took a breath and said, more softly, "I don't want to hear it. We just buried our daughter. I don't want to hear about any more death."

Ghana turned off the TV and laid the remote on the coffee table. "Are we gonna talk about Malawi?"

"No." Bet shook her head firmly. "I don't want to talk about anything."

"When are we going to talk about her? Yes, her death was tragic, but we can't pretend it didn't happen. Her story is part of a bigger issue happening across the nation. We're a part of it, whether we want to be or not."

Bet shrugged Kenya away as she tried to place her hands on her shoulders. "Ghana," Kenya said, "just leave it."

"There's another march, here in D.C., on Saturday," Ghana said. "I'm going to represent the family there. Mama, you should be there. You should come and show your support for all the black lives that have been taken."

"All the black lives?" Bet said. "I don't care about *all* the black lives. I only care about Malawi."

"Then come for her."

Bet just wanted to go back to bed. Cover her head and sleep. She was exhausted and unable to process what was happening in the world these days. So much violence. She took Ghana's hands in her own and squeezed.

"Ghan-Ghan, you are strong, much stronger than me. Please understand. I just can't. Not right now. But I ..." She inhaled. "I love you." She looked at Kenya. "I love you both. I don't say it enough, but I do. You are both so beautiful. So much like your father. Please. Just let me be. For now. Okay?"

Ghana and Kenya exchanged a look. "Okay, Mama," Ghana said, returning Bet's squeeze.

"I'm going to lay down for a bit. I'll eat something later." Bet released her daughter and went upstairs. She took another sleeping pill and snuggled under the covers. She'd feel better after a nap.

* * *

Ghana looked up the stairs as if her mother would reappear and the image reminded Kenya of when they were little, when Ghana would sit on the bottom step waiting for Daddy to come home. When Malawi was old enough to walk, she would sidle up next to her and the pair would sit and chatter until, most often, Kenya dragged them upstairs to bed.

"Let her sleep," Kenya said. "At least she knows we're here and that we care about her."

With a nod of agreement, Ghana returned to the kitchen. "I can't stay too long. I promised Ryan I'd meet him later."

"Can I talk to you about something?" Kenya turned off the stove and beckoned her sister to the settee. "Let's sit."

She ushered Charlene out to be with her brother, almost pushing her out the door despite the girl's protests that it was too hot outside. Ghana eyed her suspiciously and asked if it was about Sidney. "It's about Junior," Kenya said. She checked to make sure the sliding glass door was firmly closed then sat next to her sister and began, "He's …" Suddenly she felt strange saying the word, using it to describe her son. "He's a homosexual."

"People don't really use that word anymore. Just say gay."

Heat rose into Kenya's cheeks and she swallowed a lump. "Okay. He's … he says he's gay."

Ghana continued looking at her expectantly.

"He likes other boys," she said.

Her sister laughed. "I know what being gay means."

"You're not shocked?"

"Oh, Christ, Kennie. He's your son. He's still our Sidney Junior."

Kenya looked at the carpet and nibbled the skin around her thumb.

"Are you seriously upset?"

"Well …" Kenya could feel her cheeks burning hotter. "It's not normal."

"Nuh huh. We are not having this conversation. You are not going to sit here and speak bullshit about the gay community."

"Men are supposed to be with women."

Ghana raised her palm to Kenya's face, and Kenya swatted her hand away.

"Did you just smack me?"

"I'm afraid for him," Kenya said. "It's bad enough being black these days without being … gay as well."

"That's not what's bothering you. Admit it, you're homophobic."

"I am not." She couldn't hold her sister's judging stare and feared her sister was right. She'd always thought of homosexuals—gay people—as abnormal. Sidney had said it was a choice people made to get attention. People have said they were gay but weren't and said they weren't when they were. Kenya wasn't sure if it was a choice or genetic.

"But what do I do?"

"You can be a complete idiot, you know that?" Ghana patted her sister's knee. "Just keep being his mother. Stop being judgmental. Accept him for who he is."

Her sister went back to the kitchen and stuck a spoon into the pasta to taste it. Kenya followed her and leaned against the cabinet. "Is it my fault, you think?" she asked.

Ghana ate another spoonful from the pot. "This is good. Hey, should we be worried about Mama? You think she's gonna be okay?"

"She'll be fine." Kenya looked back at the patio doors. "But do you think it's my fault?"

"What?"

"Junior."

Ghana stopped eating, tilted her head and slowly blinked at her, then finally said, "Half of me wants to pretend you're not asking what I think you're asking, and the other half wants to smack you."

Kenya frowned unsure how to respond.

"Nobody chooses to be gay any more than we chose to be black." Ghana dumped the spoon in the sink.

"But ..."

Ghana waved her hand in the air. "No buts. Some decide to be open and honest about who they are, and others decide to keep it private, but they don't choose to be gay. What's wrong is that kind of thinking."

Holding in her irritation, Kenya watched her sister sling her bag over her shoulder and lean out the sliding glass door to say goodbye to the kids, then watched them trail inside asking about dinner, turn the television to the Cartoon Network, and argue as they always did about what show to watch. Her sister's immediate dismissal burned, but as she listened to her children she saw that nothing about her son had changed, yet everything about him had changed. The real question was whether or not *she* had what it would take to change.

36

Malcolm sat outside the house, a small one-level white stucco with a small grass yard and a concrete path up to the front door. No media trucks were here anymore. Malawi was old news. He looked up and down the quiet, unassuming street, not the place of breaking headlines. He envisioned Malawi running into the light pole, in the dark, trying to avoid a dog or cat running across the street. How familiar had she been with this neighborhood? Clearly, not so familiar to expect to be shot and killed. She'd probably been afraid. His baby girl had been afraid of the dark for a long time, longer than Kenya or Ghana. Though, sweet and sassy at three.

"Daddy, I'm just gonna lay here with you, 'kay." She didn't ask. She told him what was about to happen. "There's a storm outside and I'm gonna lay with you, now." Her body would thump its way in, not quiet and subtle, but boisterous, bouncing the bed, pulling the covers, making her presence known. She was sleeping with Daddy. Not Mama. Sometimes she slept in between them, but Bet liked her space. She didn't like to be crowded and discouraged the girls from sleeping in the same bed with them. Their bed was a haven away from the children. But Malawi discarded what her mother said and pushed her way into the bed anyway, knowing her daddy wouldn't push her out, knowing he would reach out his arm for her to grab and gently pull her in, cradling her in his chest, feeling her tiny feet push against his thighs, her warm cheek pressing into his skin. He treasured those moments and they'd made him forget all the reasons why he so badly wanted a boy.

He could see her walking up the path and knocking on the

screen door. He could see her body being thrown back onto the ground, her head hitting the stone path. He shouldn't think these thoughts, but they came uninvited and played out in his mind.

A flatbed truck was parked on the curb outside the house, and Malcolm assumed it belonged to Jeffrey Davies. A dirty green truck with rust spots spattering its sides. He imagined sticking a knife into the tires, but that would be pointless.

The weight of the handgun in his lap felt ten times its actual weight. When he had arrived at the motel, he searched online for gun shows in the area and found one in Fort Lauderdale, about an hour's drive away. The vast array of weapons overwhelmed him when he walked into the auditorium, keenly aware that he was one of only a handful of black patrons walking through the expanse of weaponry. A petite busty brunette sold him the gun. She caught his eye and flashed him a wide smile as he passed, so he stopped and looked at the selection on the table.

"What you looking for?" she said cheerily. Her face was deeply tanned with eyelashes far too thick and long to be real.

"Not really sure," he said, eyeing the array of weapons. "A handgun. Something not too complicated. Reliable."

The saleswoman pitched a variety of guns, picking each one up and displaying it like jewelry. Springfield. Ruger. Smith & Wesson. Glock. He liked the Smith & Wesson with the thumb safety and, after holding it in his hand, aiming it at the floor, he decided it would do.

He was a little surprised at how simple the process had been. He completed a form, giving his father's name and the address of the cheap motel just outside Palm Beach where he was staying. She seemed unconcerned about the paperwork when he offered cash. "Just a formality, really," she said, and threw in a dozen bullets for free.

He would only need one. Maybe two.

He sat in his car across the street from Jeffrey Davies' house where his little girl had been shot dead. The county prosecutor finally arrested the man almost two weeks after the shooting, but released him that same day on bail. So much had been said in the media about whether or not he was guilty; some believed he had a right to shoot; others said he was guilty of first degree murder. But the prosecutor cited lines from the Stand Your Ground law. Such bullshit! No man, especially one with a gun, should feel threatened by a young woman, weighing less than one-hundred-and-twenty-five pounds and armed with a cell phone that likely didn't get any service. All the words and the political posturing. It was all bullshit. The local attorney he'd hired was doing the best he could, but Malcolm couldn't wait for the court system. He knew how long that process could take. Today, he would make it right. An eye for an eye. A life for a life. Davies for Malawi. That seemed fair.

He ran his fingers along the plastic grip to the cool metal of the slide. He'd never fired a gun before but he had no fear as he imagined firing a bullet into Davies' brain.

37

The crowd was electric. Such an unoriginal description, but it was the only word that came to Ghana's mind. Electric. She could feel the energy, hot and alive, charging through the crowd on invisible wires. She felt buzzed as she looked out at hundreds, no thousands, of people chanting and singing in between speakers, and cheering as each person called for action. This must be what Martin Luther King Jr. had felt when he stood before an audience in 1963. The clock tower stood watch against the powder blue sky and the Capitol dome shimmered at the far end of Pennsylvania Avenue. Voices echoed through the loudspeakers. The Reverend Curtis Bishop had come from New York City to lead the march, his words echoing the peace marches of the sixties. He was not as tall as Ghana expected, but he held himself erect like a military officer. Reverend Bishop never rose to the status of the Reverend Doctor King, but as a young man he marched with the slain leader, and in the decades since had continued to shout for justice for African Americans wherever it appeared to have been denied. This was his march—the Peace and Justice March—organized by him along with a coalition of civil rights organizations, demanding justice for the young unarmed black men and women who had died at the hands of police, self-proclaimed vigilantes, and fearful white citizens. Ghana was proud to be standing with him and his supporters.

She was one of many on the platform at Freedom Plaza. Though she had followed the news accounts of one death after another, seeing so many survivors gathered together on the podium shocked her. Speaking now was the mother of Tamir Rice. Her son had been carrying a toy gun that the officer said looked real. The woman began to cry causing Ghana to tear up. She swallowed a lump in her dry throat and hoped she'd be able to speak when it was her turn.

She heard her name and stepped forward, placed her hands on the lectern to steady herself and took a breath. Her parents had been invited to attend, but her mother hadn't responded to the invitation, so the organizers contacted Ghana, who gladly accepted, though now, looking at the audience she feared she would stumble and appear foolish on national television. Several microphones from various television and radio stations were angled at her mouth. The organizers suggested just a few comments, five to ten minutes tops. She thought about the note cards in her jacket pocket, words she'd scribbled down, read and reread hoping they made sense, hoping she would be able to convey a message of peace.

"What a beautiful crowd," she said and a cheer blossomed around her. She took another breath and fumbled in her pocket for her cards, but decided she didn't need them; all the words were firmly in her mind. She leaned forward and said, "My sister had no gun." She paused. "No weapon. She was no threat." Another pause. "She simply needed help. And what she got was two bullets; one in the shoulder and one in the chest. Why?" She cleared her tightening throat.

Several voices rang out in the audience. "Because she was black!"

"Yes," Ghana responded. "Yes, because she was black. Simply because of the color of her skin. Because she was a black woman at a white man's door."

Yelling and cheers again filled the air.

"When are we, as Americans, going to look at one another as

human beings? Not as a skin color. Not as a religion. Not as someone different and therefore threatening. But as a people. Human beings trying to live, to be happy, to find love, to be at peace. Together. When will we be at peace with one another? When will this race war end?" She inhaled. "I don't want my sister's death to be yet another meaningless killing. I want this tragedy, this heartbreak, to have meaning, to be a path toward peace, toward ending this violence against one another. I call on every human being, every American, to demand peace."

The crowd burst into applause and cheers, and began chanting, "We want peace." Ghana stared at the faces, the placards and fists pumping the air. Chills ran through her. She stepped aside and accepted a hug from Reverend Bishop. People were smiling and nodding, grabbing her hand and thanking her. She moved near the back of the platform, her mission accomplished.

When all the speakers were done, they marched along Pennsylvania Avenue to Congress where Reverend Bishop expounded on his message of peace and justice. Ghana inhaled the cheers and the singing around her, her body tingling with electricity. Something good would come from this. Surely it would.

38

It was time, he thought, though Malcolm wasn't sure what to do with the gun. He considered sliding it into his waistband like they do on television, but that wasn't his style. He didn't want it to slip out. He imagined grabbing the gun and a bullet firing spontaneously into his leg. Instead, he put it in his pants pocket and it banged against his thigh. Malcolm removed it and made sure the safety was on. Nice and safe. He adjusted his glasses and placed a straw fedora on his head—a slight disguise—got out of the car and crossed the street, taking each step carefully, slowly. He walked up the path. At the front door, paint was peeling off the frame and the screen was dented near the bottom. To the left below a single window was a flower bed with several small green shrubs and a lawn of brown grass. He pulled the wobbly handle and envisioned Malawi doing the same. Opening the screen door to knock was hardly suspicious activity. With his fist, he pounded on the wooden door and stepped back so Davies could see this was not a young woman he could bully, but a large man he should be scared of. His throat was dry and he tried to swallow. In case Davies opened the door shooting, Malcolm was poised, ready to drop to the ground and roll into the shrubs, though it would be a dumb move for the man to repeat himself.

Several moments passed and Malcolm knocked again, hitting the wood harder, louder. Finally a voice shouted from the window. "Who is it?"

"I'm from the courthouse. We need to talk." Malcolm looked at the window but couldn't see a face, just the shifting of a curtain. He smiled anyway hoping Davies would be convinced and open the door.

"I talked to my lawyer already," the voice said. "Who are you?"

"Just need to discuss a few administrative things. It'll just take a minute."

Another moment passed and Malcolm considered kicking in the door, but unlike the screen, the wooden door looked pretty sturdy. Then it opened. Malcolm instinctively retreated a step, but the man had no weapon. He wore a striped cotton shirt, rolled at the sleeves, worn thin from wear, and loose-fitting faded blue jeans. His face, suspicious, wary, was heavily lined through his cheeks and forehead, his gray hair long to his shoulders and a thinning beard flecked with gray. He was not a young man and Malcolm was unsure, now, what he had expected. This man was old, weary.

"My attorney said not to talk to no one."

"I understand." Malcolm swallowed another dry lump. "Can I come in?"

The man frowned, hesitated then made way for Malcolm to pass over the threshold. He entered a darkened living room, a worn brown couch along one wall, a low wooden coffee table slightly askew in the middle of the room, in the corner near the front window, a large television set with an antenna sticking out the top, and a brown leather armchair positioned a few feet in front of it. The leather was cracked and Malcolm wondered if it was fake. Pleather, he thought. This was where the man was sitting when he heard Malawi at his door. Malcolm looked around for the shotgun, but it was likely hidden away, under his bed perhaps. Davies stared at him, his brown eyes too close together. Malcolm wasn't sure what to do now that he was inside.

"Well?" The man waited.

Malcolm needed to sit down. "May I?" He pointed to the couch.

Davies nodded and seemed to ease somewhat, his hunched shoulders shifted away from his ears.

Malcolm positioned himself on the edge of the couch, the inner springs squeaking wildly as if he'd squashed a mouse in the cushions. The gun was heavy in his pocket, pressing against his thigh.

Davies remained standing.

"Jeffrey Davies," Malcolm said, taking the hat and placing it on his lap. The man continued to look at him with that same tired expression. "Jeffrey Davies," he said again with more conviction, mustering up the courage to say his piece. He removed the clip-on sun shades from his glasses to reveal his face. "You killed my daughter."

For a moment nothing changed. Davies remained standing, his face stuck, then his eyes widened and he backed away, panic shifting the muscles in his face into horror. The realization he'd allowed the girl's father into his home, perhaps gauging how much time it would take to get the shotgun before Malcolm went in for the kill. But Malcolm's desire to inflict unspeakable pain had faded. He looked at the man's bare feet, his twisted toes clinging to the faded rug.

"You should be in jail right now."

"I'm calling the police." Davies grabbed a phone sitting on a small side table next to the armchair and began to dial.

Without thinking, Malcolm leaped up, pulled the gun from his pocket and aimed it at the man. "Dial the number and I swear to God, I will blow you into hell." His entire body was shaking and he hoped Davies couldn't see it. "Drop the phone. Now."

Davies had hit two of the three numbers, his finger poised to press the last one. Malcolm's large size was palpable standing in the home of this small man. He didn't need the gun. He could reach out and choke him with one hand. Watch the life in him fade away. The man's fear hit Malcolm in his chest, making him feel winded. He gripped the gun with both hands, steadying his aim, daring Davies to complete the call.

39

People were walking randomly now, not as a unit with signs held high, but as a ragged mass heading home, broken signs piled around trash cans and an occasional flyer fluttering in the breeze. Still buzzing from the event, Ghana meandered south from the Capitol building toward the Metro. No fancy Town Car to take her home like the one for Reverend Bishop.

She passed a tiny park with luscious green grass and inviting brown benches. D.C. was a beautiful city in the summer, she thought. No skyscrapers to spoil the view of white billowy clouds above the trees. Even the blocks of stone-and-glass federal buildings appeared majestic in the sunshine. On days like this she was hopeful that what good there was in the world would overcome all the bad shit that was happening. Surely, people would hear this call for peace and respond in a positive way.

Along the route, a few police officers lingered by their vehicles, casually chatting with each other, likely waiting for the crowd to completely dissipate.

Waiting for the walk sign, she spied two patrol cars parked askew half a block down the side street she was about to cross. Two officers stood on the sidewalk. Ryan was working today. Overtime because of the march. The chances she would stumble upon him were slim, but one of the cops had his height, his build. She decided to see if it was him. As she started to walk, a loud crash erupted, like the sound of a metal trashcan, and the two officers backed up. She didn't see anything. Another bang and from seemingly nowhere half a dozen men in black hoodies crowded the narrow street throwing rocks at the two cops. One man held what looked to Ghana like a metal pipe and he swung it wildly at the officers.

One officer was hit with a rock and dropped to the ground while the other pulled his gun but was hit from behind by the metal pipe. Ghana screamed. She spun around, waving her arms, looking for the numerous cops she'd seen along the route, but that was a block or two away. People glanced at her but kept walking. She turned back to see both cops on the ground, two men kicking them. In the distance she heard a siren. One hooded man ran toward her and she shouted at him, "What the hell are you doing?"

As he approached, she saw he was not a man, but a kid, fourteen or fifteen at most.

"Fuck the police," he yelled. "They're killing us. It's our turn to get them back."

Horrified, Ghana watched him run across the street and disappear into the Metro station. The siren roared louder to the scene and the remaining boys scattered, though two were caught by the arriving officers. Two police vehicles blocked the street, their doors gaping wide. An arriving officer stopped her.

"I just need to know if it's Ryan." She was shaking as if the weather was cold. "Is it Officer Evans? Ryan Evans?"

The cop, an older light-skinned man, shook his head sympathetically. "I don't know for sure, Ma'am. I need you to step back."

"I saw one of the boys who did this," she said. Her throat was closing, tears building. "He was a kid. A dumb, stupid kid."

The officer took her information in the event she may be needed as a witness, and he promised to call if Ryan was one of the officers who was attacked. But she knew he wouldn't call. He likely wouldn't remember his promise in all the chaos. She pulled out her cell phone and called Ryan's number, hoping she was mistaken, but there was no answer. An ambulance arrived from the other end of the street, and she watched as the EMTs carried the two men into the emergency vehicle. A crowd had formed now, people milling around trying to see what happened, snapping pictures. Standing on the sidewalk, she called Cass. She wasn't making any sense, her words tumbling over each other, her hands shaking, tears blurring her vision. "You have to come get me in your car. We need to follow the ambulance. I need to know if it's Ryan."

40

"Please," Malcolm said. "I just want to talk to you. That's all. Don't make me shoot you." He heard himself talking and almost laughed. They sounded like lines from a movie. This moment was unreal as if he'd slipped through the veil between what was real and what wasn't, watching himself play out a scene from a bad movie with corny lines and terrible actors. Davies placed the phone back in its cradle and sat down, deliberately, as if afraid to disturb the springs in the chair. He clasped his hands between his wide knees and eyed Malcolm warily. "What you want?" He assessed Malcolm, weighing whether or not he would fire the gun.

"What right did you have to take her life?" Malcolm said, hands gripping the weapon. He lowered it slightly, but kept his finger on the trigger, knowing the safety was still in place. He remained standing.

"I got a right to defend myself." Davies' eyes drifted to the floor, his lips opened and closed like a fish until he said, "Didn't know I was shooting a girl. Honest to God." He made eye contact with Malcolm, who could see the man's hands were also shaking, ever so slightly. "I swear to God," he said again. He pressed his lips together, thin lips that disappeared into a straight line on his face. Malcolm gripped the gun tighter. He was no fool.

"You shot her twice," he said, his anger expanding, his judgment, his authority pushing through his chest. "She was looking for help and you opened the door and shot her in the chest."

Davies nodded, short jerky movements of his head. "I know that now. But I got a right to defend myself and the court says I was within my right."

"Within your right?" Malcolm moved closer, leaning over Davies who flinched. "You said you didn't even know what was outside."

"It coulda been an intruder. We've had breakins here. My neighbor—"

"That's bullshit. You don't fire a gun unless you know exactly what you're aiming at. And you admitted you didn't know. You just fired." Davies said nothing. Malcolm was on the verge of losing all control and louder he demanded, "Why?" Again Davies flinched; his silence pricked at Malcolm's fury and he repeated his question, "Why?"

"You're right. I didn't even look," the man said, dropping his gaze to the rug. "I just opened the door and fired. It was s'posed to be a warning shot. I just saw a figure in front of me." Davies looked up at Malcolm. "I don't know why I fired again. It just happened. Wasn't till she was on the ground I realized it was a girl."

Malcolm leaned away repulsed and confused. "Shit like that doesn't just happen. What the fuck were you so afraid of? That was my little girl!"

"There's folks out there. They wanna take what you got. They come into this country and take over. We gotta take it all back."

"Take what back?"

"Our way of life. Our traditions."

"Like what?"

Davies fell silent and Malcolm returned to his seat on the couch, resting the gun on his knee. "You want to go back to owning slaves? You really think that's a better way of life?"

"It would be for me."

The man's response stunned Malcolm; he wasn't sure if he should laugh or scream.

"You really think *you* would own slaves?" Malcolm snorted. "The big hot shot slave-owner, ordering other people around. That's who you think you would be?"

This little man in his tiny run-down house thought his life would be better working for a slave master. Malcolm surveyed the room. There was nothing here to steal, yet this man was convinced immigrants were taking over, that if white men like him didn't stop people of color, all his rights would be taken away. But it was white men in power who were sucking him and people like him dry, smiling in their faces, telling them the government's got their backs—as long as they vote them into office. Malcolm didn't understand why this man couldn't see that the men he'd voted for didn't care if he had running water, if he could afford to pay his electric bills, or if he lived in a safe neighborhood. They just wanted his vote.

"You really think your right to own a gun helps you pay your bills? Helps you get the food you need and healthcare when you're sick?"

"It's my right to own a gun."

"Sure it is. And as long as you're focused on that, your leaders keep getting richer while you keep getting poorer."

Nothing Malcolm could say would change Davies' thoughts about the world he lived in. This man would die believing his rights were being trampled on because African Americans and immigrants were squeezing him out of jobs and homes. Malcolm placed the handgun on the coffee table.

"You can have this." He emptied his pocket of the bullets and dropped them next to the gun. They tinkled softly as they rolled across the wooden surface. He stood up and walked toward the door. This man may never go to jail, he thought, but he was already stuck in a hell that death would never give him. Malcolm walked back to his car without looking back.

41

Cass pulled up on the opposite side of the street and Ghana stepped off the curb, ignoring the no-walk sign. A car horn blew and she stopped as a minivan sped by her. Inside Cass's Toyota, Ghana called Ryan again. She had been obsessively dialing his number since calling Cass, listening to his voice on the answering message, hoping he was not one of the beaten officers. This time, he answered. His live voice said, "Ghana, I can't talk. I'm okay. I'll call you back." Then silence. She stared at the phone, at his picture. "Oh, fuck! Thank you. Thank you." Her body slackened in the seat and she rested her head back holding the phone in her lap.

"Where are we going?" Cass said, as a cop frantically waved his arm for her to move on. She pulled into the flow of traffic and drove north. "What hospital?"

"Just take me home. He's okay. Let's just go home."

Cass maneuvered through slow-moving traffic and Ghana felt her breathing begin to calm. He was okay. He hadn't answered because he was working. Not because he was in the ambulance. He was okay. Her hands were still shaking and she clasped them together.

"You know I love you," said Cass, breaking the silence, "but girlfriend, this traffic is shit on a Saturday and you have me out here just to take you home? You need to tell me what the hell happened because I couldn't make out one word you were saying on the phone except that Ryan was in an ambulance."

Ghana inhaled deeply but still couldn't speak.

"I gave up a damn good parking spot, too, right outside my door." Cass chuckled. "You got two seconds to start talking or I'm dropping you off at the next corner." She patted her hand on Ghana's knee. "You said he's okay. C'mon, talk to me."

Tears filled her eyes again and Ghana covered her face with her hands.

"Hey, c'mon now," said Cass. "I'm just teasing you. Just trying to lighten the tension. You said he's okay, right?"

"This whole thing is so fucked up, I can't even get my head around it." Ghana recounted what happened, telling Cass about the kid she saw, his nasty comment as he passed by, the viciousness of the boys' actions, the shock at seeing them purposely attack the cops. "Those cops didn't do anything to them." She took a breath. "That isn't what this movement is supposed to be about. It's not an eye for an eye. It just doesn't work that way." After a moment, she said, "I kept thinking, please don't make it be Ryan. I was so afraid it was him."

"Well, it wasn't."

Her mind swirled with the events of the morning, the cheering and chanting, the signs, the speeches, and then the violence toward these two police officers. "We just spent the morning marching for peace." She looked at her friend who was frowning at the car in front of them. "What do we do, Cass? What do we do to get rid of the poison in the air?"

"Maybe we need more violence. I'm not saying I want Ryan to be hurt, but maybe we need an all-out war before anything will actually change."

"An all-out war? Cass, you're crazy."

"Yeah, a civil war for real freedom, real change."

"And who do you think would win that one?"

Cass found a parking spot a block away from Ryan's apartment and they walked slowly through the busy afternoon. Young and old occupied with their lives, shopping, running errands, oblivious to the chaos on the other side of the city.

"It's not a war we need," said Ghana. "We need to vote. We need politicians willing to make real change. Someone needs to step up."

Cass laughed. "You thinking of running for office?"

"Hell, no. Not me."

"Well, that's where the real problem lies."

Puzzled, Ghana cocked her head at Cass, who said, "The right people don't run for office. And the system is so screwed up that even when the right people do get elected, they can't be effective."

Ghana wiped her wet cheeks. She had no desire to be a politician but she could speak out, write letters, and encourage others to do the same. People couldn't keep their heads buried in sand. Not anymore.

* * *

Cass didn't stay long, just until she was comfortable leaving Ghana alone. When she'd gone, Ghana called Ryan's mother to make sure she knew he was okay; Mrs. Evans screeched through the house to her husband and thanked God and Ghana repeatedly. Ghana's belief in a god had never quite blossomed into more than a fascination of good and evil represented by angels and demons. Life should be lived every day instead of spent waiting for something better to come after death. Just keep on keeping on, as Malawi would say.

Ghana passed the evening flipping from one news channel to another and taking calls from family and friends asking about Ryan—

news reports didn't reveal the identities of the cops who were attacked, though they did mention that one was white, the other black, one suffered a severe concussion, the other several cracked ribs and a broken shoulder. But they were alive. Five of the six suspects had been caught and arrested, all teenage boys, three black, two Latino.

Ryan finally came home shortly after midnight and she hovered awkwardly between the sitting room and the foyer. His anger was palpable in the slow, stiff way he walked through the apartment, taking off his gun belt, his shirt, his vest, opening the refrigerator and staring for several minutes then slamming it closed and standing hopelessly, hands gripping the counter, eyes closed. She wanted to talk but knew to wait, to let him mentally make the shift from work to home.

Without a word, Ghana cared for him in the best way she knew how. Walking around him, she pulled from the fridge bread, sliced roast beef, cheese and mayo. She cut the sandwich in half and placed it on a small plate then popped the cap off the last bottle of beer. She carried the beer and the plate to the sitting room and set them on the coffee table, settled onto the couch and waited. She could hear him inhale and then the soft tread of his bare feet coming to sit next to her. In one motion, he folded himself into her, his head snuggling into her neck, his face damp from tears, his body heavy against her. She felt his anger and frustration begin to thaw and wrapped her arms around him, stroking his hair, kissing his head.

For a long time, they sat in silence, their bodies softening into one another. She was sorry; sorry that race was still a polarizing issue, that she had vented her anger at him simply because he was a white police officer. Sorry his fellow officers were attacked because they represented *them*. That her sister was killed because she represented *us*. Everyone representing something negative to someone else, an oppressive force or an evil, invasive force. There should be no *us* versus *them*. The world should simply be *us*. One humanity.

After a while, still no words passing between them, Ryan leaned forward and ate the sandwich, gulped some beer and offered her the bottle. She took a sip and they shared the rest. A car alarm went off somewhere in the distance and the cry of a fire truck, heavy on the street below, gave Ghana goose bumps. Finally, he offered her a half-smile and said, "I can't be without you, Ghana." He looked at the floor. "I heard a lot of shit today about black and white, but those kids didn't care. All they saw was blue and that, for them, was the enemy. There's a lot of asshole cops out there doing fucked up shit, but—" He turned to her. "Ghana, there are a helluva lot more good cops doing what's right for people no matter what color their skin. We're not perfect, I know that, but we don't deserve this anymore than black folks deserve the violence against them."

She nodded repeatedly, feeling the hairs rising along her arms and neck.

"I'm just trying to do the right thing," he continued. "Just trying to do my job with the training and skills I've got. But—" He inhaled, long and deep. "I can't do it without you."

Ghana kept nodding, her throat thick and constricted, awed by his declaration.

"Baby," he said, gently tugging at her shirt, pulling her close and engulfing her in a hug. "I just can't."

She leaned into him, pressing her face against his chest, as if his sturdiness would give her the strength to find words. Finally, she said,

"I'm so sorry," but he stopped her, saying she shouldn't be. She pulled back and looked at his face. "But I am. For creating this rift between us. For letting the outside affect what we have right here."

"Shh," he said and pushed her back into the cushions then laid his head on her chest, his arm protectively around her waist. In a moment, his breathing was heavy. She should wake him and get him to bed, she thought, but instead simply snuggled him closer to her.

42

The night was quiet then the A/C unit chugged on, filling the motel room with cold air and a deafening whir, until it shuddered to a sudden silence. Malcolm was on the floor, his back leaning against the bed, drinking one shot of bourbon after another, waiting for the next onslaught of noisy cold air. He had stopped by the liquor store on his way back from Davies' house and stared at the bottle for a long time before cracking the seal. He was crying now, blubbering like one of his daughters when they were little. Wiping his nose on his sleeve, he considered getting tissues but couldn't find the motivation to move. He was a fool for having come to Florida, thinking he could storm in and kill the man who murdered his daughter. He poured another glass to half full.

He knew she was here with him. He wasn't into all that mumbo-jumbo stuff, angels and spirits, but in the still moments when the A/C was off, he felt her here. Maybe it was the alcohol. He looked at the bottle. Nah! She was with him, guiding him, stopping him from completely losing it.

"You need to visit your mother," he said aloud to the room, to his invisible daughter. "Bring *her* back from the edge."

Beautiful Bet. She had been his heart. Lured him in, her hook catching in the middle of his chest, though she hadn't been aware of what she was doing at the time. At least he didn't think so. He spotted her in the deli near campus. She often sat there in the afternoon with her nose in a book or scribbling in a sketchpad. He started dropping in whenever he was free, hoping to see her, buying a bologna or salami sandwich he often didn't eat. Took him about three weeks before he summoned the courage to approach her. What he said exactly, he couldn't remember, but she had looked at him with that same look she gave him when not the least bit interested in what he was saying. Why are you wasting my time, her eyes said, and he had almost curled into a ball on the floor. Instead he turned and walked out of the deli. He saw her again a week later and sat at the same table, across from her. Without saying a word, he pulled out a book and read silently until she asked, "Can I help you?"

"No." He glanced at her, then went back to reading.

After a while, she got up and left. Another week passed before he saw her again. This time he was already seated in the deli eating a salami-and-cheese sandwich when she walked in. He saw her look around and hesitate before coming over. He pretended not to notice when she sat down next to him, close enough that he could feel the warmth of her body and smell the floral fragrance of her perfume.

"Hi," she said. Her voice timid and uncertain.

He raised his eyebrows at her and continued eating without speaking.

"What's your name?" she asked.

He took a moment to swallow and wipe his mouth with a napkin. "Malcolm Walker," he said and offered her his hand. She shook it firmly. "I'm Elizabeth Ellis. My close friends call me Bet."

"Well, I'm going to call you Bet and hope we become close friends."

She smiled at him, a broad toothy grin, and he knew she would be his wife.

Ever since that day, he couldn't remember a time he hadn't wanted to be with her. Even when he found the love letter from Teddy. Hurt and angry, he hadn't spoken to her for several days, but despite his pain, he never imagined himself without her.

Her gloom and rage frustrated him and he wished he could take her pain away. Wished he wasn't repulsed by her grief. Wished he had the power to bring Malawi back. His daughter wouldn't want this. Wouldn't want them to give up. He took a sip of warm bourbon, savoring it in his mouth before swallowing. The A/C chugged and cold air hit his face.

For the first time in his life, he didn't want to go back to her.

43

The moment was surreal, sitting in her lawyer's office talking about her rights and what she could expect to get, as if her marriage had simply been a collection of assets. Kenya kept thinking how it wasn't supposed to be this way.

If Sidney didn't fight her, she would do okay financially. She would go back to work, though she wasn't sure what she'd do. Her lawyer was talking, saying she would draw up the divorce papers and send Kenya a copy in the next few days for review before sending them to Sidney. The words tumbled around in the air before falling, splat, on the glossy brown desk.

Kenya left the office, her body swaying slightly with the rush of activity on the street in downtown Bethesda, the afternoon's heat soaking into the buildings around her. Using a tissue from her purse, she dabbed at the moisture on her temple. On any other day, she might wander through the shops, get a mani-pedi, stop somewhere for a light lunch, check the latest releases at the bookstore. Enjoy some time for herself. Now, though, she felt unsteady and ill-prepared for her life without Sidney. For being by herself. Being a single mother to two black children, one possibly gay, in a world that seemed against people of color. The man with the tattoos who bumped her car popped into her mind; there she was thinking he might hurt her, while he was wondering if she was okay. The memory made her feel silly. She made herself a promise: that she would no longer be afraid.

Kenya smoothed her skirt and strode across the street to her car. She would be better, a better woman than she'd ever been. She wouldn't judge others based on how they looked. She'd love her children more, encourage and accept them no matter what. Knowing Junior liked boys would be tough to accept, but she'd try. She'd be a better daughter, too. As if to prove this to herself, she drove straight to her mother's house. She knew she wouldn't get the comfort she wanted, but she should make sure her mother was okay while her father was out of town. That's what a good daughter would do.

When she arrived, the front door was unlocked and the hairs on her arms and neck prickled. From the foyer, she called for her mother but only Kitty came running from the sitting room, several plaintive meows filling the silence. Nothing seemed out of order. No doubt her mother was upstairs sleeping. Kenya put food out for the cat then headed upstairs. It was time for her mother to start living her life again. She had to stop sleeping her days away. With a firm knock on the bedroom door, she pushed it open. "Mama? It's me, Kennie."

Her mother was sound asleep, laying on her stomach only half covered by a sheet. Her arm dangled over the side, and Kenya couldn't help rolling her eyes. "For God's sake, Mama, get it together." As she approached, a sour smell pinched her nose. Kenya saw vomit on the pillow and released a shriek. She wanted to move her mother, shift her onto her side but wasn't sure if that was the right thing to do. She pressed two fingers to her mother's neck but there was no pulse, then slid her hand under her chest and felt a weak heartbeat. Without a second thought, she grabbed the phone on the bedside table and dialed 9-1-1. Only a few minutes passed before the ambulance arrived, but the time seemed like forever. An empty bottle of pills lay on the table, and Kenya noticed what looked like a used condom on the floor. She bent low and peered at it, feeling a wave of shock—her father was still in Florida—then wondered if someone had plied her with the pills. She called Ghana who answered at the same time two EMTs arrived at the front door. They rushed in and Kenya directed them upstairs where they checked her mother's vitals, asking Kenya a barrage of questions, most she couldn't answer. But she gave them the empty pill bottle. Benzodiazepine, they said. The pair got her mother on a stretcher and into the ambulance. Quickly, Kenya locked up the house and followed the wailing siren and flashing lights to the hospital. In the car, she called her father but he didn't answer. She called again from the hospital, this time leaving a message to call her immediately. Sitting in the waiting room, she took slow, long breaths until Ghana arrived, and recounted what she found, leaving out the detail about the condom. Ghana's pale pallor startled Kenya and she hugged her sister tightly as if squeezing would return a flush of color back to her sister's cheeks.

They waited. Silent. Tense. Stunned. Finally, a doctor appeared and told them their mother would be fine. They'd pumped her stomach and would keep her overnight for observation, but physically she was fine.

Seeing her mother with tubes attached to her arms and nose caused Kenya's knees to buckle, and she slumped into the nearest bedside chair. Leaning forward, she gently grasped her mother's hand. "Daddy should be here," she said. Seated on the other side of the bed, Ghana agreed and urged Kenya to call him again.

She didn't want to let go of her mother's hand, but Kenya made the call. This time he answered. He sounded groggy and called her Malawi, causing her to falter. "Daddy, it's Kenya. Are you okay?"

"Oh, Kennie. Of course. Sweetheart. I'm good. I'm good. And you?"

"Were you sleeping?" It was only four in the afternoon.

"No. No, I wasn't asleep. Just … How are you?"

"Daddy, Mama is in the hospital. You need to come home."

"Your mother?" He cleared his throat. "What happened to your mother?"

His words were slurring and she decided not to give him details. "She's sick, Daddy. Can you come home? Please?"

"Okay, Sweetheart. I'll get a flight as soon as I can."

The thought that her father was drunk on an early Monday evening gave her an odd queasy feeling in her stomach, like she'd fallen down a rabbit hole—only this wasn't Wonderland.

44

Consciousness slipped in so gradually that when Bet opened her eyes she wasn't sure she was awake. The ceiling seemed miles away, and as it came into focus, she saw gray tiles, not the white ceiling of her bedroom. She jerked her head up and found herself constrained by tubes and wires all around her. Then Ghana's face filled the space before Bet's eyes, talking, asking questions. "How you feeling?"

Like the steady flow of liquid through an IV, Bet's memories ran cold through her veins. The pills. The dizziness. The wish for everything to end. She closed her eyes as a rush of embarrassment made her head feel hot. Her throat was dry and sore when she spoke and the words were husky as they tumbled out. "You must have better things to do than be here with me." Ghana scowled and Bet instantly regretted her words. She tried to think of something more positive, but couldn't.

After a moment of silence, Ghana explained that Kenya had been here, too, but had left to get the kids. "She's bringing back coffee and breakfast." Bet offered a slight nod. Encouraged to keep talking, Ghana leaned forward, her hand lightly touching Bet's arm. "She called Dad. He's coming home. He's getting a flight today to come home." Her warm hand pressed into Bet's skin, yet another flush of cold rushed through her. Nausea bubbled in the bottom of her stomach as she remembered the young man—a boy really—with the sleeping pills, who touched and kissed her. She'd vowed she wouldn't see him again, but ... Embarrassment brought heat from her neck to her cheeks. She wanted desperately to erase everything from the last week. Two weeks? Three weeks? Bet wasn't sure. Ghana asked if she was okay. No, not really, but she nodded. Her throat hurt like hell and she pressed her fingers to her windpipe.

"They pumped your stomach. Put a tube down your throat," Ghana said, giving Bet's arm another squeeze. "It must hurt."

Bet frowned and closed her eyes.

A nurse arrived, a young woman with shiny black skin wearing pink scrubs. "Good morning," she said, flashing a bright smile. "How are you feeling?"

Stupid, Bet thought, but shrugged her shoulders and gave a half-hearted smile in return. The nurse checked a monitor and made a note on a clipboard. "Dr. Freeman will be in later to chat with you." The doctor will ask if she'd taken the pills on purpose, if she'd wanted to die. Yes, and yes. Now, though, Bet was glad she wasn't dead. She was glad Ghana was here. Glad Kenya was on her way. And even more so, glad Malcolm was coming home.

She knew she'd pushed him away, and maybe she'd done it on purpose, pushing all that was good in her life as far away as possible, because why should she deserve to have a good life when Malawi's was cut so short. She was responsible. The voice, small inside her head, had been on replay for weeks. She was responsible. This voice, small as it was, she thought, told the truth.

"When can I go home?"

"Let's not rush things," said the nurse. "We'll see what the doctor says, but we may have you stay another night for observation."

They wanted to make sure she didn't try again to end her life.

As the nurse exited, Kenya and the children came in. Kenya carried a cup holder with two coffee cups and two paper bags of food, talking in a rush like hard rain: "You're awake. How are you feeling?

What were you thinking? Why didn't you call me?" Bet didn't want to look at her daughter's judging eyes. As Kenya leaned over the bed, passing one cup and one bag to Ghana, Bet offered a smile and beckoned to her grandchildren, but it was Kenya who bent forward first to kiss Bet's cheek. "You look terrible," Kenya said. Charlene followed with an awkward embrace.

"We were worried about you, Grandma. You okay now?"

Bet cradled the girl's face and kissed her hair, breathing in the fruity fragrance. "I'll be fine, Honey. I feel better knowing you're here with me."

Junior nudged Charlene and squeezed in for a kiss. "I'm so glad you're okay," he whispered. Bet blinked away tears and looked up to see Caroline in the doorway. Instinctively, her skin prickled.

"I heard the news and had to come see for myself," the woman said.

"Be nice, Mama," Kenya said into her ear. Charlene cheered, "Grandmama," and moved away from the bedside to give her great-grandmother a hug. Bet wasn't ready for her mother-in-law but she swallowed a scratchy dry lump and promised herself not to get upset. She focused on her grandson, asking him how he was enjoying the summer break. "It's okay." He rested his head on her arm.

Caroline walked around to the other side of the bed where Ghana sat and said, "I have flowers being delivered. They should come today." Ghana gave her grandmother a kiss and offered her chair, but Caroline remained standing. She was doing that thing, Bet noticed, chewing on her mouth as if eating invisible candies. The prick of irritation plunged deeper into Bet. No one spoke. Only the sound of the machines, beeps and flashing lights until Kenya suggested she and the kids take a walk to the cafeteria for more creamer. "I'll come too," said Ghana, and the crowded room emptied suddenly, except for Caroline.

"Is this what you meant?" Bet asked, looking at the floral pattern on the woman's skirt. She didn't want to acknowledge that Caroline may have been right. After a moment, she made eye contact with her mother-in-law. "You said I'd lose more than my daughter. Is this what you meant?"

Caroline glanced around the room then looked back at Bet, placing both her hands on Bet's forearm. "Kenya says Malcolm is coming home." With one hand she patted Bet softly. "You can push through this. I know you, Elizabeth. You will be just fine as long as you don't take anything for granted."

Bet covered one of Caroline's hands with her own and gave a wan smile. "You are right. I'm so very lucky. To have all of you."

* * *

The room was dark, but low lighting filtered through from the hallway. Caroline, Kenya and the kids were gone. Ghana slept in the chair next to the bed, her hair a mass of twine resting over her shoulders and chair. Bet made a silent promise to do better by her middle child.

A familiar shadow filled the doorway. Not the doctor. He came closer, looming over her. She inhaled, feeling tears forming. Malcolm had come back. He'd been such a blessing to her, and she'd been awful. Just awful.

"I hear you're feeling better," he said, his voice soft and tentative.

"Yes. I don't know why they're keeping me here," she said. "I just want to go home."

"In time."

Ghana stirred and exclaimed a shriek of joy at seeing her father. They exchanged a firm embrace, then she leaned into Bet, kissing her cheek and asking if she needed anything. "Gonna get something to drink."

Malcolm's arms hung motionless by his sides and he watched Bet for a while before taking the seat where Ghana had been. He looked tired. Hungover.

"You just got back?" she asked.

"Yes. Came straight here from the airport."

She wanted to say so much, but felt awkward. Foolish.

"I talked to the doctor." He snorted. "What were you thinking?"

His disappointment smacked her, and she covered her mouth afraid she would dissolve into a sobbing mess.

"I feel responsible," she said. "Like it was all my fault."

"What? What was all your fault?"

"Malawi."

"Don't be ridiculous, Bet." He leaned forward and took her hand, fingering the lines in her palm. "That had nothing to do with you."

"There's something I need to tell you."

He narrowed his eyes at her and she looked away. She didn't want to tell him but she had to. "When I got pregnant." She withdrew her hand. "When I first got pregnant with Malawi, I wasn't going to tell you."

Malcolm said nothing and continued to watch her; she couldn't read his expression. "I didn't want you to know." Her heart was thudding, a captured bird trying to escape. "I was going to get rid of her without you knowing." She saw a slight frown shadow his face but then it was gone. Maybe he didn't understand. "I was going to have an abortion, Mal. I made an appointment and everything, but the car wouldn't start. Remember that old Tercel? It didn't start, and I missed the appointment. I rescheduled, but by then you'd guessed I was pregnant. And you were so excited that I couldn't go through with it. You were just so excited."

His gaze drifted away from her and he reclined, silent, contemplating her confession.

"I was going to kill her, Malcolm, and now she's dead, and it's my fault."

Dread rattled inside her for a long time, rolling around like a loose marble while he said nothing. Finally, he focused on her and asked, "Do you wish you had gone through with it?"

His question surprised her. "No, of course not. I was unhappy at first. I wanted to go back to art school and get my master's. But I loved her." She felt lightheaded. "Sometimes, I was frustrated. I admit that. All the girls. They were a lot. Sometimes I just couldn't cope, but you always helped me. And they were good girls. Really, they were. They were good girls, all three of them."

She studied his face, willing him to speak. To say something. The silence went on too long and Bet began to speak just as he did. "It's not your fault, Elizabeth." He inched forward in the chair. "You didn't go through with it. You didn't do anything wrong. We had three beautiful girls. They're still beautiful. Malawi will always be beautiful. And we have two still here with us. We can't forget them." He paused for several moments. "We have a beautiful family, Bet. We always did."

She reached for him and he tightened his grip around her fingers. "We going to be okay?"

He nodded. "Yeah. We'll be okay."

45

Kenya placed the fruit platter on the back seat on the driver's side and the paper grocery bag with cookies and bottled water on the floor. The mid-August evening was still humid, and she flicked on the A/C to high. Already in the trunk was a flask filled with hot water, tea bags, a coffee pot and coffee with creamer and sugar. She should make it to the downtown library around six, barring any issues with traffic. The first meeting of Malawi's Sisters was scheduled to start at seven. Kenya had booked a room in the library's basement, and Ghana recruited her friend Cass, who worked for a marketing company, to get the word out about the event. Cass said to expect fifteen to twenty people.

Kenya had been skeptical about Malawi's Sisters and her role in it, but Ghana had put her in touch with a woman whose gay son, a student at Howard, had been beaten to death in an alley a few blocks from Howard's campus. She'd met the woman—Destiny—at a coffee shop near the university. Destiny had fake burgundy braids, dark lipstick and wore a low-cut pink blouse that exposed a generous cleavage. She gave Kenya a bright smile and a firm embrace that almost consumed Kenya. There had been a time Kenya would have dismissed this woman, thinking her ignorant and a waste of time, but as she listened to Destiny talk about her son, about her experience, she appreciated the woman's life and wise perspective.

"He was flamboyant and people didn't like it," said Destiny. "There's no information on who did it." As the woman talked, Kenya felt the fear for her own son expanding inside her stomach; she had wanted nothing to do with Ghana's support group and started preparing a speech to convince Junior to keep his feelings for boys to himself. Just don't be gay, she wanted to scream at him. But then Destiny said something that stopped the roll of thoughts in Kenya's head and made her listen.

"My son was simply who he was," she said, her voice soft and plain. "Whether made by God or some gay gene or whatever, he was a person who loved clothes and music and dancing. He was studying art, and no one had the right to take his life away from him. Nobody." She fell silent, then after a moment, "We need to support each other. And we need to speak out against this kind of violence to save all the young ones coming up now so they can walk in their own light without fear."

Destiny had offered a tissue and wrapped her arm across Kenya's shoulder. They had sat in the corner of the coffee shop quietly sobbing together. Kenya thought of Junior and her desire that he be able to *walk in his own light without fear* no matter his race or sexual orientation. So, she signed on with the notion that Malawi's Sisters could grow into a platform for much more than simply supporting women and their grief.

At seven-thirty only two women had wandered in; both Kenya and Ghana practically pounced on them, offering tea or coffee, cookies or fruit.

"Well, let's go ahead and begin," Ghana said, glancing at the entrance. Just then Destiny came rushing in, apologizing for being late, and Kenya accepted the woman's enormous hug.

When Ghana opened her mouth nothing came out. Her eyes searched the ceiling as she gathered her thoughts, then she looked at Kenya as if to say she couldn't speak. A moment of sudden emotion and Kenya felt it too, the air so thick it suffocated, but she cleared her throat and said, "We lost our sister." The room was quiet and when one of the ladies coughed, the noise bounced off the bare walls. "Malawi Walker. She was twenty-seven. She was shot by a white man who said he thought she was an intruder. She was defenseless." Kenya's heart was in her throat. The three women—Destiny, Monica, and Shayla—nodded in understanding. Kenya fell silent unable to continue.

Then Monica said, "I lost my sister. Trina Blackmon. She was thirty-one. She was shot by a white man on the highway. He said she cut him off and he followed her and shot her at a stoplight."

Shayla's voice was low. "I lost my boyfriend. Ralph Dickson. He was forty-five. He was shot by a police officer for resisting arrest. He was unarmed and had one blunt in his pocket."

Kenya could feel the burn of tears and blinked rapidly hoping they would disappear, but several drops slid down her collarbone. The small group talked about feeling helpless, lost and unprotected.

"Our community is under attack," said Shayla.

"Can we pray?" Destiny asked.

"Of course," said Ghana, finally finding her voice. They reached out and clasped hands.

"Jesus Lord," Destiny said. "Please, Lord, give us strength to face each day without our loved one. Lord, help us understand those who have done us wrong and help us forgive them."

Kenya's chest tightened. Forgiveness was a place she wasn't ready to visit. Jeffrey Davies. Malawi. Her husband. Though she was impressed with Destiny's declaration to try, Kenya didn't know why any of them deserved her forgiveness. When the prayer was over, their voices echoed, "Amen." Everyone stood and offered one another an embrace; firm, supportive hugs that left Kenya feeling uplifted.

Ghana apologized for the small turnout and explained that this was their first meeting.

"It starts with one at a time," Monica said. "I appreciate you both for this. It helps to share. I'm not alone." She gave both Kenya and Ghana another tight hug. Shayla and Destiny did the same before leaving.

Just as they were packing up the food a young girl, perhaps fourteen or fifteen entered the room.

"Can I help you?" Kenya asked.

"This the group for people who've lost a loved one?"

Kenya nodded, and the girl took a few steps forward.

"My name's Stacy. My mother was shot. She went out to get something from the corner store and never came back."

Kenya beckoned the girl closer and took a seat, patting the chair next to her. Ghana pulled a chair up forming a triangle. Kenya asked how long ago this had happened.

"Last week."

"What do you need?" Ghana asked, her hands open on her lap.

The girl shrugged. "We staying with my grandmother. Me and my little brother. I saw a flyer upstairs and thought I'd come in." She stared at the floor for a moment, then added, "I don't know what to do."

"What was your mother's name?" asked Kenya.

"Cecilia. Cecilia Jones. She was beautiful." With a nod, Kenya encouraged the girl to speak. Stacy talked about her mother for a while, saying where she worked (at a diner in Adams Morgan), how she liked to sing in her church and loved to knit sweaters in the winter. Stacy started to giggle and said, "She was a really bad knitter. Everything was too big or too small, but she kept making stuff anyway."

Kenya laughed and told about the time she tried to knit an afghan for Junior and it came out skewed. "I can't even knit a square," she said chuckling. Before they knew it, the three of them were laughing and sharing stories about their mothers.

Ghana looked at Kenya and asked, "Do you remember Mama taking us to the carousel on the Mall?"

Kenya thought for a minute. "Yes! Malawi was still a baby." She explained to Stacy that a carousel had been on the National Mall since the 1920s, replaced in the early 80s by a new one.

"Mama didn't want to get on it, but we begged and pleaded," said Ghana. "So, there she was clinging to Malawi with one hand and to the pole coming out of the horse's neck with the other, as if at any moment she was about to get thrown off. Her face. A picture of fear. Me and Kenya just laughed."

"And after the ride ended," Kenya continued, "Mama laughed, too. All of us sitting on a bench eating ice-cream and giggling like there was not a worry in the world." She looked at her sister. "We did have some good times, didn't we?"

When a library attendant came in to say it was almost closing time, Ghana and Kenya gave Stacy a group hug, their arms overlapping around this heartbroken young girl. For a moment Kenya imagined Malawi in her arms, remembered their group hugs, remembered wiping ice-cream from Malawi's lips, kissing her forehead and gripping her hand as they walked through the neighborhood. The three musketeers, Daddy called them, sending Kenya to the encyclopedia to find out what a musketeer was. Malawi had been so annoying, and yet … Kenya couldn't imagine her childhood without her sisters.

Kenya watched Stacy disappear out the door. Yes, this was what the group was all about. Giving women a chance to remember, to laugh and feel connected to someone else who understood. This was how she would honor her baby sister.

46

Malcolm sat in a metal chair in the church basement, surrounded mostly by people he didn't know. Mostly black. Mostly alcoholics. A few suffering from other addictions who were welcomed by the group. Bet clasped his hand in her own and smiled, an encouraging smile, a happy-he-was-with-her smile. He wasn't excited to be here, but he was willing. After her ordeal with the overdose, Bet had been seeing a therapist every week and had gone back to church where she learned about the weekly Alcoholics Anonymous meetings. She kept telling him he should go too. "You'll be surprised," she'd said. "It's not a religious cult. It's not a bunch of weirdos sharing their most intimate secrets. Just normal folks trying to make it through each day without falling off the wagon."

The wagon. Like this was some kind of Wild West saga. And maybe it was. You hit a bump in the road and went flying into a ditch.

Bet was talking to the group. Sharing a story about what she did when she was struggling against numbing her feelings. He'd watched her do this. She would stop in the middle of whatever she was doing, get on her knees and pray with her palms together, head down, eyes closed, lips moving in silence. "I talk to God," she said to the group. "I talk to Malawi. I tell them I'm struggling, and it helps. I know they're watching me, and it helps me stay focused."

He was proud of her, and tried to tell her often. She needed him to communicate more. So he was trying. He needed her to give him space, and she was trying. They were enjoying each other, laughing and touching again.

He knew he had a ways to go.

In the last few months he'd tried to stop drinking, but had found it more challenging than he expected. He wasn't an alcoholic. That's what he told himself, yet not drinking didn't feel normal.

"You count the days," Bet kept saying. "Sometimes the hours." He hadn't had a drink in nine days. She'd been without any pills for almost three months. Prayer and the meetings helped, she said. So he figured he'd give it a try, the meetings, at least. He wasn't ready for prayer. Joe had given him a book on meditation, so he was trying that, letting his thoughts fade away and just being present. Sometimes he thought about Jeffrey Davies. Such a pathetic man. Driven by fear of the changing world around him. Malcolm wanted him in prison, but in many ways, he was already there, in a hell created by himself.

It was hard to stop his mind roiling, not to think about anything at all, but in those brief moments of silence, when his brain got quiet, he could feel Malawi there, encouraging him, being silent with him, and he enjoyed those moments.

"I'm proud of you," Bet whispered, squeezing his hand.

He offered a weak smile and said, "It's better than being in a ditch."

47

Bet was trying to make amends, but the one thing she had yet to do was reach her brother. She'd been bounced from one person to another until finally reaching a woman who said Will was in Houston. She'd given Bet his number and it had sat on the kitchen counter for several days. Finally ready to call, the number held her gaze for a long time before she dialed. A man's voice answered giving the name of a church.

"I'm looking for William Ellis. Do you know him?"

The man seemed confused for a moment then realized she was referring to Willie, the church's janitor. "What you need him for?"

"I'm his sister."

"Is that right?" The man paused. "Hold on."

The wait went on so long, Bet thought she'd been forgotten. She settled at the kitchen table and rehearsed what to say, but every iteration rang false. Then another voice, her brother's voice, came on the line and she lost her own.

"Elizabeth? This Elizabeth?"

"Yes, Will. It's your sister."

"Well, I'll be damned."

He'd been working with the church for five years now, not entirely sober, but managing. Renting a room in a nice house in a decent neighborhood.

"Why you calling me? Someone die?"

The room started spinning and she grabbed the table. "We lost Malawi over the summer." She paused. "But that's not why I'm calling. For years, I criticized you for your drinking and your unstructured ways.

And I want to apologize. I'm sorry for not being more supportive. You didn't deserve to be treated badly. And I'm sorry for that."

"Well, ain't that some shit." He chuckled, without malice. "You know what, sister, it's all good. I forgave you years ago. We're all good. I'm glad to hear from you."

They talked a little while longer until he had to get back to work. He gave her his cell number and she promised to call again soon. Maybe even visit him in Houston.

* * *

Memories lingered like rain clouds ready to drown the earth, but instead of a deluge only a few drops fell, one at a time smacking the ground, stinging the skin. There was no way to forget. Her three little girls. Stair steps in height, sitting on the floor of her studio. Kenya, the oldest, with her arm hanging loosely around Ghana's shoulders; and Ghana holding Malawi, still a toddler, wriggling between her sister's legs. The three of them dressed in red and white, posing for pictures that Bet would use for their annual Christmas cards.

Standing in the basement with her eyes closed, she could almost hear them giggling. But when she opened her eyes there was only the hum of the furnace warming the house. Mid-October had brought a sudden drop into the low forties, and the cold air seemed reluctant to leave her basement studio. She stared at the cardboard box sitting on the worktable, the box from Malawi's home in Florida; the box Kenya and Ghana had packed up after the protest march. She should have gone with them, no matter how difficult it would have been.

Now, what seemed like a lifetime later, she pulled off the tape and opened the flaps. Immediately, she could smell her daughter; the scent took her breath and brought tears. She took a moment to settle the sudden thudding in her chest. Covering everything was a yellow blanket trimmed with satin. Bet's mother, God rest her soul, had bought the blanket as a gift before Kenya was born, wrapping it around a yellow crocheted outfit she'd made herself. Her mother never lived to see Ghana or Malawi, but the blanket was passed down to them both, staying with Malawi, who'd clearly cherished it for all these years.

Bet ran her fingers over the satin teddy bear covering the lower left corner of the blanket. She was surprised at its condition; only the edges were frayed and the fabric was worn thin, but overall it looked good. Settling on a nearby stool, she could hear her girls giggling. Hear them running through the house playing hide and seek. Too often she'd dismissed or ignored their activities, had tried to quell their enthusiasm. Images arose … Kenya, in such earnest, changing Malawi's diaper, feeding her, playing mother. Ghana instigating trouble, leading Malawi out of the yard to do God knows what, and Kenya screaming at them from the lawn. Bet smothered her face with the soft blanket allowing the memories to dance through her.

As the images faded, an idea bubbled in their place. Nothing could change her past choices, the burdens her children had to bear because of her selfishness, nothing could bring back their sister, her daughter, but a thought emerged of something that could represent her memories and her love. Still holding the blanket, she rummaged through her files to find a business card and headed upstairs to call an old friend.

48

Kenya almost skipped through City Hall out to her car. She had just registered Malawi's Sisters as a non-profit organization and couldn't wait to see Ghana's face when she showed her the official papers at the meeting tonight. It'd been a long time since she'd done anything not related to her children, her husband, or her house. It felt good. Over several weeks, she and Ghana had worked on a mission statement, developed bylaws and created a strategic plan to make it all official. The next step was to file for tax-exempt status.

When she'd reviewed the website Ghana designed, seeing the name, Malawi's Sisters, large on the screen, filled her with emotions she couldn't quite place. Already they'd made a difference for the few who had come to the meetings. And these meetings, these women, had helped Kenya, too. Had given her strength to follow a path of her own, to be a single mom, a divorcée, a working woman again. She was waiting to hear back from a small law firm about a part-time position. Sidney called sometimes and they talked. He held out hope for a reconciliation, but he was her children's father. That was all. Nothing more.

She had talked to Malawi almost every night since the funeral; in the beginning she didn't hold back her anger, but now she was moving slowly toward forgiveness. Her therapist said forgiveness would release her from her anger. Dr. Collins said she didn't have to condone the behavior to forgive the person. Kenya wasn't sure, but with Malawi at least, it seemed the right approach. She was still working on her thoughts of forgiveness toward Sidney and Jeffrey Davies—that would have to come later. If at all.

Kenya arrived at the library for their third monthly meeting just a few moments before Ghana, who had brought cookies, water and tea, scaled down since the first gathering. Though last month, the group had grown to a dozen women.

Waving the manila folder in the air, Kenya giggled. "It's done. We are official!"

Ghana screamed with delight and looked at the papers of registration. "Now we can apply for grants and funding."

"Yep. Now it's for real."

With chairs and food in place, they waited, nervous for what would happen. A few minutes before seven they heard voices outside and Monica and Shayla arrived with another woman. Stacy came in with her little brother and grandmother, and behind them five new faces, then eight more and Ghana went to get extra chairs. Then Destiny arrived and more after her in ones and twos until twenty-six women sat in a ragged circle. Standing, Ghana introduced Kenya and herself, then in a loud, strong voice said, "We lost our sister. Malawi Walker. She was twenty-seven. She was shot by a white man who said she was breaking into his home. He didn't ask any questions. He just shot her."

The woman to Ghana's right stood up and told her story, and each woman followed, each one naming their family member, telling how they died. Many cried and held each other but by the end there was some relief. The heavy air had been lifted.

As the women filed out of the meeting room, a young Latina carrying a notebook approached Kenya and introduced herself as Lisa Herrera from the Washington Post. She had heard about the organization from a friend and asked if she could interview Kenya and her sister for a possible article.

"A news story?"

"Yes. I'm not sure yet that it will run, but it could make an interesting feature story. If you're both willing to talk to me?"

Kenya looked at Ghana and they both chuckled. "Sure."

Lisa acknowledged Malawi's death and the protests and marches in her name and those of so many others. She asked why they decided to start a support group and Kenya deferred to Ghana to respond.

"There are too many women suffering the loss of a loved one to violence," said Ghana. "This group isn't for people losing a family member to a disease or illness; this is specifically for women dealing with the sudden, violent loss of a loved one. And, especially in the black community, there are a *lot* of women suffering."

"And what about the men? Don't they need support, too?"

"Of course," said Kenya. "Men are more than welcome to attend, but we find that women who are grieving are more inclined to want to talk and share with each other."

"And what about your parents, how are they coping?"

Kenya exchanged a glance with her sister, then said, "They are struggling with the loss, just as we are, but they're finding their way."

"Your father hasn't returned to the bench. Does he plan on returning at all, and if so when?"

Kenya shifted in her seat. "I'd like to leave our parents out of this story, if you don't mind. We don't know his plans. Our parents are proud of what we're doing, but they're not involved in Malawi's Sisters."

Lisa was quiet for a moment, then smiled, "Of course." She said she'd return to the next meeting with a photographer. "Do you have a business card?"

"Um, not yet," said Ghana. "We need to get them printed."

"Oh, and please be sure to get permission from the participants to use their name and image," said Kenya. "We don't want anyone feeling uncomfortable about being here. We want to create a safe space for everyone to be free to talk openly about their experiences."

The women shook hands and Ghana offered thanks for Lisa's interest in the group. After she'd left, Ghana cheered and did a little dance, waving her hands in the air. "This is truly amazing," she said, giving Kenya a tight hug. "And look at you, getting your lawyer on."

Kenya rolled her eyes and laughed. "This is more than I imagined. And *you* are amazing. This is all you. I'm so proud of you."

* * *

When the article was published, a picture of Kenya and Ghana, both looking purposeful, eyes directed at the camera, was on the front page of the Features Section. The story was passed around on social media and Kenya received congratulatory calls from neighbors and friends.

"We're famous," she said.

Ghana screeched like a child on the other end of the phone. "If this spreads, we can be more than just a support group. We can be a much larger organization offering all kinds of resources with the ability to push for real change."

"Slow down, there," Kenya said with a laugh. "Let's just make sure we have more food for the next meeting."

49

Bet listened to the television news while folding laundry—she needed clean sheets for Kenya and the kids coming to stay, and Ghana and her boyfriend may spend a night. Eventually she turned off the TV. It was too much. Images of death. Endless analysis of race. Black versus white. It was just too much. It was Christmas Eve for goodness sake. She turned on the radio station that had been playing Christmas music since Thanksgiving and stood, looking through the sliding doors in the den, folding towels and sheets that had come out of the dryer last night. She watched the bare trees that bordered the property line with the Johnsons and wished it would snow. Christmas seemed more special when it snowed, but the weather this year was unusually warm. A slight breeze tickled her legs as it crept through the eroding seal on the patio doors that Malcolm had yet to fix. But it wasn't important anymore, she thought.

She didn't hear her husband come down the stairs and slip into the kitchen until the refrigerator door opened. She didn't look; simply imagined him there, leaning on the open door, letting out the cold air, mulling what he wanted to eat and drink. People didn't see this side of him, padding through the house in his socks and sweatpants as if he had no responsibilities in the world. Judge Malcolm Walker. Her Malcolm. He had returned to work a month ago, and she could tell he was happier for it.

"Did you eat breakfast already?" he asked.

"Uh huh." She didn't look his way but heard the crunch of corn flakes and knew he was standing in the archway between the kitchen and the den, watching her, holding a bowl in one hand, shoveling food into his mouth with the other.

"What's the matter?"

She shook out a towel and glanced at him. "I'm fine."

His head cocked to the side and he came closer. "What is it?"

Bet shrugged. "Everything changes, yet nothing changes." He kissed her forehead and turned back to the kitchen. A chair scraped the floor, and the rustle of newspaper stirred the air.

"When are the kids getting here?" he shouted.

Bet paused, inhaled slowly and continued folding. Not everyone would be here. So much change. Yet nothing changes. People die. People continue to fight.

"Huh? When is everyone getting here?"

She snapped a pillowcase in the air, folded and placed it neatly on the pile on the couch then ambled through to the kitchen. "Why are you shouting through the house? I'm right here."

"You were supposed to wake me," he said, grabbing at her. She swatted his hand away and he laughed. "Huh? Why didn't you wake me?"

She rested her hands on his shoulders and leaned in to kiss his cheek. He pressed his right hand on hers and she hugged him.

"You okay? Talk to me," he said.

They'd begun again, the two of them. Attending AA meetings together at her church. Working through the steps. She never told him about the young man with the pills, and never would, though Kenya knew. Her daughter had come by the house one afternoon and hemmed and hawed until she finally said she'd found a condom in the bedroom. Bet's blood had thinned leaving her dizzy. She'd said nothing and Kenya explained that she cleaned up the house before her father had come home.

After several moments of silence, Bet had said, "It was a foolish mistake."

"Is it over?"

"Yes, of course." Shame had rushed back heating her cheeks. "It wasn't really anything at all."

Her daughter's understanding surprised Bet.

Kenya had taken both her hands into her own and said, "It's okay, Mama. We all make mistakes. Nothing good will come of me telling anyone." Flustered, Bet hadn't known how to respond. All she could say was, "Thank you."

Bet was learning to find God again. To see Him in all things around her. Some days were harder than others, but her grandchildren especially brought her a profound joy. She'd been painting again; though it was coming slowly, she could see potential in her sketches. Sudden tears blurred her vision and she blinked them away.

Malcolm pushed back from the table and wrapped his arms around her. "Shh, it's okay. It's going to be okay."

She didn't want to cry anymore, but couldn't stop; some days the tears brought a moment of relief from the chaos inside. News coverage of protest marches, no indictments for the guilty, and more shootings rubbed like sandpaper on her wound.

Malcolm released her and she grabbed a piece of paper towel to blow her nose. "Everyone should be here this afternoon," she said. "It's going to be so strange. You know, without …" She'd been thinking this for days. Christmas without Malawi. She gripped the back of a chair to stop herself from falling, and added, "And without Sidney, too."

"No chance of them getting back together?" Malcolm poured

himself a mug of coffee then sat back down at the table, scanning the newspaper.

"I don't think so. Kenya didn't share details, just that he cheated again." Bet pulled out a chair and gestured for Malcolm to get her coffee, too.

He frowned, but got up and poured her a mug. "He and I never got along that well, anyway," he said. "I'm not going to miss him that much."

"After all these years, that's all you have to say?"

Malcolm jerked his shoulders.

Bet filled her coffee with cream. "Ghana is bringing Ryan. He's going to have dinner with us tonight and then spend tomorrow with his family. I think she's going to spend some time with them, too."

"We should meet them. Don't you think?"

"His parents? You think so?" Ghana's relationship with this Ryan had seemed so vague and distant. Almost secretive. Or perhaps Bet had never made more of an effort. She would.

"Yeah." Malcolm adjusted his eyeglasses and peered at the newspaper. "Seems to me it's getting serious."

Bet pondered this for a moment. She had no excuse for the years past, only for the last few months. She'd been wandering through each day wrapped in gauze, everything hazy and out of focus. She'd do better with her daughters.

* * *

Kenya was the first to arrive with Charlene and Junior, who rushed in with hugs and kisses for both Bet and Malcolm. Junior wanted to start setting up the train track around the Christmas tree right away, and Malcolm grinned. He'd already gotten out the box and had tested the equipment to make sure it would work smoothly, but pretended he'd forgotten and wasn't sure they could do it.

"Maybe tomorrow?"

"No! Grandpa, we have to do it right now. It has to be all ready for Christmas morning."

"Right now?"

Junior pleaded, getting on his knees and placing his hands in prayer position. Malcolm chuckled. "Well okay then. You lead the way."

Kenya and Charlene joined Bet in the kitchen; Kenya was tasked with peeling potatoes and washing and cutting the collard greens while Charlene grated the cheese for the macaroni. Bet prepared the turkey. Christmas Eve, the beginning of their three-day celebration of Christ and family; Bet wondered how much of either she had ever truly embraced. She'd always been stressed throughout the season, buying gifts and preparing meals to impress. In the early years, Christmas Eve had been her day to prepare dinner for family, and then on Christmas Day, she and Malcolm would traipse over to his parents' house on 16th Street. After Malcolm's father passed away, Bet continued to cook on Christmas Eve and prepared a small ham on Christmas Day with Caroline spending the three days with them.

The doorbell rang and Bet heard Charlene running to the door. "Grandmama is here."

Bet's shoulders tightened. Caroline breezed in carrying several bags, one filled with various pies and another with two large tins of popcorn, much to the grandkids' delight. She gave hugs and kisses to

Charlene and Junior and offered a light hug to Bet. "You're looking well," she said warmly, before heading to the sitting room to place gifts under the tree. The woman wasn't so bad, really.

A short time later, Ghana's laughter filled the front foyer and Bet heard her argue with her niece. "Not until tomorrow. No. Not until tomorrow." Ghana breezed into the kitchen and dumped two bags of wrapped gifts in the corner. Bet dried her hands on a towel. "Those go under the tree, my dear." She'd only met Ryan once or twice before, brief encounters she barely remembered, so today she wanted to make sure he felt welcome. His chosen profession wasn't getting much love in the press, and police officers—the good ones at least—deserved respect. As they fussed with the gift bags, Bet saw the contrast between the two: her wild child with her dreadlocks and tattoos, and this tall blond white man, wearing a gray sweater and black pants. A complete opposite of Ghana. Bet still struggled to see the beauty in her daughter's style, but she was trying. Perhaps this man would influence her to tone down her wild ways. But then, maybe that's what he loved about her. Perhaps, in their opposites, they brought balance.

She hugged Ghana close and tight. For too long she'd taken her children for granted. When she let go, Ghana seemed surprised. Her daughter stared for a second then turned and said, "You remember Ryan?"

Bet opened her arms to him and felt his lips soft against her cheek. As she released him, he said, "Thank you so much for inviting me to share in this family gathering," and offered her a small deep red poinsettia.

She accepted the gift with a smile. He was soft spoken, gracious and gentle, just like Malcolm. "You are most welcome," she said. The world needed more young men like him.

When dinner was ready everyone pitched in to get the bowls and dishes to the dining room, and Bet made sure the candles were lit. As was the family custom, Caroline gave the blessing before they ate. She asked God to bless the food and the family as she always did, but asked Him to hold Malawi close in his care. The words, "Hold her, oh Lord, in your care," poked at Bet's heart and she bit her lip, pushing back a gasp. She wouldn't break down. She wouldn't.

* * *

The house was full of warm and loving energy and Bet enjoyed this feeling, a sensation of love and excitement she hadn't felt in many months. Even Caroline's presence wasn't oppressive. Lounging on the couch, she admired the shimmering white lights on the Christmas tree and Johnny Mathis singing seasonal tunes in the background. Dinner was settling heavily in her stomach, yet she couldn't wait for some apple pie and ice-cream. Malcolm and Ryan appeared to be having as much fun with the train set as Junior, with all three of them hunched over the miniature tracks. Kenya and Ghana were in the kitchen whispering and tittering with each other. And Charlene was on the loveseat playing a game on her tablet. Bet shifted from the couch to sit next to her granddaughter.

"What're you playing?" She peered at the screen and saw it was a word game. This made her smile.

"You don't have to be sad anymore, Grandma."

"Why's that?"

"Everyone is happy. And Aunt Mowie is with God. So that's not so bad, right?"

Bet chuckled. "True. Sooner than expected, but she is at peace." She patted the girl's lap. "What are you most happy about?"

"That we're all together and we're all happy."

"Aren't you sad that your daddy isn't with us?"

"Yes. But he gave me a phone and I can talk to him anytime I want to." She pulled an iPhone from her pocket and flashed it at Bet. "We talked this morning, and I'll call him tomorrow, too." She paused to look at her phone then looked back at Bet. "Mommy is happier. They were sad together. It's better now."

"My goodness. How old are you?" Bet pressed her lips to her granddaughter's forehead.

When the girls came in from the kitchen, Kenya settled on the couch next to Malcolm and Bet got up, letting Ghana sit in the loveseat behind Ryan; her daughter's hand caressed his head as she passed him. With everyone here, Bet decided it was time to present her special gifts.

"Okay, okay," she said. "Girls, I have something for you." She got on her knees and fished out two bags from under the tree, then settled on the couch in the space next to Malcolm.

"I was wondering who those bags were for," said Kenya, leaning forward and clapping her hands together. She and Ghana burst into laughter like little girls.

"I finally went through Malawi's things." Bet paused. "And I saw the yellow blanket. Takes my breath away that it's still around. My mother gave it to me and each one of you cherished it." Bet inhaled sharply, remembering her mother's death just after Kenya was born. "Anyway, I met this woman some years back who made teddy bears out of clothing of loved ones who had passed away. I found her card and asked if she could make something with the blanket."

Kenya and Ghana sat grinning, Ghana bouncing like a toddler.

"So, here." Bet reached across Malcolm to hand a bag to Kenya and stretched out to Ghana, who moved from the loveseat to sit by her mother's feet. The sisters rummaged quickly through the tissue paper and pulled out, almost simultaneously, a small yellow teddy bear.

"They're called memory bears," Bet said, "and they just seemed like a fitting memorial to Malawi. The blanket has a part of each of you and, well ..." Bet fell silent, tears filling her eyes. Both Kenya and Ghana each emitted a screech of joy. Each bear had a ribbon around its neck with a small tag with their names on it.

"Mama they are beautiful," Kenya said, wiping her eyes.

"So, so beautiful," Ghana echoed.

"This is the best gift ever, Mama," said Kenya. She leaned over her father and gave Bet an awkward hug and a kiss on the cheek. "Just perfect."

Bet grabbed a tissue and blew her nose and Ghana rested her head on her mother's lap.

"I haven't been the best mother," Bet said, stroking Ghana's hair. "I'm going to do better. I promise."

Charlene chimed in that she wanted to see the gifts and positioned herself on the floor next to Ghana, who gave her the bear. Charlene ooohed and cuddled the bear. Bet was overwhelmed with a mixture of joy and grief. She blew her nose once again and passed the tissue box to Kenya.

Just as she was about to suggest some apple pie, Ryan stood up and gave Malcolm a look. In response, Malcolm offered a slight nod.

"Um," Ryan began. "I, uh, don't want to spoil the moment, but figured this would be a good time to say thanks to you all for being so welcoming to me." He looked at the floor and stuffed his hands in his pants pockets. "I had a chat with Mr. Walker earlier this evening to make sure I had the all clear."

Bet started to smile and watched Ghana's face, her damp eyes widening in suspicious surprise. Ryan continued. "Ghana and I have been together now for about two years, and …" He fumbled with his pocket and pulled out a small box. "I would like to ask for your hand in marriage." He got down on one knee and looked at Ghana who was still on the floor, her hands covering her open mouth, tears glistening her cheeks. He opened the box, revealing a small diamond ring. "Ghana Walker, will you marry me?"

A moment of silent anticipation passed until Ghana nodded emphatically and everyone erupted into cheers. Ryan pulled the ring from the box and slipped it onto Ghana's finger. Tears splashed Bet's cheeks and she swatted them away with a laugh.

"This calls for a glass of champagne," said Malcolm, rushing to the kitchen where he uncovered two bottles of Dom Pérignon and two bottles of sparkling cider that he must have hidden earlier in the back of the fridge. Bet pulled out champagne flutes from the cupboard and smacked Malcolm on his arm when he came back. "You knew this was happening?"

He gave her a wicked grin. "He called me a few days ago and we met at the courthouse. Said he wanted to do it right and asked my permission, but said he wanted it to be a surprise."

There was a glow in her house that Bet had never felt before.

A warm glow keeping the darkness of night at bay, and she wished the family could have experienced this every year, this joy that had nothing to do with race or culture or religion, or even age. Just family loving each other.

Bet stood next to Malcolm and raised her glass. "To love," she said.

Yes, to love.

50

Malcolm finished his sparkling cider and settled into the cushions of the couch. He was tempted to have a glass of bourbon, but resisted. Bet shifted toward him and he draped his arm over her shoulders as she snuggled closer. Ghana and Ryan were on the floor playing with Junior, though Ghana was mostly admiring her engagement ring. Kenya was on the loveseat with Charlene, playing with the bears, and his mother was nodding in the armchair. And Malawi. She was here, too. Life didn't get any better than this.

"Do you think it's true?" he said.

Bet looked up at him. "What's that?"

"That love will conquer all."

"Where's this coming from?" She chuckled and he laughed too, feeling embarrassed by his melancholy.

"I don't know," he said. "Looking at these two. Seeing the love between them. Thinking about all that we've been through, and we're still here. Still together."

Bet squeezed his thigh. "Yes," she said. "I think love can conquer all, but only if everyone accepts it into their hearts and makes it a way of life. A thing they live instead of a thing they do when they feel like it." She paused. "If I've learned anything this year, that's it."

Malcolm had learned more than he could ever express, and wondered if he could live love every day.

Junior rose from the floor, stretching his arms into the air above his head and asked if he could watch a movie. Malcolm saw his mother in the shape of Junior's face, in his smile, though he had his father's stocky build and eyes.

"Yeah," Ghana said, jumping up. "Let's all watch a movie."

Ghana and Junior ran off to the den, leaving Ryan on the floor by himself. He laughed. "I could sit here and play with this all night."

With a grin, Malcolm leaned forward and patted the young man on his shoulder. "There's nothing more fun than a cool train set no matter your age."

Ryan slowly got up and followed Kenya and Charlene as they ambled out of the room. Leaving his mother sleeping in the armchair, Malcolm helped Bet collect the dirty glasses and as they carried them to the kitchen, Kenya cried out for them to come quickly. They dumped the glasses on the counter and saw the image of a church on the television. Malcolm walked through to the den and leaned his hands on the back of the settee. A news announcer was explaining that a lone shooter had killed twelve people exiting a church after a Christmas Eve service in a small town in Virginia. All twelve victims were African American and the shooter was a young white man, who had been taken into custody. The room was quiet except for the news account coming from the TV. Terror filled everyone's eyes and Malcolm was afraid to move, fearing his body would crumble.

Breaking the silence, Charlene asked: "Grandpa, what does this mean? Why did he do that? Why are people still killing black people. Killing us?"

The ground beneath Malcolm wavered. He could think of nothing to say to reassure his grandchildren, his family. He stared at the television screen and wanted to smash it to pieces, knowing it would make no difference to what was happening in the world.

His mother stepped into the room and took his hand. "We need to love each other," she said. Her voice even, simply stating a fact. "We need to be a family and take care of each other, be here for one another."

Junior was frowning. "But that doesn't stop people from killing us. We should fight back. Shouldn't we?" He looked at Malcolm, who shook his head. He didn't know what to say. He looked at his mother who squeezed his hand.

"Fight, yes, but not with violence," Caroline said. "Not like that."

The television screen showed police cars and yellow caution tape around the front of the church.

Kenya cradled Charlene, whose sobs came in small bursts like hiccups. Caroline released Malcolm and put out her hands for Junior to come to her and he did, slowly. She held him close. "Revenge isn't the answer," she said. "Violence only creates more pain. Dr. King said we should love our enemies. Only then can we transform a world of violence into a place of goodness, a place of love."

"A place of love?" said Kenya, her face crumpled. "I'm not going to love my enemy for this. This makes me feel like there's no love in the world anywhere. I'm so sick of all this killing. I'm sick of it."

"In this family, we have love," Caroline insisted. "In this family we have each other. As a people, we should be coming together and organizing in a non-violent way to stop this madness. As a nation, we need to respect one another and stop viewing others as the enemy, but instead, embrace them."

Malcolm looked at Ryan whose eyes were closed, a frown wrinkling his forehead.

His mother continued. "We may never rid the world of people

like him," she said, looking at the shooter on TV. "But we must try, and it begins with us. If we can't love those who come from the same blood, then we will never love and accept those we view as different. So here, here in *this* house, in *this* family, we will love each other." She looked at Bet. "We won't let this kind of violence destroy us."

Caroline grabbed Junior's hand and reached her other hand to Kenya. Malcolm followed her lead and reached for Bet and the family formed a circle. His mother bowed her head and began to pray, asking God for the strength to fight evil, not with violence but with love in their hearts, and to bless the families of the victims.

He listened, admiring her faith in prayer. But in his heart, he believed change came only when people put their prayers into action and practiced love and acceptance of one another. Practiced respect for everyone no matter their race or religion. His mother was correct: they had to love each other. When she said, "Amen," Malcolm looked at his mother, his wife, his daughters, his soon-to-be son-in-law, and his two precious grandchildren. Each one had a role to play. Each one would do what was necessary to make the world better. But for now, he wanted only to enjoy this time with his family. He snatched the remote from the arm of the couch and turned off the television.

Kenya and Ghana have been with me for many years, their voices mumbling, often incoherently, in my head so that I couldn't figure out their stories. Then in 2014, Renisha McBride was shot and killed by a white man, and the horror of this tragedy got stuck in my brain. Eventually, Kenya whispered, "Our sister was killed the same way." And Ghana said, "Yeah, help us share that story."

So in 2015, with the kernel of a novel and the help of family and friends, I journeyed to Bali, Indonesia, for a month-long writing retreat. In this gorgeous oasis, this book blossomed into more than mere whispers in my head. My deepest gratitude goes to my workshop leader, Bernadette Murphy, for her encouragement and guidance that pushed me forward when I didn't think I could reach my first-draft goal of 50,000 words. Much love and thanks go to my Bali Scribe Tribe Sisterhood. And thank you, Mastin Kipp, for organizing this magical retreat.

Heartfelt thanks go to so many who held me up through the writing, the rewriting, and the literary agent rejections. To name a few: my writing group, D. Marietta Williams, Cheryl Head, Savanna Jeordan, and Celeste Crenshaw. To Mary Eno for the inspiration during the first draft. To Michon Lartigue for your insight and friendship. To Carolina Cabanillas for your creative eye. An enormous thank you to David Haynes and Kimbilio, and especially to Edwidge Danticat for selecting this work as the inaugural Kimbilio National Fiction Prize. To the team at Four Way Books: Martha Rhodes, Ryan Murphy, Mari Coates, and Clarissa Long.

And thank you to Chris and Amanda for your ongoing love and support.

Melanie S. Hatter is the author of *The Color of My Soul*, winner of the 2011 Washington Writers' Publishing House Fiction Prize, and *Let No One Weep for Me, Stories of Love and Loss*, a short story collection. She is a participating author in the PEN/Faulkner Writers in Schools program in Washington, D.C., and serves on the board of the Zora Neale Hurston/Richard Wright Foundation.

Kimbilio is a community of writers and scholars committed to developing, empowering and sustaining fiction writers from the African diaspora and their stories. Kimbilio is grateful to the English Department and to Dedman College at Southern Methodist University for the generous support that has helped to make this and other Kimbilio projects possible. kimbiliofiction.org

Publication of this book was made possible by grants and donations. We are also grateful to those individuals who participated in our 2018 Build a Book Program. They are:

Anonymous (11), Sally Ball, Vincent Bell, Jan Bender-Zanoni, Kristina Bicher, Laurel Blossom, Adam Bohanon, Betsy Bonner, Mary Brancaccio, Lee Briccetti, Jane Martha Brox, Carla & Steven Carlson, Caroline Carlson, Stephanie Chang, Tina Chang, Liza Charlesworth, Andrea Cohen, Machi Davis, Marjorie Deninger, Patrick Donnelly, Charles Douthat, Emily Flitter, Lukas Fauset, Monica Ferrell, Jennifer Franklin, Helen Fremont & Donna Thagard, Robert Fuentes & Martha Webster, Ryan George, Panio Gianopoulos, Chuck Gillett, Lauri Grossman, Julia Guez, Naomi Guttman & Jonathan Mead, Steven Haas, Lori Hauser, Mary & John Heilner, Ricardo Hernandez, Deming Holleran, Nathaniel Hutner, Janet Jackson, Rebecca Kaiser Gibson, David Lee, Jen Levitt, Howard Levy, Owen Lewis, Sara London & Dean Albarelli, David Long, Katie Longofono, Cynthia Lowen, Ralph & Mary Ann Lowen, Jacquelyn Malone, Fred Marchant, Donna Masini, Catherine McArthur, Nathan McClain, Richard McCormick, Victoria McCoy, Britt Melewski, Kamilah Moon, Beth Morris, Rebecca Okrent, Gregory Pardlo, Veronica Patterson, Jill Pearlman, Marcia & Chris Pelletiere, Maya Pindyck, Megan Pinto, Taylor Pitts, Eileen Pollack, Barbara Preminger, Kevin Prufer, Vinode Ramgopal, Martha Rhodes, Peter & Jill Schireson, Jason Schneiderman, Jane Scovel, Andrew Seligsohn & Martina Anderson, Soraya Shalforoosh, James Snyder & Krista Fragos, Ann St. Claire, Alice St. Claire-Long, Dorothy Tapper Goldman, Robin Taylor, Marjorie & Lew Tesser, Boris Thomas, Judith Thurman, Susan Walton, Calvin Wei, Bill Wenthe, Allison Benis White, Elizabeth Whittlesey, Rachel Wolff, Hao Wu, Anton Yakovlev, and Leah Zander.